SUMMER SISTERS

Jan Dirksen

This is a work of fiction. All of the characters and events portrayed in this novel are either products of the author's imagination or are used fictitiously.

Cover photo by iStock photos (used with permission).

ISBN 13: 9798711627975

Kindle Direct Publishing

Printed in the United States of America

Dedication

To my wonderful mom. What a beautiful example of a Godly woman.

Table of Contents

CHAPTER 1 1
CHAPTER 2 4
CHAPTER 3 7
CHAPTER 4 11
CHAPTER 5 16
CHAPTER 6 20
CHAPTER 7 23
CHAPTER 8 28
CHAPTER 9 30
CHAPTER 10 33
CHAPTER 11 38
CHAPTER 12 43
CHAPTER 13 45
CHAPTER 14 50
CHAPTER 15 54
CHAPTER 16 60
CHAPTER 17 66
CHAPTER 18 69
CHAPTER 19 74
CHAPTER 20 80
CHAPTER 21 86

CHAPTER 22 90
CHAPTER 23 94
CHAPTER 24 103
CHAPTER 25 109
CHAPTER 26 113
CHAPTER 27 116
CHAPTER 28 122
CHAPTER 29 126
CHAPTER 30 134
CHAPTER 31 140
CHAPTER 32 143
CHAPTER 33 147
CHAPTER 34 152
CHAPTER 35 161
CHAPTER 36 167
CHAPTER 37 172
CHAPTER 38 180
CHAPTER 39 193
CHAPTER 40 197
CHAPTER 41 204
CHAPTER 42 211
CHAPTER 43 218
CHAPTER 44 224

CHAPTER 45 231
CHAPTER 46 242
CHAPTER 47 251
CHAPTER 48 260
CHAPTER 49 268
CHAPTER 50 278
CHAPTER 51 284
CHAPTER 52 293
CHAPTER 53 299
CHAPTER 54 305
EPILOGUE.. 313
ACKNOWLEDGEMENTS.. 319

CHAPTER 1

GRACE

How blissful is this! A summer—the *entire* summer—at our family cabin with just my sister. Days of sunshine, lying out on the beach, paddle boarding, jet skiing, boating, and happy hours in the evening with really nice wine. And definitely an added plus--no cares, no responsibilities, and no contact with the outside world. Wait—that's not true. We do have our iPhones.

First of all, let me tell you that Ellie and I are summer girls through and through. If ever there was anyone destined to have a summer birthday, it was me.

It's like God looked down from heaven and said, "You are the perfect person to be born on August 1," (even though I was due the middle of July). Just don't ask my mom about that.

Even when I was a little kid and didn't get to bring treats to school on my birthday, it was a small price to pay for being a summer girl. My sister is definitely a summer girl also, even though her birthday didn't quite cooperate. Her birthday at the end of March might seem like spring or summer in some parts of the world, but in the Midwest, we're usually hanging on to winter as if it's never going to die.

But birthdays aside, summer is our time to shine. We both probably should've been diagnosed with Seasonal Affective Disorder, before it was even a thing. Winter was torture. But what could be better than lying on uncomfortable lawn chairs, with lemon juice in our hair, and baby oil with iodine slathered all over our bodies? The station on our transistor radios would tell us when it was time to turn over (every 30 minutes), so that our SPF zero didn't totally fry us. We would do this for hours, every day. We have two older sisters—Ann and Katie, who would try to tan on occasion. They gave it the old college try, but didn't love it like we did. We also have a younger brother, Dan, who spent every day at the city pool with his friends—a cooler way of being a summer kid.

But I digress.

When Ellie called me this morning and said, "What are you doing this summer?" I didn't think much of it. She said, "How about you and me—a summer at the cabin?"

My first reaction was no, I'm way too busy. And who goes on a vacation for the whole summer? I'm a mom (with two married kids, who have their own lives). I also have seven grandchildren that I love to spend time with (even though they're getting too busy to have much time for me). And last but not least, I have a husband that I love dearly (but works way too many hours and is rarely home). I work very part-time as a nurse (when the mood strikes me), and I have great friends (who won't come out of their houses due to the latest pandemic). Our mom at the age of 88 lives in a retirement home nearby, and even though she loves to see me, she never makes any demands on my time. You know, maybe I'm not that busy.

Even though my first thought was, "this will never happen," it becomes really appealing to me as the afternoon wears on.

"I'll talk to Mike tonight, to see if he has any plans. And by the way, what brought this on?"

Her reply, "Time... You know, it's been a while since Will passed away, and I decided it's finally time to enjoy summer again."

CHAPTER 2

ELLIE

So here I am, just Ellie. Actually, my real name is Elizabeth. I didn't love it, because back in the 60's long historic names weren't really in style. There was a lot more of the Carol, Linda, Nancy, or Jane variety. When I was in sixth grade I informed my family and friends that from then on I would be known as Ellie, not Elizabeth. I was a dark-haired kid with a bunch of siblings and two loving parents living in the suburbs of Grand Rapids, Michigan. I had a normal life–great parents, four siblings, and eventually, a marriage to a nice guy with whom I had three kids. Normal until he dropped dead of a heart attack at the age of 55. That's when you find out who your true friends are. Everybody was really nice at first–too nice. People came out of the woodwork. In about six months you knew who was going to stick by you and who wasn't. The latter list was a lot longer.

So here I am, at the age of 62, living in a small northwest Iowa town, with nothing more than being known as the widow of "that really nice college professor—you know, the one who died on Main Street?" I've been widowed for a while, but am just now starting to feel like there's a life here—that I'm not destined to live out the rest of my life as "poor Ellie." And what better way to resurrect a life than a summer in our parents' cabin?

Here's the story on the cabin. Our dad was a financial wizard (or so he said) that made his way in the credit card business. In the early 70's, his company made the move to South Dakota, where taxes were extremely favorable for this type of business, and as an added incentive, no state income tax. A double bonus! The company did well, he did well, we as a family lacked for nothing, and life was good. When you have some money, it's time to buy a vacation home, right?

Great thought, but there aren't a lot of gorgeous lakes around Sioux Falls, South Dakota. You're going to have to drive a bit. Lake Okoboji looked fine, but it was too busy and the land values were going through the roof. To the south is the town of Yankton, through which the Missouri River runs. Lewis and Clark explored the area, back in the day. A dam was built, a lake was made, and water sports now abound. So do huge, spacious campgrounds with lots of trees, and golden sandstone bluffs around the whole lake. I'm often amazed at how beautiful it is. Dad saw the potential in this, and had a large cabin built on the lake in a gorgeous cove, with a big dock, lake access, and sunsets that couldn't be rivalled anywhere.

This cabin was a godsend to us. Our parents came from poor backgrounds, so having a summer home was something very foreign to them. And wow, did we make it enjoyable! Mom would cook delicious meals, dad would fish, and also taught the kids and grandkids how to waterski, along with some wild tubing rides. Summers there were something that my parents would've only dreamed about when they lived on Iowa farms as kids during the Depression. We enjoyed so many summers there. But when Dad died of cancer at the age of 70, the cabin lost some of its joy.

Don't get me wrong, life went on and life was good. Mom was a trooper and tried to pretend everything was as it should be. We gathered at the cabin for big summer events, but as the years went on our times there together became more infrequent. Mom started going to Arizona for the winters and spent less time at the cabin in the summers. Basically, it hasn't been used for the last five years.

That's when I decided, "It's time!"

CHAPTER 3

GRACE

The phone call from Ellie really excited me. A whole summer at the lake! How long has it been? I don't bother to try and figure it out, but I do know that it has been way too long. I put on one of my little summery sundresses, make a great dinner of grilled ribeye steaks and baked potatoes. I pair it with a great pinot grigio. And I know, red wine goes better with steak, but we're not big into drinking red wine.

And then I wait for Mike to come home. I really won't have to bribe him, because he always gives in to what I want, but I think I should at least make a good effort.

Mike can be described in one sentence: "He's a hard worker."

Certainly there's a lot more to him than that, but I have never seen anyone work so hard. He grew up doing construction with his dad, his wonderful, sweet dad who became the best father-in-law I could've ever asked for. His dad had these cute little sayings for our son like "you can't learn any younger," "you'll be a man before your mother," and my personal favorite, "well, anything is possible." Because some of the ideas I came up with during our house remodeling projects did seem kind of impossible.

Mike is cut from the same cloth as his dad. He can fix or build anything. However, that's not his full-time job. As if he didn't work hard enough doing construction, he decided he also wanted to become a full-time firefighter and paramedic.

"Oh, just a little something to do on the side," he said.

What? On the side? How many hours are there in your day?

So that's his life. He can be up all night completing a 24-hour shift and then spend the next day doing some handyman jobs or remodeling our house, incorporating my 18th idea that I've had this year. By the way, the house looks awesome.

In years past, Mike also did some work on the cabin, in his spare time, of course. Dad hired someone to build the cabin, but Mike has made some nice updates to it over the years. It's nothing fancy, but it's a really nice-looking place. Thank heavens it's not a dump. This poor girl would've never survived in a run-down cabin with mice and bats. I literally have rodent nightmares, even though the only rats I've ever seen are on TV, and luckily my interactions with mice and bats have been kept to a minimum. Not sure where my extreme phobia comes from. I'm sure my mother's hysterics whenever she saw a mouse had something to do with it.

The cabin is set back from the shore just enough to have a nice green lawn before the sand of the beach starts. It has cedar siding with a welcoming front porch. Screening in the porch was a necessity because the bugs in South Dakota can be brutal. The inside is pretty typical—one nice great room divided from the kitchen with a peninsula (it was built in the 80's, remember). There's an open stairway to the upstairs on the back side of the great room. Upstairs—four bedrooms with two bathrooms. My parents had a master suite (which was pretty snazzy in those days). They must not have wanted five kids using their bathroom. Once a few grandkids started showing up, Mike turned the attic into a huge bunkroom with a "community-type" bathroom. Multiple sinks, showers, and toilets. All in all, a really nice place to vacation.

When Mike comes in for dinner, I make small talk and then finally bring up what's on my mind.

"Ellie called today and she said she's going to the cabin for the summer. She was wondering if I wanted to join her."

Mike's immediate response is, "Well, I have way too much work to take the summer off. And you know I only get four weeks of vacation."

"Umm, she was really thinking of only her and me going."

I could see the wheels turning in his head. We have never been the type of couple to take separate vacations, and I rarely go on "girl trips."

"And you could always come down for a few days if you have any downtime—we won't kick you out!" My feeble attempt at a joke.

Mike is very practical, but he's also very loving, and I know exactly what his final response will be.

"Well, you know I've always loved your sister, and I think it's great she's finally going to do something fun. If you can be the one to lift her spirits, you should go for it. Just don't plan on me being there much—you know how busy my summer is going to be."

News flash—really?

CHAPTER 4

ELLIE

Grace and I have timed our trips so that we arrive in Yankton at the same time. Her drive from Sioux Falls and my drive from Iowa are exactly the same distance. We meet at the local sub shop for one of their famous sandwiches, talking with our mouths full about how much fun we're going to have and how tan we're going to get. No sunscreen for the Anderson girls!

And then it's a quick ten-minute drive and we're driving down the hill to our second home. There are a lot of homes on the bluffs above us, but we're the lucky ones—we're right on the water with our own private beach. (Not exactly private—there are three cabins that share the cove and the beach that goes with it. We're the middle one). And we're basically hidden from the cabins above us by all of the pine trees in between us. The lawn looks pretty good—nice and green at the beginning of June. The beach has been raked and the dock looks to be in great shape.

We weren't exactly sure what we'd find. I'm just so excited to think about the wonderful hours Grace and I are going to have here together just lazing in the sun. It's somewhat of a solemn moment when we walk up the front stairs. It's been so long, and it seems kind of weird with just the two of us. We find the hidden key and open the front door, which creaks as it moves. We're practically pushing each other out of the way, we're so anxious to see inside.

"What the heck?"

"Holy crap! Are you kidding me?"

We just look around and can't believe our eyes. Obviously our wonderful upstairs bathrooms have sprung a leak, and this didn't happen just recently. Pieces of ceiling and insulation are hanging down everywhere. Much of the sheetrock looks a little damp. The moisture in there is definitely the mold-making variety, with everything covered in a blackish-greenish fuzz.

Grace stands there in a stupor and says, "This is so not what I want to see right now."

I just look at her and the tears start.

"I was really pumped about our summer. I just hate to think it's not going to happen. This was something I really needed."

GRACE

I call Mike with the bad news. One of the things I love about him is his eternal optimism. After he hears my tale of woe, he soon says, "Don't worry—we're going to get this taken care of. Your summer isn't over yet. Take out a bottle of wine, sit on the porch, enjoy the view, and I'll call you later."

Another thing I love about Mike is the fact that he knows a lot of people, has great connections (even in a town 80 miles away), and everyone definitely owes him a favor.

It takes a little while, but eventually he calls me back.

"I've got plumbers lined up first thing tomorrow morning."

What? An actual miracle has just taken place in Yankton, South Dakota? Thank you, Jesus!

"I also called your mom, to ask her if she had anyone looking after the place. She said she just had someone looking after the exterior, since she thought everything inside would be fine."

Well, how stupid of us kids to expect our 88-year-old mother to take care of this. What were we thinking?

"Sorry to say, you're going to be living in a construction zone for part of the summer, but it'll get done. I've got people."

Sounds a little like the mafia, but in a good way.

Like the good girls that we are, we obey our orders and Ellie and I take our bottle of Sauvignon Blanc out on the porch. We sit there and try to be the eternal optimists that we were trained to be. We rock on the porch swing that has been there since the cabin was built. It was actually inherited from our grandparents' front porch. It's a swing that got a lot of use from our entire family—grandma and grandpa, aunts and uncles, and lots of fun cousins. Ellie pushes the swing with her feet while my feet dangle. There's a bit of an inconvenience to being 5'3."

We reminisce about the swing, and especially about Grandma. I was the fortunate one to be named after her—Grace. Actually, both of our grandmas' names were Grace, but our maternal grandma was the really fun one. So even though as a kid I hated my name (it was an "old lady" name), now I love it. How I wish she was still around so I could tell her how honored I am by being named after her.

We then talk about Grandpa, who was a sweet, quiet guy.

I reminisce, "Remember him sitting in his recliner, chain-smoking cigarettes? It's kind of weird, since we are not a cigarette-smoking kind of family."

Ellie responds, "I think he picked it up in the war. I can remember sitting by him when we were just children, watching in fascination as the ash on his cigarette grew longer and longer. He'd always knock it into the ashtray just before it was going to fall. Impressive to a kid, I guess."

We continue on with great stories about our family and the fun times we've had at the cabin. It's therapeutic, and definitely takes our minds off the disaster waiting inside.

Our family is a little different in that none of us siblings look alike. We love to tease our mom about that.

"Really, Mom? Dad, the milkman, the postman, the next-door neighbor, *and* the ex-boyfriend?"

She absolutely hates that joke. We have dark brown hair, light brown hair, red hair, and blond hair. We also have a height difference going on. We run short, tall, short, tall, and short. Since I'm number three, I'm one of the short ones. Ellie is much taller than I am, and when we were kids it really ticked me off that everyone thought she was older than me. It was always, "little Gracie."

In first grade my teacher made us stop playing "Red Rover" on the playground, because I basically got strangled every time I tried to run through the line. Some of my classmates who loved to play the game thought that the punishment was way too harsh. "Just don't let little Gracie play" would've been their solution to the problem. Can't say as I blame them.

As we sit here, trying to enjoy the wine and the view and be positive about it, our minds are swirling with the state of the cabin. Do we just give up and go home? But we have such a great summer ahead of us! And Ellie really needs this! As we're sitting there, actually feeling a little sick to our stomachs, Ellie suddenly blurts out, "We need a plan!"

Oh my, I haven't heard those words in a while. We used to hear them all the time, when we spent a lot of time with Ellie and Will.

Even before he'd greet us with a hug or kiss, the first words out of his mouth were always, "What's the plan?"

I don't think dying of a heart attack on Main Street at the age of 55 was his great plan, but obviously it was God's.

CHAPTER 5

ELLIE

As we're sitting here watching the boats going by and trying to come up with a plan, something else comes into view. Or should I say, "someone."

We're both surprised to see a guy mowing our lawn. It's hot and sunny, his shirt is off, and he looks better than anyone should look while they're mowing. He looks to be in his late fifties, hair totally shaved, and guess what—he must not believe in sunscreen either! We just sit and watch him, and he doesn't see us through the screens. If we were polite we would've jumped up, introduced ourselves to him, and told him he didn't have to mow our lawn.

But we are relaxed, drinking our wine, and are busy trying to come up with "The Plan." Truthfully, it's just fun to watch him. After a good hour of watching him mow, he finishes and shuts the lawnmower off. That's about the time he realizes he has an audience.

We decide we're not totally rude and go down to the lawn to meet him. He introduces himself as Lucas, and says he's so happy to finally meet us. Wait, what? Well, it turns out he's the guy that Mom hired to take care of the lawn and beach, since he lives right next door. His cabin is right to the east of us, with our lawns, beaches and driveways adjoining. His place basically has the same look and feel as ours, just on a slightly smaller scale.

I proceed to thank him for all of the work he's done.

Lucas is very gracious and says, "It's no big deal. I've lived in my cabin for years. Mowing your mom's yard and raking her beach is just a continuation of mine, and makes my property look better."

I'm sure that's the truth. If Mom hadn't put any thought and work into this, our place would've been the haunted house of the neighborhood. We really failed mom miserably—why didn't we help her line this up, or at least ask her about it?

Lucas asks us, "I've been doing the upkeep on the outside, but I'm just curious to know who's been doing the upkeep on the inside."

Grace and I look at each other, mortified at what we have to say.

I just blurt it out, "No one."

Lucas raises an eyebrow but doesn't say a word. I start spewing words like a blubbering idiot,

"We didn't know nothing was being done or being looked after...it's a mess...I can't believe we didn't take care of it...we should've helped our mom...the ceiling is hanging, the sheetrock is falling, the place stinks like mold...it's a disaster..."

I just kind of trail off from there, with Lucas looking at us like *we're* a disaster.

He stares at us for a minute and eventually says, "Hmm. So...what's the plan?"

GRACE

As the old saying goes, you could've knocked us over with a feather. Ellie and I just look at each other, totally speechless.

Lucas says, "Well, should we go in and check out the damage?"

We let him lead the way, and he's the one that turns speechless when he sees the mess. Actually, now that we're seeing it for the second time and the shock factor is over, it's not quite as bad as it initially looked. Oh, believe me, it's still a mess and it'll be a lot of work, but like Mike said, "I have people."

The great room has taken the biggest hit. The bathrooms are right above it and that's where the major damage has taken place. The kitchen actually doesn't look too bad, and the half bath and mudroom are pretty much left unscathed. But the place just reeks. We're looking at mold remediation, a new ceiling, new sheetrock in numerous places, a complete paint job, a major cabinet cleaning or replacement, new furniture, and new flooring, because who wants carpet in a cabin?

So now our summer of lazy bliss has turned into a project.

Wait—a project? Who doesn't love a project more than Ellie and I do? We both have remodeled our houses so many times over and relished every minute of it. Our husbands, not so much. The wheels are turning in both of our heads. This is our time to shine!

We check out the upstairs. The bathrooms are total gut jobs—who did this plumbing in the first place? The bedrooms are fine. Check for mold and paint them. Get rid of the carpet—gross! Laminate flooring is the way to go in a cabin. Up to the attic. Absolutely no problems there, except do I see a little bat poop? That's definitely going to need to be checked out.

As Ellie and I chatter about this and that, come up with new ideas and reject other ones, Lucas just looks at us, a little stunned.

Eventually he says, "Well, I guess you have a plan."

CHAPTER 6

ELLIE

I must admit, hearing those words come out of someone else's mouth is a little unnerving, to say the least. But he's right—we do have a plan. Just not an immediate one—like, for instance, a plan for tonight. I think we would do fine to stay in the attic. Wash up some bedding and we're good to go. Grace thinks otherwise. She refuses to stay there until an exterminator has been there and declares it a "critter-free" zone. The reality is that we both could drive back to our homes. What's 80 miles? But now that we're here together, it feels like giving up if we go back home.

A hotel room in Yankton seems like our best bet. Two minutes later and we have the reservation. We say goodbye to Lucas, finish our wine, and drive into town. We visit a local

Mexican restaurant that has been here for years, and then call it a night. Or I do, and Grace sits up and reads for hours.

We're both pretty good at sleeping in. We inherited that trait from our mother. Now that she's in a retirement home she doesn't let herself sleep in longer than 8:30 AM. She thinks her neighbors would regard that as being lazy. Who cares? I'm not as good at it as I used to be. Probably a menopause thing. I still know that I'll never be a "rise and shine" kind of person. But Grace has got me beat, hands down. Her excuse is that she's a nurse and works the night shift, so she's a good daytime sleeper. The only problem is that she hasn't worked a full 12-hour night shift for years, but still can sleep in better than anyone. If she has to be anywhere before 10 AM, she has to set an alarm. This morning I'm awake at eight, and wait for Grace to finally get up.

She looks at me with one eye open and says, "What? It's not like we need to be anywhere."

She's right, but I do want to get to the cabin since the plumber is coming today. I just want to hear about the extent of the damage. We quickly eat the continental breakfast at the hotel and head out to the lake. We see Lucas in the water, for something we would call an early morning swim, even though it's almost 11 AM. We give him a wave and head in to see what the plumber has to say. We hear pretty much what we expected to hear. Toilets leaking, pipes burst, total floor rot underneath—no big surprise. The good news is that he could have it all fixed in two weeks, give or take. So far so good. Another truck drives up. Pest control.

I look at Grace. "When did you make that call?"

"I told Mike to put that at the top of the list. You know that's a deal breaker for me."

"And to be honest, it is for me too."

Grace's phone rings and it's Mike calling her with an update. A mold remediation crew is showing up tomorrow. They'll have to hang lots of plastic while they're working and then we'll have to stay out for a day. Once that's done, we can sleep in the attic. A construction crew will be showing up after that, and things will be taken care of. Then Grace and I can do the fun part–picking out colors, flooring, furniture, light fixtures. Umm, just wondering, who's paying for this? Time to give Mom a call.

CHAPTER 7

GRACE

"Hi Mom. I'm down at the cabin with Ellie."

This is spoken at a decibel level that can be heard throughout the entire lake region. Mom has state of the art hearing aids, but they seem pretty worthless over the phone. She does so much better face to face. I suspect there's a lot of lip reading going on. I explain to her the state of the cabin. She's shocked.

She says, "We were just there!"

Yeah, half a decade ago. I'm a little nervous to broach the subject of the cost of the repairs. Mike and I do okay financially, but we're not loaded. The looming retirement years make you look at your bank account a little differently than previously. And Ellie and I have talked and know that our siblings won't be ponying up for anything cabin related—they never go there. Ann is in Des Moines, Katie's in Phoenix, and Dan is in

Michigan. Can you blame them? Mom does fine financially, but she could live to 100 and assisted living doesn't come cheap. After trying to make small talk, I get up the nerve to tell her how much the repairs are going to cost. She asks me to repeat that. Uh oh, not a good sign. But then she goes on to pooh-pooh the whole thing, and tells me that Dad set up an account for the cabin and any repairs or updates it might need.

"We never used that money, and, come to think of it, the last time I looked at that account, it had grown to quite a tidy sum."

Ellie and I just look at each other and shrug. Really? We take care of all of her accounts--this one must've passed us by. She tells me to keep track of everything and she'll write a check at the end. Wow—one huge hurdle crossed!

Another question crosses my mind.

"Mom, did you hire Lucas to take care of the boat and jet skis also? We checked out the fuel gauges and it shows they're all full of gas. And we're not mechanics, but they look to be in pretty good shape."

"Oh yeah, that's been taken care of for years. But not by Lucas."

"What do you mean?"

"Before your dad died, he had a whole list of things that I needed to take care of and pay for. One of those things was writing a check to AMI, in May and September."

"What's AMI?"

"Andy's Marina Incorporated."

"What? I always thought that was some American mutual insurance thing. Mom, Ellie and I are your executors. Why didn't you tell us you were paying for the watercraft to be serviced and stored every year when we weren't using them?"

Mom gets a little cranky.

"Just a few comments here, Grace. First of all, you weren't our executors when Dad died. I was. He gave me strict instructions on all of the financial stuff, and I'm not an idiot. Second of all, we had a lot of money invested in the boat and jet skis, so I wasn't going to just let them sit there and rot. And third of all," and now I can hear a little humor creep into her voice, "aren't you glad that they were all gassed up and ready to go when you got there?"

I have to smile. "Thanks, Mom, you're the best. You're still really good at taking care of us. But from now on, let Ellie and me, or basically Mike, take care of it. One less thing for you to worry about, right?"

"I will gladly turn that over to you. I never liked being out on the water anyway."

No truer words were ever spoken.

I hang up and give Ellie the good news. And now that some worries are taken care of, we decide to do what we came here to do in the first place–lie in the sun. We take a look at the lawn chairs in the shed. They're dilapidated and full of spider webs. Way too gross for our liking. So instead we just grab our beach towels from our cars and lie on the beach like we did as kids. This is heaven. A rare cloudless sky, too early in the season for gnats and mosquitoes, a light breeze, and the sound of construction going on behind us. We could live without that last part. But even that's a good sound, because things are getting done.

Lucas gives a wave from next door, and we somewhat self-consciously suck in our stomachs. What are 60-year-olds doing in a two-piece swimsuit? Granted, they're definitely more matronly than what we used to wear, but still maybe not our best choice. Like most post-menopausal women, we've added some pounds over the last few years. I've gone from always wearing a small to having to bump up to—don't say it—a medium. Oh, the horrors! I keep vacillating between "so what, I'm 64 and who cares" to "oh my goodness, I can't believe I look like this and I have to go on a diet right now!"

It doesn't help that most of my calories come from wine and go straight to my stomach. Mike loves to tell people, "She eats like a bird but drinks like a fish." Ha ha—really funny.

Lucas saunters over and we make small talk. We get on to the important things, like are you single? As far as I'm concerned, that's really the only important thing, because it's time for my sister to find a man.

ELLIE

"Are you single?"

This comes from my sister who can make small talk with a fish, and this is what she comes up with? How embarrassing! There are other parts of the conversation, none of which I can seem to remember. But I do remember his answer to the single question, which was yes. Interesting.

To be honest, I think I've done a pretty darn good job of being a widow. I'm self-sufficient, I can make minor home repairs, I don't bug my kids about not coming to see me enough, I babysit the grandkids whenever I'm asked. I'm actually rocking it. But I'm lonely. Oh, so lonely. Thank goodness for Netflix, which has provided me endless friends over umpteen episodes and countless opportunities to cry over sad movies. So yes, to hear that the handsome guy from next door is single does raise my spirits just a little.

We also learn that he's basically retired after selling his car dealership, and likes to do handyman jobs in his spare time, just like Mike. Wow—a match made in heaven. Possibly I'm getting just a little ahead of myself.

Lucas says he needs to get back to his project (whatever that is), and we head back into town to shower, eat dinner at the other Mexican restaurant, and call it a night. Well, at least I do. My sister the night owl will watch TV and read and play games on her iPhone until she finally gives in to sleep. Then I'll have the joy of trying to get her lazy butt out of bed in the morning.

CHAPTER 8

GRACE

Ellie and I are big fans of the home decorating network. We've seen almost every show on that channel, but we're mostly interested in the ones where homes are getting remodeled. These people can make something awful into something really stunning. We go for the more modern, contemporary results, not so much the country, shabby-chic look. Even though we've spent hours watching these shows, we really just like the last ten minutes, when you see the spectacular results. I don't need to know about every pipe that burst or that the whole house needs rewiring, or worse yet, that you have mice in the walls. Just get to the good stuff.

And that's why I'm not going to bore anyone with the details of our remodeling project. The crews came–plumbers, carpenters, mold remediators, pest control, floor installers, painters, and more, and they did their various jobs. Ellie and I picked out stuff, and it's done.

We wanted to keep it light—no dark knotty pine for us. Light gray walls, white kitchen with quartz countertops, gas fireplace with white-washed shiplap running up to the ceiling, comfy furniture, seafoam and teal accents, beachy throw pillows and artwork. Laminate flooring, gray planks that look like worn beach-wood, which is exactly what I wanted. Laminate flooring sounds kind of cheap, but they've made that stuff look really nice. We can seat oodles of people in the great room with lots of leather seating and a big screen TV. It's still a cabin, we didn't pick out high end appliances or the most expensive furniture, but it's pretty impressive, if I do say so myself.

Ellie and I have done a lot of projects over the years, but this one was different in the fact that we hired professionals for the work that was done. I must say, working with all of these contractors did get a little stressful this past month, but it was a whole lot easier than doing all of the work ourselves. I think we're on to something here. Maybe the home decorating network will be calling us soon for our own remodeling show. It could be called "Trashed Cabins by Neglectful Daughters That Turn Out Okay." Okay, maybe not. But the best thing is, we still have two months of the summer left.

CHAPTER 9

ELLIE

Oh, to wake up in a glorious king-sized bed. The nice part about having a cabin full of mold is that we had to replace all of the mattresses, pillows, linens, towels. You name it, it's new. And it feels like heaven. We had a little discussion about who got the master suite. Grace was gracious (don't you love that) and decided since my life basically sucked the past few years, that I deserved the master suite. I didn't fight her on that.

Then she added, "And who knows...maybe Lucas will join you someday."

I stopped her right there. No use getting too far ahead of ourselves.

Now that the whole month of June was basically wasted with the remodel, July is here and we need to plan a big 4th of July celebration. Grace's daughter Emily was born on the 4th, so we've usually celebrated together as a family. We make our calls and find out who can come. Mike is coming for the weekend, and is bringing Mom along. She's excited to see the cabin. Emily and her family are coming too, so she can get as much attention as she can as the birthday girl. That was not kind–she's an amazing girl, funny as heck, has a wonderful husband and four great kids, and I love her to death. Grace's son and family can't make it–golfing plans with friends instead.

My daughter Abby and her husband Greg and two kids will be here. No big surprise since Abby and Emily are best friends and complete each other's sentences. My son and my other daughter, as well as their families, won't be able to make it–too many commitments on a long holiday weekend.

Once again, we're lying out on the beach and Lucas saunters over. We talk about our 4th of July plans.

"Why don't you plan on spending the day with us? We haven't been to Lewis and Clark Lake on the 4th for quite a few years, so it'll be fun. If you can put up with a bunch of kids."

"I have to tell you, holiday weekends on this lake have gone totally crazy. There are an incredible number of boats and jet skis out, and too many of those drivers have had way too much to drink. Basically, it's a recipe for disaster."

Okay, maybe boating won't be our first choice of activities. Instead I come up with the idea of the Anderson Olympics. Fun ideas like paddle board races, running races with flippers on, water balloon fights, bean bag tournaments, swimming races–basically anything that will keep the kids entertained enough to curtail any whining about the fact that we're not actually boating. If the weather doesn't cooperate, it'll be a cooped-up cabin of kids. Not good.

Time to plan the menu–it'll be the usual. Burgers, hotdogs, salads, chips, water-melon, birthday cake. Oh wait, they're all going to be here two days. Let's add some breakfast stuff, lunch stuff, snacks and food for another dinner. We start making lists on our phones and keep adding to them throughout the day. The list is growing by the hour.

We finish up the day with a glass of wine (huge surprise), watching a gorgeous sunset, and then a sappy movie, and hitting the sack on our super-comfy pillow top mattresses. All in all, a great day, just like we envisioned the whole summer to be.

CHAPTER 10

GRACE

Grocery day. What kind of a relaxing day is that? But we hit the store with our extensive list and try to make it somewhat fun. I'd much rather be lying out on the beach. We start out with one cart and I end up going back for another. Besides our list, Ellie keeps throwing in all of this "fun stuff." Fun stuff to her is different cheeses, crackers, meats, sushi, fruit, chips, dips, nuts, pizza ingredients (when did that turn up on the menu?).

As you might have guessed, Ellie is a great cook. She's adventurous, has great presentation, and truly enjoys it. Me, not so much. For one thing, I'm a picky eater. For another, I just don't think it's worth all the work. You spend hours preparing something that you can eat in ten minutes. The ironic thing is, my friends tell me that I'm a great cook. I just don't choose to do it very often.

Another thing about Ellie–she doesn't like using paper plates. And she doesn't even have a dishwasher in her home! Those are two things that would make my life miserable. It's bad enough having to cook all of this stuff, but to do dishes afterwards just adds insult to injury. Needless to say, I'm throwing a bunch of paper plates and plastic silverware into the cart, because I'm not doing dishes for a houseful of people on my vacation, even though we thankfully have a dishwasher.

Our next stop is the bakery to pick up the traditional red, white and blue birthday cake for Emily, chocolate of course. After that, it's time to drop a few hundred bucks at the fireworks store (and yes, fireworks have been legal in South Dakota for as long as I can remember). I remember throwing sparklers and firecrackers at each other when we were as young as five years old. Things must have been a little more relaxed in that day and age, or else our parents just really wanted us out of the house.

We get home, unload umpteen grocery bags, fill up two refrigerators and the entire pantry. By this time, the afternoon clouds have rolled in. What a bummer. If it rains this weekend, we are so screwed. But all is not lost. We raid the refrigerator and pantry and come up with a delicious supper. We spend the rest of the evening in front of the TV. Umpteen channels and nothing worth watching. Time for bed. Funny how being out in the sun and fresh air really does make you sleepy. Maybe I'll even get to sleep tonight without taking an Ambien.

In the morning, Mike shows up with Mom. She's amazed by the transformation of the cabin, as well she should be.

She keeps saying, "It looks so different!"

Well, that was kind of the point. I give Mike a hug and a kiss (it's really good to see him relaxed), and he brings Mom's bag up to her bedroom. She walks with a cane since her stroke two years ago. She can do stairs well if we just let her take her own pace. Ellie and I are so happy to have her here. The woman is a saint. Our dad was a little work-driven, to put it mildly. Between business during the day and client meetings at night, he was never home. Even though we thought we were model kids (perfectionism seemed to run in the family), I'm sure the five of us drove her crazy at times.

About the time we sit down on the porch to just sit and talk with Mom, up drives a Suburban with Emily, Chris and their four kids. They are so excited to be here, because to be honest with you, some of them are young enough that I don't think they really remember being here before.

The three boys and their younger sister come running up the steps yelling, "Grandma, Grandpa!"

They're still young enough to give us rib crunching hugs without embarrassment, even though the oldest two are teenagers. They proceed to check out the attic bunk room, and can't wait for their second cousins to arrive. That doesn't take long, and soon all of the kids have put on their swimsuits and are jumping off the dock. Nothing like water to entertain kids.

We women sit out on the porch with Mom. Abby and Emily are so good with their grandma, and Ellie and I just enjoy listening to their conversation. Mike checks out the construction to make sure it was done to his standards. Most of it passes his inspection.

The afternoon passes with lots of swimming and snacks. Grandpa Mike takes the boat out and gives one tube ride after another. One of the things that makes it interesting is that Lucas asks to join him. Ellie and I smile at that.

I make the kids happy by giving them jet ski rides. Actually, they're the ones doing the driving, and I just laugh while I hang on to the strap and hope I don't fall off. But of everyone there, there is no one that loves jet-skiing like my oldest grandson Caleb and I do. We have two jet-skies and Caleb is old enough to drive one by himself. We catch a sweet boat wake that is just perfect. We spend a really fun time criss-crossing the wake, both of us getting air-born over every wake jump.

"Caleb, that is literally the most fun I've had this whole summer!"

He totally agrees. But eventually the boat goes in to shore (bummer), so Caleb and I head in too. Pretty soon Ellie goes into hostess mode, and brings out the hors d'oeuvres and cocktails. Mom accepts one glass of white wine, her limit for the next week or so.

When we were growing up our parents never had one drop of alcohol in the house, except for some horrendous cough syrup concoction that our pediatrician prescribed when I had a bad cough for weeks.

I ask Mom, "Do you remember that cough syrup you made for me as a kid? It was made up of equal parts of honey, lemon juice, and whiskey. It was awful! I used to run and hide from you so you couldn't give it to me. That guy should've been disbarred! I was eight years old!

Mom laughs. "We couldn't get by with that in this day and age. I remember he told me that if the concoction didn't help your cough, that Dad and I could drink the whiskey straight so at least we could get some sleep. By the way, we didn't do that."

The rest of the evening is spent stuffing ourselves over dinner (that's where the pizza ingredients come in handy), watching the kids play outside, and trying to get the kids settled down in the bunkroom after being revved up all day. All in all, a great day. Not relaxing, but still, summer at its best.

The next morning we wake up to July 4. Super sunny, just a little muggy, with a forecast of a gorgeous day, highs in the upper 80's. Mike and Ellie are already up and at it—making breakfast for the whole crew. Emily comes stumbling down the steps a few minutes after I do.

"Happy birthday!" we all yell.

That wakes her up a little. She loves her birthday more than anyone else loves theirs. Her kids give her their homemade cards and gifts, and they and their dad smother her with hugs and kisses. A good start to the morning.

Mike and Ellie are in their element. Drinking coffee with mom and hauling stuff out of the fridge. They love making breakfast, eating breakfast, anything associated with breakfast. Basically Emily and I hate breakfast. We don't like eating in the morning, eggs make us nauseous, and the cleanup with all of those pans and griddles is so not worth the fuss. But it's a fun time and everyone is in a great mood. The kids are dying to go swimming and are out on the lake the second breakfast is done.

CHAPTER 11

ELLIE

Other than Christmas, the 4th of July is the best holiday of the year. Having family together, being out in the sunshine, swimming in the lake, and of course, the fireworks. I love fireworks. Actually, our whole family does. Some people can take it or leave it, but not the Andersons.

The day will be awesome. It's already started out really fun. Making a big breakfast for a big family with a guy in the kitchen is my kind of morning. Even if the guy is my brother-in-law. We've got things all cleaned up (I even allowed paper plates) and go sit out on the beach, waiting for the parade to start.

Yankton does make a big deal of the Fourth. They have a 5K run and half-marathon at 7 AM. I don't know who would ruin a perfectly good holiday by getting up early and running, but to each their own. Sounds like absolute torture to me. The boat parade starts at 10 AM. It's kind of hokey with people decorating their boats with streamers, balloons, and flags, but it just gives you that "feel good" feeling, you know?

After the parade is done, it's time for the Anderson Olympics, a new, hopefully annual, event. We pick teams and find we're minus one person. Duh. You'd think by now I'd be used to being the fifth wheel, but it always catches me off-guard. Grace tells me to run over to Lucas' cabin and ask him to be my plus-one. I hesitate a minute and then decide, what the heck, and run over to ask him. Being the nice guy he is, he agrees. I think he was secretly watching us out of his window.

"Let the Olympics begin!"

We let the kids light sparklers in place of an Olympic torch, which they all think is quite exciting. We set up the obstacle course for the flipper races, race paddleboards out to the buoys and back, see who can shoot Silly String the farthest, and play a bean-bag tournament. Some of the kids wanted to do a jet ski race but we decided that was a little much. The teams are neck and neck, but a winning team is declared and Mom gets to present them with a trophy that we found at Goodwill. Mike had taken the grandkids to Goodwill one afternoon for that purpose. Naturally they picked out the biggest and gaudiest trophy they could find. The older kids and Grandpa Mike decorated it with "Anderson Family Olympics" and any other idea they could come up with. It'll be a traveling trophy, and the kids are fighting to see who gets to take it home with them. The parents aren't quite as excited.

We spend the rest of the afternoon swimming and just hanging out. We grill hotdogs and burgers for dinner, with six ravenous kids. We light the candles on Emily's birthday cake, throwing on some sparklers for good measure, and have that for dessert. After that, the kids get to light off the fireworks we bought, with Mike lighting the big ones. Lucas seems to be enjoying himself, but is a little quiet. But what do I know? We haven't spent that much time together.

Finally it's close to ten o'clock, the best part of the 4th. We haul out a pile of blankets, because the best way to watch fireworks is lying flat on your back. We spray a little bug spray around and lay all the blankets on the grass. Everyone finds their spot, except Lucas, who's just sitting on the edge of a blanket near me.

I smile at him. "You know you have to join us in this, right?"

He nods and lowers himself on his back next to me. He puts his hands behind his head and settles in.

The fireworks start with a big bang. Let me clarify—I mean the actual fireworks shooting up above us. The kids ooh and aah, and yell if it's an exceptionally loud bang. My granddaughter Brooke snuggles up to me and that makes my day. But then on my other side, I feel a hand reaching out to mine, and that really makes my night.

GRACE

Another big breakfast is in progress as I make my way downstairs. Seriously, two mornings in a row? Could we just throw some cereal at the kids and call it good? Everyone is in the post-holiday mode. Kind of grouchy, kind of sad, a little tired. Mom decides to ride back to Sioux Falls with the kids, because surprisingly, Mike has decided to stay another day. Big hugs and kisses as everyone leaves, and then, amazingly, peace and quiet.

Putting our feet up on the porch, Ellie announces it's time for mimosas. Who are we to argue? Mike yells at Lucas to come over. As we're sitting there drinking our mimosas (who are we kidding–it's champagne with some orange juice for coloring), I can't help but think it just feels right to be sitting as a foursome again. It's been too long.

It's one of those totally lazy days. We don't do much, and that's okay. But it feels comfortable. I'm so glad we're here.

It's about five o'clock, and if we don't put some food in our stomachs soon, it's not going to be pretty for any of us. Lucas suggests a shrimp boil–have we ever done it? No, but it sounds really good.

"I've got the boiling pot and all of the ingredients. Get cleaned up and come on over. It's going to be fun."

As we head on over, I just can't help but feel this is the perfect way to end the weekend. Mike and I are together, and Ellie doesn't have to cook. And it is fun.

Lucas starts by bringing the water in the pot to boiling, and then throwing in some potatoes and onions with Cajun seasoning. A little later he adds different kinds of sausage, later still some corn on the cob, and finally, some crab legs and shrimp. He's got a tablecloth thrown over his picnic table and proceeds to throw the whole pot of food on it.

He drizzles melted butter over everything, gives us each a fork, and says, "Have at it."

Delicious! Not only does it taste great, but it took a little time while we just sat and talked. He got to know us, and we kind of got to know him. He's really a nice guy, but not a big sharer. But that's okay—it just takes time.

CHAPTER 12

ELLIE

What a weekend. It absolutely could not have gone any better. Is it the sunshine that's making me so happy, or is it more? Too soon to tell.

Mike has to leave this morning. He thinks we should go out for breakfast before he leaves, and proceeds to go upstairs to wake up Grace. Grumpy Grace comes down 15 minutes later.

"What—it's not enough that you made breakfast two days in a row? Now we have to go out for breakfast?"

Mike's playing a dangerous game. Waking Grace up early and making her eat breakfast is not a smart move. I just smile.

"I'm going to go over and see if Lucas wants to go along."

I can't believe I'm saying that but yet it feels good.

We take two vehicles so Mike can head for home after we're done and the three of us can go back to the lake. Grace and I order light—we're going to be huge if we keep eating like this—and the guys order the "big man's breakfast." Who named it that on the menu and why are guys proud of ordering it? It comes time to pay at the counter, and of course everyone wants to pay for everything and nobody will let anyone do it. Mike and Lucas go to the counter to split the bill.

Before I explain what the girl at the cash register says, I guess I should explain that basically Mike and Lucas look very similar. They're both very tall, bald (or I guess it would be more complimentary to say that they shave their heads), and are 100% Dutch. They look more like brothers than Grace and I look like sisters. We came to find out yesterday that Lucas is a little older than we thought, and he and Mike are only two years apart in age. They're ready to pay the bill and the girl says, "Are you guys brothers?"

Without missing a beat, Lucas says, "No, he's my dad."

We all burst out laughing, and we leave the girl trying to figure it all out.

The next few days are spent doing what we expected when the summer began. Basically doing nothing besides sunning and reading. We're very gifted at that. Everyone has to have a talent, you know.

CHAPTER 13

GRACE

In the middle of feeling very complacent, lazy, and loving every minute of it, I get a phone call from Emily.

"Mom, Abby and I were just talking about how much fun we had last weekend. It was so awesome! It was so relaxing, the cabin looks amazing, and would you mind if we invited two others couples to come up with Chris and me, and Abby and Greg this weekend? No kids, just an adult weekend away. Everyone thinks we have the greatest moms and would love to spend time with you."

Yeah, right. A weekend in a newly remodeled lakeside cabin is appealing even if there are two old mothers thrown in with the deal. But they're smart enough that they can see some advantages in that, in that one mother likes to cook, and the other mother is a pretty fun hostess, if I do say so myself.

"Well, of course. Let me talk to Ellie, but I'm sure it'll be fine."

Ellie and I just look at each other and shrug our shoulders. Summer sisters will do anything for their kids.

Friday arrives and so do the couples. At least it's in the evening so we don't have to cook dinner. Emily and Abby are both in their element. They are fun-loving, witty, and pretty darn cute. They'll enjoy being the hostesses this weekend. And the feeling will be mutual—these couples love to hang with them.

What wonderful daughters Ellie and I have raised. Both of them are talented, hard-working, have great husbands, and are super-moms. Abby looks exactly like Ellie looked 25 years ago—tall with dark hair and striking eyes.

People say Emily and I are exactly alike. I don't see it—maybe the fact that she's blond and about eight inches taller than me might have something to do with it. But there must be something there. Her friend Janna has even taken to calling us Emily Junior and Emily Senior.

We love the fact that the two of them are great friends. They're so much alike in personality. As much as Ellie and I are "summer sisters," they are most definitely "summer cousins." They love the beach and all that goes with it as much as we do.

In come the four couples, bringing in enough luggage, food and wine that you'd think they were staying a week. I've met the other couples before—Ryan and Kristie, Ethan and Janna. Nice people. I had forgotten that Kristie is pregnant.

"No wine for me!" she exclaims.

I ask her when her due date is and she tells me it's in two weeks.

"One last hurrah before this baby is born!"

We give them the tour and Ellie and I say goodnight. They're old enough to be on their own.

Morning comes and even though Ellie and I both know that Emily and Abby are great hostesses, we feel like we have to do a little hostessing ourselves. No big breakfast, thank goodness. The kids brought bagels, fruit, granola and yogurt. My kind of breakfast, if I ever ate one. We do make our famous mimosas and everyone loves them, except for poor Kristie, who's not allowed to have one. Bummer for her.

From then on they're on their own. Boating, jet-skiing, swimming. They can do whatever they want. In the meantime Ellie and I lie on the beach. And then Lucas walks over.

The three of us sit there, making small talk. I get up and give them the excuse that I'm going to give Mike a call, which I do. He's working on a new deck in our backyard, which is a huge project. Most of our house remodeling projects are my idea, but this one is totally his. He tells me that he's gotten lots done today—something about braces, or trusses, or floor joists, whatever—this whole project has been hard for me to envision. It's going to be amazing, but the scope of this project overwhelms me.

He tells me, "I should probably tell you that I'm fine."

"What does that mean?" I ask.

"Well, yesterday I fell down the hill into the gully and cut up my leg. But it's fine—no stitches needed."

"Is this really worth it?" I ask him.

It doesn't help that this has been one of our hottest summers on record. Great when you're sitting by a lake, but not so great when you're doing physical labor.

Jan Dirksen

ELLIE

Okay, here's something that hasn't happened in 40 years—someone asks me for a date. Naturally, that someone is Lucas. Once Grace leaves to go and call Mike (a little obvious, I think), the two of us are actually pretty relaxed with each other. We chat about the weather, the cabin, my kids, the local news, the national news. Wow, we're really getting somewhere.

Finally he blurts out, "Do you want to go out for dinner tonight? Maybe Murdos?"

I'm familiar with it, and it's a fun place. Nothing fancy, but it has the best fried walleye ever. Plus it has a nice patio that has a great view of the river. For those of you who are into history, the Gavins Point Dam was built in 1957. It holds back the water to make the Lewis and Clark Lake to the west of it (upriver), where our cabin is situated, and below the dam, to the east, the Missouri river continues. Picture the Hoover Dam in your minds, but on a much smaller scale. Murdos is located on the river below the dam, so envision slow moving water, paddleboards, kayaks, and fishing boats. Really pretty and calming.

On another note, our kids and grandkids have never been allowed to say the word damn, so they have gotten years of howling laughter by talking about the dam road, the dam fireworks, the dam resort, the dam campground, the dam ice cream shop. The possibilities are endless.

I get ready by not overdoing it, and just do some low-key makeup and a nice sundress. I come down the stairs and Abby gives me a look. Not a bad look, but a "I'm happy for you and have a good time" look. That's one hurdle conquered. Hopefully her brother and sister will feel the same.

Lucas shows up at the door about the same time and we're on the road. Time will tell.

CHAPTER 14

GRACE

You can tell the couples are having a great time. Lots of laughing, lots of storytelling. Abby and Emily fix a huge meal with Chris and Greg doing the grilling, and they all hang out on the porch. They certainly don't need an old lady hovering, even though they're all very complimentary and beg me to stay. Nice kids. I say my goodnights and make my way upstairs. Ellie still isn't home—way to go, Ellie!

I have just fallen asleep when Emily comes bounding into my room. "Mom, Kristie's water just broke."

My first stupid thought is "thank goodness for laminate floors," and then I'm fully awake and run downstairs with Emily.

Kristie is standing in the kitchen, in a puddle of fluid. I've been a labor and delivery nurse for 30 years, and I know the signs. There are true signs, and then there are those that are so ridiculous they're laughable, I once had a patient come in who thought her water had broken.

I always say, "Tell me the story."

She went on to say that while she was taking a bath, she suddenly felt "extra wetness."

I tried to keep a straight face.

I said, "While you were sitting in a tubful of water you felt extra wetness?"

Then I asked her if she'd had any leaking since then and she said no, only while sitting in the tub. I kid you not—I can't make this stuff up. Being the nice person that I am, I tell her that it was great she came in to get checked out, no she doesn't need to be embarrassed, come in anytime (even though she's been here six times already), while in my head I'm screaming, "*Are you kidding me*?"

Needless to say, I sent her home 30 minutes later.

Well, Kristie has the true deal. I know what amniotic fluid looks like, and I know what it smells like. I know that Kristie has two other children (in fact, I was her nurse at one of her deliveries, and her second labor went pretty quickly). She's leaning over the countertop, moaning with a contraction. Truthfully, she's more than moaning. She's in "full-on" screeching mode and screams, "the baby is coming."

I yell at Emily, "Let's get her upstairs."

Ryan is trying to help (basically he's worthless) as we try and help Kristie up the stairs. We bring her into the master suite.

Emily cries, "Mom, we can't let her deliver in Ellie's bed. She'll destroy the mattress."

"We're not putting her in the bed, we're putting her in the walk-in shower. We can wash most of the mess down the drain when we're done."

For any of you that don't know a Labor and Delivery nurse, let me tell you that we thrive on adrenalin. Give us a three-day induction and we're bored to tears. Give us a C-section, and you spend the whole time worrying that you're breaking the sterile field. But give us a fifth-time mom who comes up screaming and tells us the baby is coming, we're all over it. We strip off her clothes, throw her on the bed, check her to see if she's crowning, and if she is, we call the doctor. But in our hearts, we kind of hope the doctor doesn't make it because we love delivering the baby ourselves. The fact of the matter is that usually those deliveries are super easy with no complications. But I can brag about the fact that one time a baby was crowning, the cord was tight around the neck twice, I had to clamp it, cut it, unwind it from around the neck, and then delivered a screaming, healthy baby. We love our stories.

I tell Chris to call 911 as we make our way into the shower. Emily throws in some of our nice new, white, fluffy towels to give Kristie something comfortable on which to lie back on or sit. Those things will be going in the trash once this event is over. Emily is a nurse also but works in the ICU, and those ICU nurses hate OB. Kristie is screaming, I tell her to stop. Chris pops his head in and informs me that he's boiling some water. Not always sure why that's such a big deal in the movies, but whatever works to give people something to do I guess is a good thing. I tell Kristie to give me a push. Instantly I see a headful of black hair, and in one push it's over. Out comes a pink, healthy-looking baby boy that starts crying immediately. I tell Emily to see what time it is (that'll have to go on the birth certificate). I tell her to grab some dental floss and a scissors. Not ideal, but it's the best we have at the moment. I tie the cord in two places and I let Ryan cut the cord in between those ties.

Like I said, these fast deliveries almost always go well. Ryan is overwhelmed, and immediately all of us start crying. Even though the odds were good that this was going to have a happy ending, many times it doesn't. I put the baby up on Kristie's chest and we're all in awe. It never gets old.

A few minutes later the placenta comes out with a gush of blood. For being a nurse, Emily looks a little squeamish.

I just look her and say, "Aren't you glad we put her in the shower?"

CHAPTER 15

ELLIE

We're in Lucas' Jeep, with the top down, enjoying the five-mile ride to Murdo's. Fortunately it's not a fancy place, because the ride does havoc to my hair. I finally give up and just pull it back into a scrunchy. Casual's good, right? We walk into Murdo's, and everyone calls Lucas by name. I remember this place well, but haven't been here in ages so nobody recognizes me.

Behind the bar, Ron calls to Lucas, "I saved your favorite patio table."

Lucas must've called ahead, which impresses me. We make our way out onto the patio. The place is packed, except the last table on the end is empty. Lucas must enjoy a little solitude when he's here.

It's a perfect night for this. Still a little warm, plenty of sunshine, a nice breeze, no bugs yet. We order drinks—tap beer for Lucas, and a nice chilled rose' for me. Talk is easy and relaxed. We order—shrimp quesadillas for me, and the walleye basket for Lucas. Sounds a little fishy, but our meals are served quickly and are excellent.

We continue to talk as our second round of drinks are served. Nothing deep or earth-shattering. We discover we both absolutely love watching NFL games. His favorite team: the San Francisco 49'ers. Mine: the Kansas City Chiefs. We can both live with each other's favorites. They're not teams that either one of us have hated in the past. Now if he was a Green Bay Packer's fan, that might've been tough to take.

He asks me about the kids and grandkids, trying to figure out who's who.

"I know you're a widow. Do you want to talk about it?"

"Not really tonight," I tell him, "but sometime soon."

For some reason he offers up absolutely zero information about himself and his family. It takes me a little while, but I finally dare to ask him.

"What about your family?"

"My parents are elderly and live in a nursing home here in town. I have two sisters who both live out west."

That's it. Riveting conversation. No mention of an ex-wife, kids, hot love affair—absolutely nothing. I don't press the issue. But other than his lack of details of his life, we have a fun time talking and getting to know each other. Finally he asks if we should head back. We drive back to his cabin, and we can hear that there's a lot of fun going on next door. Good for the kids!

We sit on the couch, scrolling through the TV channels together, trying to find something decent on. No such luck. Too early for preseason football. Who needs TV, we decide, and go sit out on his deck. The perfect evening continues, and we sit side by side as we await the sunset. You can tell it's going to be a good one. To make a good sunset it takes just the right amount of horizontal and interestingly-shaped clouds, and since it takes place over the lake, it'll be even be better yet. We've got all of that going on tonight, so it'll be worth waiting for.

And we were right. It's funny how you sit there waiting for the sun to set. It seems to take forever, and then boom, it's falling faster than a rock. Tonight the sunset rivals anything the tropical islands have to offer. We're sitting on his wicker couch together, and it just feels so right, you know? No conversation needed, just comfortableness. I haven't felt this comfortable with anyone since Will died, and it makes me feel almost giddy, as I'm trying to sit there quietly and just absorb the sensation.

Until we hear the ambulance siren. It keeps coming closer and closer, and we're both amazed when it pulls up on our shared driveway. What in the world is going on? We see paramedics rush out with their stretcher (don't ever call them ambulance drivers—I learned that from Mike) and run into the cabin next door. Our cabin!

GRACE

Chris yells upstairs, "The paramedics are here!" He sends them on up the stairs.

Kristie is cuddling the baby and Ryan is still in a state of shock. We wrap her up in some blankets and the paramedics get her situated on the stretcher.

As they're carrying her down the steps, Ellie and Lucas come racing in the front door, as Ellie is shouting, "What in the world is going on here?"

They take one look at Kristie and the baby on the stretcher and figure it out pretty darn fast. Abby fills them in on a few details. The paramedics stop for a few minutes so everyone can ooh and aah over the baby. Ethan and Janna are so bummed.

"I had my kids by C-section so I would've loved to have watched the delivery."

"We'll save that for next time," I tell them.

Even though so many people think it's great, I've never felt comfortable with the fact that deliveries have turned into a spectator sport.

Someone cleaned up the big wet spot on the kitchen floor and we all gather around the island, just to get over our shell-shock. I'm really okay with how the whole thing went down, but it is a little sobering when you know you're the one in charge and a life could be hanging in the balance.

But as they say, "All's well that ends well." Other than the fact that this baby was born on a shower floor, without a doctor present, and not in a hospital, it ended as well as it could have. And he's perfect! That's really all that we could ask for—to have a healthy mom and baby.

Once the adrenalin wears off, I'm more than ready for bed. Ellie walks Lucas out. Quite the end to that date. Hopefully it's a "first date" story that we'll hear for years. The kids are all still quite pumped—it'll be a while before that group settles down. They're on their own.

ELLIE

The couples are up on time, hanging around in the kitchen and snarfing up whatever food they can find. Surprisingly, none of them look the worse for wear. The excitement of the events of the previous night must have been more enthralling than drinking too much alcohol. Their plan is to get packed up and take off to the hospital to see baby Max (how cute), and of course Kristie and Ryan. These women are going to have the best story to tell to all of the other moms once school starts. They'll get their story straight, embellish it a lot, and will be the envy of everyone else who doesn't have an exciting summer story to tell.

Grace and I decide it's time to give this place a cleaning. Starting in the kitchen, we do the dishes, wipe the counters, mop the floor (a must), and then head on to the bathrooms. Next it's time to launder sheets and towels. Like Grace said, the towels from the delivery are going in the trash. White towels saturated with blood are never going to come clean. I must say, I'm so glad Grace put Kristie in the shower instead of in my bed. Just the thought of it is so gross.

While I'm cleaning, thoughts of last night keep running through my head. The Jeep ride, the quiet table on the restaurant patio, the sunset, the easy conversation. If the birthing debacle hadn't put an abrupt end to our evening, would he have kissed me? I'd like to think so. It's just something fun to think about. And it's been a long, long time since I've even remotely thought about something like that.

CHAPTER 16

GRACE

The next days pass exactly as planned. On some of the mornings we take a paddleboard ride, other mornings a jet-ski ride. After a light lunch, we usually either lie on the beach, or if it's too hot, paddle around on the air mattresses just to cool off. It's been a typical July in South Dakota—sunny, 90's, muggy, some days windier than others. We buy or rent books on our book readers and then trade them with each other. Nothing too heavy—a lot of fun summer beach reads with some murder mysteries thrown in for variety.

Mike gives me a call and says he's starting his four days off on Thursday, and for once he's actually going to take those days off and not do any handyman jobs this week. He must really miss me! The feeling's mutual.

We see Lucas come and go, usually with his pickup loaded with tools. Most evenings he comes over and sits with us on the front porch for happy hour. Sometimes he stays for supper, other nights he just heads on home and we don't see him until the next day. I love watching him and Ellie make conversation, joke around with each other, giving each other playful jabs. I would love to record all of this on my phone and send it to Emily and Abby, but I guess that wouldn't be appropriate. But it's so tempting!

As promised, Mike shows up on Thursday. He was up most of the night at the fire department, but heaven forbid he would take a nap. We ride the jet-skies together, and then spend the afternoon lying out on the air mattresses. Ellie has decided we need to have a big supper tonight, so she's gone to town to get groceries. Lucas comes home and decides to join us in the water. It's hot! Oh wait, I meant the temperature. But if Ellie was here, she'd think it was hot too.

Ellie arrives home with more bags of groceries than anyone should ever need. I run to help her carry them all in, and ask her what's on the menu. Chicken marinated in olive oil, soy sauce, and red wine vinegar; twice baked potatoes, asparagus, French bread with an olive oil and garlic dipping sauce, and Caesar salad. For appetizers, bruschetta with tomatoes and basil, and a crab dip with assorted crackers. Accompanied by a crisp Sauvignon Blanc or a chilled fruity Rose.' Really, who talks like this? I would've said chicken, potatoes, a vegetable and salad. I can tell this is going to be Ellie at her finest.

Since it is going to be an Ellie meal, I go out to the lake to talk to the guys. I inform Lucas that he better be planning on staying for dinner, or else we're going to have a lot of food that won't truly be appreciated. Lucas readily agrees. Oh, big surprise!

The meal is delightful, as Ellie always says. I think that is a word that has never come out of my mouth. And even though I think my family is delightful, and that our mom is delightful, I know that none of us have ever called anything that.

"The chicken is delightful, the bread and oil are decadent, and the wine has a wonderful bouquet."

Mike just says, "Yeah, it's all really good."

Kind of my thought.

The guys switch to bourbon, and Ellie and I stick with the wine with a wonderful bouquet, and we all bring our glasses out to the porch. It's still a little warm and muggy out, but no one can stand the heat like the Anderson girls. We turn on the ceiling fan for the guys' sake. The conversation is fun and easy. The guys seem to get along well, and if there is a lull in the conversation, Ellie and I quickly make up for that. We don't do the silence thing well. Definitely not introverts.

My chair is situated so that it puts Lucas' cabin in my direct line of vision. All of a sudden I get an inspiration.

"You know what you need by your deck, Lucas? A tiki bar!"

Ellie jumps on the bandwagon. "You are absolutely right! The vibe would be perfect, it's close to the beach, and think of the parties you could host there!"

My thought immediately after that is that we don't know if Lucas is a "party-hosting" kind of guy, but it's still a great idea. Ellie and I start throwing ideas around--what would look really cool and what wouldn't, and as we get more excited, both Lucas and Mike start to warm to the idea also.

ELLIE

Last night was fun! The meal was delightful, if I do say so myself. And what happened afterwards, well, that's Grace and me at our finest. It kind of bugs me that Grace was the one to come up with the original idea, but once the two of us got on a roll, the ideas came fast and fierce.

"Do we make it look like a tiki bar, with bamboo on the sides, and a grass roof, or do we make it look more like a jerk chicken shack, with corrugated tin on the sides and a metal roof?"

Lucas and Mike have gotten caught up in the idea and the different options. With both of their construction knowledge, at this point we'll let them decide on the building options and we'll decide on the finishing touches. Mike is pretty excited about the whole thing. God knows he wouldn't have been able to sit around for four days. But ultimately it's Lucas' decision. We all tell him that we're not pushing him into anything, and he just gives us this happy look.

"Let's do it!"

They start drawing up plans, go over to measure things out, and come up with a material list. Bright and early the next morning, they're at the home improvement store picking up all of the lumber, nails, screws, tin, siding, metal roofing—whatever goes into the makings of a Jamaican jerk chicken shack. It'll have a cement countertop with a canteen window (a huge piece of wood that encloses the front of the bar, but then lifts up and hooks up above, so that the whole side of the shed is opened up). It'll be big enough to hold a refrigerator, a gas grill, an icemaker, and plenty of outlets for blenders, griddles–any electric appliance you can think of.

The guys are pumped, for a few hours anyway. Like I've said before, July can be a scorcher, and of course this day is the hottest day of the year yet. The temperature has reached 95 degrees, with a heat index of 103. If you don't know what a heat index is, it basically means that the humidity is so high that it makes being outdoors beyond miserable. Grace and I try to keep them pumped up by bringing them lots of sports drinks and basically trying to be the cheerleaders that we grew up being. By four in the afternoon, we tell them to call it a day. It doesn't take much to talk them into quitting. We go into the cabin, because not even the porch will work for today. They need air conditioning, and they need it now.

Once they have a chance to get rehydrated with plenty of water and sports drinks, and their nausea and heat exhaustion have calmed down to an "I can live with this" feeling, we sit and relax and try to come up with something for supper that sounds remotely appetizing to them. They both just sit there in a stupor.

"Do you have any fruit, and any leftovers from last night?"

You bet. You ask, we deliver!

We haul anything out of the fridge that might look remotely edible, and let them have at it. They get their second wind, and end up demolishing a lot of food. Did it have the four basic food groups? Don't know, don't care. We sit down to watch a little TV, and within twenty minutes both guys are snoring. Grace and Mike are cuddled up on one sofa. I think that looks pretty good, so I sidle up to Lucas on the other sofa, as he continues to snore. I take his hand, and relax into him. This feels so nice.

CHAPTER 17

GRACE

I hear Mike get out of bed. Oh man, it's way too early! I just want to sleep for a few more hours. But I know I have to be supportive, since he and Lucas are doing all of the work and all I had to do was come up with the idea. Ask Mike—this has been the story of our marriage.

Our marriage—unbelievable to say that we've been married almost 45 years. How did that happen? When I think of all of the people at our wedding ceremony, when the two of us were at the ripe old age of 19, did any of them think we were going to make it? I don't know, but I can tell you this—I did. I believed that with all of my heart.

We were brought up in a very religious family. We went to church twice on Sunday and went to a private Christian school. That might sound restrictive to people, but I just felt every day that we were blessed. Blessed by God and the faith our family shared. I still feel that to this day.

Mike and I had an interesting start. When my dad decided that Sioux Falls was the place to grow his business, I was not a happy camper. It was the summer before my senior year of high school. Who has to move before their last year of high school? My thought was, certainly not me! There were tears, begging, cajoling, pleading, praying that I wouldn't have to move. Dad and Mom were adamant—you're coming with us. Do you know what really made a sad story even more pathetic? We moved on August 1—*my birthday*! I must say that my mojo as a summer girl that summer was seriously lacking.

A week later, I'm introduced to Mike at a softball game by a girl that I met at church. I come to find out that he lives right across the street from me. A few days later he asks me out. The date is not earth-shattering. Do you know how hard it is to make conversation with someone when you don't know one single person he knows and you have absolutely nothing in common? And the guy is kind of shy and quiet?

But here's the thing. He's the nicest guy. Why would I turn someone down for a second date just because the first one didn't rock my world? That's the difference between me and my sister Katie. If she went on a date with a guy and she didn't fall madly in love, it was over. I never got it.

"You have to give it time," I would say.

Her response would be, "Life is too short. I'm not going to waste it on a guy that isn't 'the one.'"

Well, how can you tell he's the one if you only spent two hours with him?

I gave Mike a chance and it was the best decision of my life. Probably the worst decision of my life was the fact that we got married in January. People are amazed when they hear that a summer girl like me got married in the winter. What were you thinking? I guess we just didn't feel like waiting until summer. Looking back, we were young and stupid and a four-month engagement seemed perfect at the time.

And truly, it was perfect. Oh, not the January wedding—that was a disaster. We had an ice/snowstorm the day before, and the temperature didn't get above zero that day. A lot of people couldn't make it to the wedding due to the weather. That was a little bit sad for us, but in hindsight, it didn't really matter. Back in those days you rented the church, you rented the reception hall, you had ham buns, potato chips, and wedding cake, and it was a done deal. No big drama and the best part, no big bills.

Mike frequently says that that whole day was one big blur for him. He said he had no idea what he was doing, why he was doing it, and how did I talk him into it? Well, he does tell me that the fact that I'm a master manipulator might've had something to do with it. Who, me?

As I lie here reminiscing, under the comforter with a box fan running for white noise, I do feel pretty blessed.

CHAPTER 18

ELLIE

The guys are sitting at the island, drinking coffee, when Grace comes stumbling down the steps.

"Morning," she mumbles.

We all laugh. Even Lucas has come to know that "early morning Grace" is something you put up with for an hour or two until she becomes "now this is the Grace we know and love!" Too bad the woman hates coffee. She could use a little morning "pick-me-up."

I'm busy making my famous egg sandwiches. English muffins, ham, bacon, eggs, cheese. Everyone else calls them by a famous name, but since I'm sure that name is copyrighted, we won't go there. The guys and I go through a pot and a half of coffee until they finally stand up, stretch, and decide it's time to get to it. Neither one seems overly energetic at the moment, but they'll hit their stride soon enough.

The oven blast hits us as soon as we step outside. Wow, it's a hot and muggy one today. The Weather Channel tells us it's going to be the hottest day of the year so far. The guys are moaning.

"Let's just finish this project this fall," is their first thought.

But they're big, rugged guys, and a little heat is not going to do them in. Hopefully!

They get the shack framed up. It's going to be so cool—the perfect entertaining spot. Right now Mike and Lucas are working on the south side of the shack, so the sun is beating down on them mercilessly. It's about one o'clock and we order them to come in and cool off. It doesn't take much convincing. They slump down on the comfy couches. I don't know if we'll ever get them up out of there again. Grace and I serve them a light lunch, which they barely even touch. But the water and sports drinks are going down by the gallon.

Mike informs Lucas, "I don't know about you, but it seems like I always pick the hottest days of the year to work on these crazy outdoor projects. I'm getting way too old for this!"

Lucas agrees with that sentiment. They finally make their way to a standing position, and slowly walk out to the shack. Grace and I hit the air mattresses out on the lake. Maybe not the best decision, but what are we going to do, stand there and watch them all afternoon?

Lucas and Mike keep working relentlessly. It almost makes us sick to our stomachs to watch them work so hard in this heat. We keep urging them to quit, but they're good stubborn Dutch boys and will stick with it for the day. They have a daily goal in mind! Today's goal is to basically complete the entire shack, and use tomorrow to pour the concrete bar top. Grace and I quickly hop out of the water to get them their drinks of choice. Water, for both of them. Boring but smart.

After downing their bottles of water, both Mike and Lucas go into the cabins. We're presuming they want to cool off in the air conditioning. But they both come out minutes later with their swimsuits on, and go running down the dock and jump into the water. It's a crazy time full of splashing and dunking each other. Grace is so corny—she has to plug her nose every time someone pushes her head under the water. A couple of her granddaughters have inherited this unbecoming trait from her. But to be honest, I wore nose plugs until the age of twelve, every time I went swimming, so I don't bother to bring up the subject.

We paddle around and tread water for a while, until the guys are finally cooled off. And then just for something fun, the four of us jump on the two jet skis and take off. Either the guys are really tired, or they're too lazy to care, but they encourage Grace and me to drive. We take off fast, kind of racing each other, but really not. Because we all know how this will end. One of our jet skis is newer and has more horsepower than the older one. Why try to prove the obvious? Both Lucas and Mike are smart enough to know better than to hang on to Grace and me—we could spin and throw them off in a heartbeat. Of course, they would probably take us with them. But they're experienced enough to hang onto the strap across the seat, which they could hold onto for dear life if need be. The way we women drive, it could come to that.

After a little bit of fun, we slow down and start cruising around the lake. The sun is starting to go down, shining on the sandstone bluffs. The bluffs look like they're illuminated from behind—just beautiful.

We're coming up close to the marina, and Lucas yells in my ear, "I'm starving and dying of thirst. Let's stop!"

We navigate our way to the marina dock and tie up the jet skis. The marina restaurant has a sign posting "Inside seating—shirts and shoes required. Outside seating—swimsuit attire acceptable." Well, I guess that's us. We'd hate to be inappropriately dressed at what would basically be described as a sea shack.

A pretty little waitress comes out wearing, well, I guess you would have to call it swimsuit attire. Personally, I would call it triangles and strings. They must have a Brazilian wax policy for their staff. Good idea.

Drinks are ordered, drinks are brought. Food is ordered, food is brought. Another round of drinks is ordered, another round of drinks is brought. You know, Grace is on to something. I guess you don't have to work in the kitchen for hours on end just to have some good food and fun. Time to head home while there's still some daylight left.

GRACE

We climb into bed, with Mike moaning and groaning. "I'm too old to be working this hard. And the heat was a killer!"

I commiserate with him and give him the appropriate compassion and attention he deserves. He's in the process of scrunching the pillows exactly the way he likes them. I know he'll be snoring in two minutes.

Before that happens I ask him, "What do you think of Lucas? Is he fun to work with?"

Not the true information I'm looking for or what I'm really wondering, but it's a start.

Mike knows me too well and knows what I'm thinking because he replies, "He's the absolute best thing that could ever happen to Ellie."

My thoughts exactly.

CHAPTER 19

ELLIE

Another day dawns bright and cheery. The cheery part might be a little bit of an exaggeration. It's downright hot. And it's only 8 AM. Whoever invented air conditioning was a genius. I quickly feed Lucas and Mike some breakfast, and they head out before the temperature gets too hot to work with concrete. We don't wait for Grace. She's still sleeping, she doesn't eat breakfast, and she's not going to be doing any physical labor today. Let sleeping dogs lie.

The guys build the forms for the concrete countertop. I help them in any little way I can, plus I like learning this kind of stuff. My construction knowledge is pretty much nil, except for decorating, so it's fun watching them discuss their options, come up with the best plan, and proceed from there. We decide on what color we want to add to the concrete, so it's not just plain old gray, and from there they start mixing and pouring and smoothing and voila'—there's a countertop! Pretty amazing.

About this time Grace comes out and is very impressed that the countertop is done.

"Wow, I can't believe it's done already!"

A couple of things here. It's 10:30 in the morning, and the guys have been at it for a couple of hours already. Yeah, a lot of people get all kind of things done in the morning. Just not you.

But I have to be fair here. Grace is not a lazy person; she just operates on a different time clock than the rest of the world. It's amazing the stuff she gets done at midnight or after. I've gotten texts from her at 2 AM, trying to make plans for our kids or our mom when I finally have to say, "I'm trying to sleep. Please stop!"

We ooh and aah over the entire shack, with the guys pointing out what turned out great and what they wish they would've done a little differently. Overall, the result is outstanding. When you put two handymen together, you know it's going to be done right.

GRACE

Mike wakes me up the next morning at eight—ugh—and tells me that he should really get back to Sioux Falls today to finish up a handyman project that he's working on.

"Seriously? Do you really have to go? I was thinking that we should christen the jerk chicken shack with the four of us tonight. And maybe we could have some jerk chicken."

I'm definitely reminiscing about a trip we took to Jamaica a few years ago.

"Stop calling it the jerk chicken shack. I asked Lucas what he wants to call it, and it's just going to be 'the shack.'"

"I get that. Makes sense. But you can't leave. We really have to do this up right tonight."

Mike gives it a moment of thought and gives in. He just can't resist my pleading, you know? All of a sudden a thought rushes into my head, and I run downstairs to Ellie, who's drinking coffee in the kitchen.

"Ellie, I talked Mike into staying another day, so we could have a christening of the jerk chicken shack, sorry, the shack, tonight. But we need stuff! Decorations, barstools, lights, the works."

Being my sister and loving to decorate, Ellie decides it's an excellent idea. We run over to Lucas' place. He's outside by the shack, finishing up a few minor details. We tell him that, #1, since we talked him into building the shack; #2, that it's on his property; and #3, that we hope to have lots of parties there—that he should let us help decorate.

"We need dishes, silverware, lights, décor, a fridge, microwave, blender, griddle..."

He looks at us, just a little overwhelmed. We offer to go and buy all of this stuff (isn't he lucky), and even better yet, we'll pay for it all (even luckier yet!)

He looks at us like he was hit by a tornado, but says, "Yeah, whatever."

That's our green light. And we're off

We head into town with lots of ideas. We hit downtown first. They have a number of boutique and antique shops. We enter one of the boutique shops. They have oodles of "beachy" stuff. Some of it's great, some of it's a little too much. No lighthouse décor for us. The nearest lighthouse to Yankton, SD, is probably at least 1500 miles away. No ocean décor for us. No sharks or whales in Lewis and Clark Lake. We do settle on a clock that's surrounded by nautical roping.

From there it's on to an antique shop. The instant we walk in the door, we see it. A pair of antique water skis, hanging on the wall. Perfect for the back wall of the shack. Our family was, and still is, big into water-skiing. The most precious item that I ever gave to my son-in-law and grandsons is my slalom water-ski. I was pretty good at it, until some vision problems ended my skiing career at the age of 61. My grandsons frequently text pictures of them skiing with it. It's a girly ski—it has a butterfly on it—but they all say that they're manly enough to handle it.

We walk farther into the store and spot a ceiling fan with a filament light. Chances are, it's going to get a little warm in the shack on the hot summer days that we have, so we need a fan. We talk to the guy and make a deal for both items. I think we made out well. The truth of the matter is, downtown Yankton's traffic is a little sparse, so I'm pretty sure the dealer was just happy that he finally had some customers.

Next it's off to the local department store. Though it's not quite the end of July, everything in their housewares' department even remotely connected to summer is on clearance. We stock up on plates, bowls, platters, silverware, water glasses, wine glasses, shot glasses, napkins, candles. You name it—if it was on clearance, we got it.

Our next stop is the home improvement store. We find some bar stools that are built for outdoor weather and are actually quite comfortable. Then it's on to appliances—boring but necessary. Oh, and lights. Strings of lights for the outside, and yeah, probably for the inside too. Okay, I think we're done here.

We come driving down the driveway. I toot the horn just a little to get Mike's attention. Actually both guys come walking out. I push the button for the hatchback on the SUV. Mike just looks and rolls his eyes, while Lucas looks amazed. I don't think he's used to what goes on to decorate a place properly, and will he like what we've picked out?

I'm a little bit nervous. I've done some decorating in the past for other people. Usually they're friends of mine, and I always take them along shopping with me. That way I get their reaction upfront and can discover what they truly like and dislike. I can just hold something up and see the reaction right away. A hit or a miss. It makes things pretty easy for me, and the client is usually happy with the results. We'll just have to wait and see how Lucas responds to all of this.

As Mike helps me unload all of the stuff, he just shrugs his shoulders. He's used to this drill. He knows what's coming—he gets to hang up all the decorative stuff and help me put everything else away. Lucas and Ellie help haul everything over to the shack.

The guys are impressed by the ceiling fan and light. That's definitely a must, they agree. Mike starts with that, and it's up and running in no time. From there on it's on to the skis. Mike wants to hang them so much higher than what they should be. An ongoing saga in our marriage. He's six foot five, and I'm five foot three, and our height difference makes it a little difficult to come to an agreement. I always bring up my home decorating sites that say "lower is better." The guys continue on with everything that we've bought.

Lucas' observation is, "Why did you buy a clock? We're on lake time!"

CHAPTER 20

ELLIE

While the three of them were busy unloading and decorating, I went and got groceries. And yes, we are having jerk chicken. And don't ask me for my recipe. (Even though I got it online and it has 5500 likes.) The chicken has to marinate for at least three hours, so I quickly get that prepared. I'm also making black beans, coconut lime rice, and the best thing of all, grilled pineapple.

Grace comes rushing in beneath a load of boxes.

"We have to wash all of these dishes and glassware before dinner tonight."

I start running water in the sink and she gives me a look and says, "What in the world are you doing?"

"We're going to wash the dishes."

"We have a perfectly fine dishwasher. These dishes will all be done in two hours without us having to lift a finger. I'm putting my foot down!"

Sometimes you just have to go with the flow. In two hours the dishes are done, she hauls them all out to the shack, and stacks them on the floating shelves that were just installed.

Soon it's time for dinner. I've made a rum punch with a Jamaican spiced rum. The four of us sit by the bar on our new bar stools as the sun slowly starts to set. Mike then proceeds to grill the chicken and the pineapple. Well, he thinks he's doing the cooking. We all know that he never watches the grill closely enough, so we all keep an eye on it. We haul out the rest of the food and enjoy our delicious meal at this delightful shack. Who would've known summer could be this good?

As comfortable as the bar stools are, we finally decide to go sit on the porch, since the mosquitoes are coming out in full force. So are the moon and stars, which glow nicely over the lake. A truly beautiful night. We are so blessed to be here.

Even though we're having a great time, Mike finally tells us, "It's time for bed. I should've driven back tonight, but that's a done deal. So it's up early for me tomorrow morning."

He and Grace say their goodnights, and then Lucas and I just sit there quietly. The cicadas, crickets and frogs are making a racket, but it's a comfortable noise.

Finally Lucas breaks the lull with a question.

"I'm curious. Tell me about Will."

Well, I guess it's time. It definitely has gotten easier to talk about as the years go by, but sometimes it hits me harder than others. We'll see how it goes this time around. Okay, Lucas, here's my story...

Will and I met my freshman year of college. I decided to go to the private college in my hometown. It has a great reputation and I guess I wasn't a traveling girl. I decided to major in social work, so I could "help people." A little naïve at the age of 18, but who isn't?

Much to my dismay, a social work degree has a few requirements, such as, the ultimate worst, chemistry. When would I ever use chemistry as a social worker? I bemoaned that fact, as did my good friend, Carma. We had our first day of chemistry class on our first day of school, and were assigned as lab partners. Probably not the best choice, but at least we were in this together, right?

As we walked into the lab and were assigned to our spots at our lab table, we both knew we were in over our heads. The Bunsen burners, the terrible smell, the beakers, the test tubes, the goggles, the periodic table. Not encouraging. And by the way, who made up that periodic table? I understand CA for calcium, but AU for gold? Come on! We fumbled through our first experiment, not getting the results we were supposed to get. Oh well, first day jitters.

A few more lab days went by. Not any better. They had some graduate students who were running the labs and helping out anyone who needed it. We were probably on the top of that list. One of the them came over and asked us if we needed any help. You think?

"Hi, I'm Will."

We introduced ourselves, and he proceeded to show us what we were doing wrong. Many things; so, so many things. He was very non-condescending, and just seemed to enjoy helping us. He knew we were only in this as a requirement, and told us his goal would be to just help us get a passing grade for the semester. Carma and I were ecstatic. Maybe there was hope for us after all.

Will was so helpful to both of us, but as the semester wore on, I could tell he was honing in on me. Which was pretty flattering, to say the least. Carma was seriously dating a sophomore, and it's amazing she could focus on any class at all. When Will asked me out, of course I accepted. Who could be anyone nicer than someone who tutors you through chemistry class? Especially when he's tall, has curly blond hair, blue eyes that are almost iridescent, and a smile that goes on forever? He seemed golden, or AU-en to you chemistry nerds.

He took me out to dinner at one of the local pubs. It was a little noisy, but we did manage to make some conversation. I asked him what would possess anyone to major in chemistry? A very legitimate question, I thought. He just looked at me in astonishment. Who wouldn't love chemistry? My initial response was, well, maybe Carma and I, or anyone else who's normal, for that matter? But I didn't say that. I just let him go on about how he loved all sciences, but that chemistry made so much sense, and on it went. He told me he would be done with his master's degree in December, and his plan was to go on to get his doctorate. He couldn't wait to teach chemistry to college students. If I would've known him better, I would've stuck my finger down my throat and pretended I was gagging. A chemistry professor?

Even though I couldn't stand his profession, and he thought mine was a little bit of a joke, we kept seeing each other. Only with his tutoring, Carma and I both managed to pass chemistry. We did throw ourselves a little party when we got our grades for the term. Our grades weren't stellar, but good enough. Carma continued down her road towards nursing, and

I graduated with my degree in social work. Will and I dated all four years of my college career and got married the summer after my graduation. He got tenure at the college we attended and life went on from there.

And life was excellent. It turns out I was a little more fertile than I thought was necessary, and we had three kids in the span of four years. I worked full-time at the hospital as a social worker, but then went to part-time, and even less-time, as the kids were born. We spent the next number of years busy with the kids: first, changing diapers, then chasing after toddlers, then sending them off to school, and then flying from one of their sporting or music events to another, night after night.

And just like that, those years were over. It was such a joy to see Will walk both of our daughters down the aisle. Our son eventually got married also, and then we sat back and waited for grandchildren to arrive. But then things took a tragic turn.

I was weeding our garden. I heard the sound of the ambulance siren, and my first thought was a prayer, "Dear God, please take care of the person who needs that ambulance right now."

I went back to weeding. What a thankless job.

I heard the phone ringing in the house, and was going to ignore it, but at the last minute I decided to run to pick it up. It was Dr. Carlson from the hospital. I knew him well since I worked at the hospital for most of my adult career.

"Ellie, you should come to the hospital. It's Will."

Okay, I thought. Will is always out walking or running. I suppose he tripped and broke an arm or leg. It only took me five minutes to drive to the hospital.

I walked into the ER and said to the desk clerk, "I'm here to see Will."

I've known her for years, but she wouldn't look me in the eye. Weird, I thought. She must be having a really bad day. But then Dr. Carlson walked through the double doors, and he just shook his head. And then he started crying. Oh man, that's a horrible sign when the doctor starts crying. He just took me in his arms and hugged me tight.

"I'm so sorry, Ellie. Will collapsed on Main Street. Bystanders started CPR immediately, and they called the ambulance right away. The paramedics worked on him. We never got him back."

I don't know how long we stood there together, both of us sobbing. How do you go on from that?

I'm crying as I tell Lucas the story, and he's crying too.

He has his arms around me and just keeps saying, "I'm so sorry."

He tells me he's sorry for me, he's sorry for my kids, he's sorry I had to go through that. He does a good job, but truly, there are no words for any of it. After my tears subside, I tell him that I'm shot and I have to go to bed.

He kisses me on the forehead and tells me again, "I'm so, so sorry."

CHAPTER 21

GRACE

The alarm goes off at 5 AM. I don't even know what 5 AM looks like. Mike gives me a little jiggle.

"Sorry, babes, I have to leave now to get to work at seven. Go back to sleep and I'll call you tonight."

I do take orders well—I fall right back to sleep. I get up around ten. I look out the window. Usually it's a bright, sunny morning, but today it's raining. If I look out the window and it's cloudy or raining, I fall into a deep funk. I know we need rain once in a while, but could it possibly just rain at night and be sunny all day?

I make my way downstairs, and—this is a first—Ellie is nowhere to be seen. Weird. I see her coming downstairs about a half-hour later, and I have to tell you, she looks like crap. Her eyes are puffy and red, and her whole demeanor is off.

"What the heck, Ellie?"

I walk to her and give her a big hug. She stands there, sobbing in my arms, for what seems like forever. Soon I'm sobbing with her, not sure what we're crying about. But if she's unhappy, I'm unhappy.

"Last night I told Lucas about what happened to Will. Needless to say, it was a little emotional."

I totally get that—no need to explain. The dreary day doesn't help our mood in any way.

I ask her, "How about we make it a movie day?"

We have a pile of DVD's from back in the day. I realize that we could just as easily watch any movie on streaming, but there's something about watching a DVD that we've watched as a family for years that makes it a little more nostalgic. We make some hot chocolate and snuggle under some comforters. Definitely a chick-flick kind of day.

We settle on Pretty Woman and Dirty Dancing to start. We have watched these movies umpteen times with our daughters. Okay, maybe they were a little young when we let them watch them for the first time, but they can't learn any younger, right? And how can you not cheer at the last dance on Dirty Dancing? Most definitely a memorable moment. About five o'clock we hear a knock on the door. It's Lucas, just checking up on us.

————————

ELLIE

Lucas comes walking in, and just looks me in the eye. A look of compassion. It makes me want to cry again. But I don't—I'm so glad he's here. Grace starts bustling about the kitchen.

"Can I get you drink? Are you hungry?"

Too much nervous energy there. But it's kind of fun to see her in action.

Lucas responds, "Umm, a beer? And I no, I'm not terribly hungry."

She grabs him a beer and throws a pizza in the oven. She is a fun hostess, even if we don't operate in the same way.

"It's movie night. Ellie and I are watching chick flicks, but I'm sure we can find a movie that you'd like."

Lucas makes his way to one of the sofas. Grace, with the pizza, makes her way to the other. I feel like I'm in junior high. Do I go and sit by Grace or make a move and sit by Lucas? I decide to join Lucas. Even though the sofa is eight feet long and I sit on the opposite end as he does.

We decide on a movie. Not a chick-flick. A shoot-em-up, high action film. We snack on pizza, and then popcorn, as the movie progresses. It's very comfortable, but you can tell the vibe in the room is different. Between Lucas and me.

Grace makes an exaggerated yawn. "I'm just wiped out. I'm going to bed."

Who are you kidding? You'll be reading for the next four hours. But it is thoughtful of her.

I ask Lucas if I can make a drink for him.

"I make a mean Old-Fashioned."

He tells me that sounds great. Don't know if he's just being nice or if he really means it. I'll be having a glass of red wine. No brown alcohol for me. I can't stand that stuff.

We settle in on the sofa. Still on opposite ends but with our feet up, facing each other.

"Okay, Lucas, it's time you tell me a little about yourself. Your background, your family, what makes you tick. Are you a felon? You know, the usual stuff."

He smiles at that. I smile back, but nowadays you can't be too careful, you know?

He starts talking.

CHAPTER 22

LUCAS

My parents were farmers, not too far from here. They owned a decent-sized farm, but do you know how hard farming is? When I was a little kid, we raised hogs. The stink is beyond anything you can imagine. It gets in your clothes, in your house. It's a smell that never goes away. It seems to seep out of your pores. I was always self-conscious as a kid that other kids would smell that on me. And the flies that go with it—it's like an infestation that you can never get rid of. I remember sitting at the dining room table, eating supper, with fly strips hanging above the table. They're long, yellow sticky things that if a fly was unlucky enough, he'd fly into it and be stuck forever. Terribly gross, now that I think about it.

The hog market is always up and down, pretty much like the stock market. It's always a gamble. Ultimately one day, my mom had reached her limit. We three kids were in the living room watching TV, when we heard my dad come in from outside. My mom just started yelling that she couldn't stand the smell, she couldn't stand the hog pens on the yard, she couldn't stand the flies, and she absolutely was not going to live like this anymore. Dad could take his pick—it was her or the hogs. Quite the ultimatum, especially when you hear it as kids. What would Dad do?

It was a tense meal at suppertime. Mom was throwing things on the table and Dad was giving her the silent treatment. As kids, we didn't eat much that night, knowing that a big decision had to be made, and it was going to affect all of us.

The tension was incredibly high for the next few days—everyone walking on eggshells. I think I was about nine years old, with one sister older than me, and the other one younger. We tried really hard to stay out of my parents' way. None of us kids cared about the pigs; we were all pretty much in agreement with Mom in that respect. But we also knew that the responsibility of making a living was on Dad's shoulders. What would the outcome be?

We came to find out years later that Mom was really smart. She hit Dad with this ultimatum when the hog market was at its absolute worst. He was tired—tired of the work, tired of the smell, tired of working his butt off with little or no profit. So he capitulated. He got rid of the hogs, and tore down the hog pens. He still kept farming, though, just doing crop farming. I guess God always looks out for you. About that same time, the price of corn went through the roof. We were never rich, but we always had enough.

By the time I was in high school, I definitely knew that farming was not for me. I was not a straight-A student, but I did well enough. I looked for a part-time job, and was offered one at the car dealership in town. I loved it. I loved the new-car smell, the feeling of detailing used cars, and the excitement of seeing the line-up of the next year's cars coming into the dealership. Sometimes I would hear the deals that were going down and see the salesmen in action, and I thought, "I want to do that someday."

The owner of the dealership, Jerry, took notice of me and the interest I took in the whole operation.

"Lucas," he said to me, "you have a knack. You're a young kid but you have potential. But don't just slide into one small promotion to another one here for the rest of your life. Get an education, and we'll see where this leads us."

Wise words. I decided to go to college, and even got some small scholarships. Since I was going to college here in town, I kept working at the dealership. I didn't think so at the time, but looking back, the four years passed in a hurry. Jerry sat me down and told me that he was starting to look at retirement, but he wasn't quite there yet. Would I stick with him and see where things led?

I was patient, and in the meantime, decided to get my MBA. Couldn't hurt, right? And if the future goal was for me to own the dealership, it would definitely help me in the long run.

ELLIE

I'm sitting there thinking—this is good stuff, good for you. But in the back of my mind I'm thinking, this is a beginning, but he's definitely not telling me what makes him tick, besides cars. And don't get me wrong, I like cars too. I have been fortunate enough to be able to buy some pretty nice vehicles, once Will and I got past the minivan stage.

"So, how about your family? Are your parents still living? What about your sisters? And what happened to the farm?"

He tells me that his parents eventually sold the farm when it got to be too much for them, which netted them a nice income for their retirement. His sisters both took off as soon as they were old enough, and live out west—California and Arizona.

"Yeah, if we ever run into my parents, I'll introduce you to them."

Okay. His parents live in a nursing home, and we're supposed to possibly just "run into them?" He must not consider me the "meet the parents" type yet. A little sobering, but the summer is young. And for now, this is enough.

CHAPTER 23

GRACE

Another rainy day. Oh, the horrors. How do people in Seattle do it? If it's a rainy or cloudy day, I would do much better by never waking up. Just let it be tomorrow, with sunshine, please?

I eventually decide that I might as well bite the bullet and get up. Ellie is drinking what is probably her fourth cup of coffee this morning. That makes her somewhat more cheerful than I am. I tell her that the only thing more depressing than a rainy day is a rainy day at the lake. Such a waste. She's on the same page. Even though she has a caffeine high, she hates the rain as much as I do.

"I think I'm going to head into Sioux Falls for the day. You know, see Mike and the kids."

Even though my grandkids aren't babies, or even toddlers anymore, I still love them and miss them immensely.

Funny thing about living in Sioux Falls. Other than the locals and extremely intelligent people, no one knows how to pronounce it. I've gotten phone calls where they need to verify my address.

"And you live in Sucks Falls, South Dakota?"

"Actually, it's pronounced Sue, like the girl's name."

"Hmm. And is that close to Sucks City, Iowa?"

My goodness, don't they teach geography and American history anymore? If they do, there seem to be a lot of people that aren't retaining anything that they've been taught.

Ellie decides to go with me.

"I can stop in and see Abby and the kids too. And if they're not around, we could always go shopping."

I agree with her. Shopping has always been our thing. And I'm a pro at shopping for other people. There are many husbands, including our brother, that put a foot down when it came to their wives shopping with me. I can't tell you how many times I've come home from a shopping trip with almost next to nothing, and the other women come home with an abundance of overloaded shopping bags.

Ellie runs over to Lucas' house just to inform him that we'll be gone for the day. And maybe overnight, if this rain keeps up. We don't want to have him worrying about us. Good neighbors, aren't we?

We get in my car and make the 80-mile drive to Sioux Falls. A quick trip, especially when you're listening to our favorite oldies station. Lots of singing–you just can't help it! For me, the ultimate best–the Carpenters. I'm a strong alto, ala Karen Carpenter. Not to say that my voice is awesome–not even close. But I do have a good ear, and can pick up harmony on basically any song. Ellie's a really good soprano, and picks up the upper harmony. We should be cutting our own record. Umm, probably not.

We drive up to Abby's house, and thank goodness, she and the kids are home. The kids come running out in the rain. They're so happy to see their Grandma Ellie. I tell her we'll talk later and decide if we're going back to the cabin tonight or tomorrow.

I drive to our house and walk in the door. I had tried to let Mike know that I was coming home for the day, but it went straight to voicemail. His pickup truck is home, but it's pretty quiet when I walk in the door. Unusual. I walk upstairs to our bedroom, and he's just crawling out of bed. It's noon. Highly unusual.

"Hey, babes, what are you doing home?"

I sit on the bed beside him and give him a big hug and kiss. I tell him I couldn't stand the rain at the lake so decided to come home for a day.

"Are you sick? What are you doing in bed?"

He shrugs his shoulders and says he had a busy 24-hour shift.

"I'm beat. I decided I should maybe just give in and catch up on my sleep a little. Must be getting old."

A shocker to be sure. He's been a paramedic since 1981 and I can probably count on one hand the number of times he's gone back to bed after being up all night. I always encourage him to go to bed when he gets off work, but he's one stubborn cuss and he thinks that's being a pansy and it's a waste of a day. But he's always been more than supportive of me sleeping all day when I've worked a 12-hour shift the night before. That's just the type of guy he is. Got to love him.

I ask him. "Do you have any plans for the day?"

"I was planning on working on the new back deck."

We have a couple of big decks on the back of our house that go into the trees and out over the gully. Built by him, of course. There are not too many backyards like ours in Sioux Falls. Total privacy. Our house is very average, nothing huge or fancy. But I will say, we have done some nice improvements to it. My ideas, Mike's sweat equity. However, it has four levels to it. Someday, when our knees give out, we'll have to give it up for a boring one-level home. Thankfully we're not there yet. And going up and down stairs all day keeps you young and fit, right?

"Can I talk you into lunch?" I ask him.

He grumbles a little about his plans for the afternoon, but soon it's a done deal. The rain has stopped but it's still not a "sit on a patio" kind of day. We decide to go downtown to our favorite restaurant that has the most impressive salad bar. It's even been rated highly in some national magazines. Justly deserved.

After lunch we text Emily and Jason to see if they or the kids are available for the afternoon or evening. Emily answers instantly and I can hear the kids talking in the background. She says they'll be over soon–the kids are excited. They're over within the hour. It takes Jason a little longer to text back. Understandably. He's a sports medicine physician with one of the local colleges. The fall sports are just starting to gear up with practice sessions.

"I'll call Michelle. I don't think she has anything going on so just plan on us for dinner tonight."

Our kids, kids-in-law, and seven grandkids are all at our house by 6:00. Not much to eat in the house, so we decide what kind of carry-out we're in the mood for. Chinese food, it is.

Mike goes to pick up Mom, who lives less than a mile from our house. She's happy to be here and everyone is excited to see her.

The fourteen of us sit around our table, dishing up rice and noodles and fried wontons and every entrée that are our favorites. One of them is almond chicken without vegetables. The first time we ordered that the waitress was appalled.

"What, no vegetables? Just chicken and almonds?"

I know–it's weird. To be honest with you, I've never been a vegetable fan. My parents used to make us eat all of our vegetables as kids, and pickled beets were the worst! I vowed that when I became a parent I would never force my kids to eat things they didn't like. And I didn't. Needless to say, my kids never learned to eat vegetables, and that's been passed down to the next generation. I feel a little responsible, but life's too short to feel guilty about that, right?

It gets a little noisy. We have high ceilings and it does echo when we're all talking over each other. I've been told that when you wear hearing aids that too much background noise is a problem. Basically, this is all background noise. I know Mom isn't hearing one snippet of conversation, but I also know that she's enjoying being around her family. And she is totally awesome, one on one. No problems there. As they say, getting old is not for the weak. She's proven that many times over.

I hear my phone ringing over all of the noise–it's Ellie.

"What are you thinking? Are we driving back tonight or are we heading back tomorrow?"

"I'm thinking tomorrow. The kids are still here and we're having a great time. Are you okay with that?"

Ellie responds, "I'm fine with that. My grandkids want to watch movies and have a slumber party with me. Fun times for everyone."

We decide to go out back for a bonfire. Even though Mike's working on building the new, bigger deck, the old one is still in working order, with a fire pit. He helps two of the grandsons put in kindling, newspaper, and then criss-cross the logs over top. Lucky Keegan is the one who gets to light the match, and he throws it in perfectly. We let the fire build up and it's roaring in no time. Leave it to a firefighter to build an amazing fire. The kids start throwing in the colored flame packets. They're called "magic fire" or something like that, and are little packets that contain some chemicals that cause the flames to be different colors. Red, green, blue, purple—it truly is magical, and we all think it's pretty impressive. We used to throw in old Christmas light cords. They basically worked the same, but we thought the black smoke that came rolling off the fire might be a little toxic.

I guess it's time to make s'mores. This is one tradition of which I'm not overly fond. You all know the routine: melt the marshmallows, put them on a graham cracker with a chocolate bar, and then add another graham cracker. Sounds easy, right? Well, someone has to be sitting there with a plate on her lap, breaking the graham crackers perfectly, breaking the chocolate bar to the perfect size, and then putting the whole gooey mess together.

There are a couple of key words here: perfect and gooey. My s'mores have to have chocolate that fits the crackers to the millimeter, and that's all fine. But then it's putting the sticky marshmallow on and squishing it together that kind of does me in. As far as I'm concerned, it's one major mess that I could do without. I don't even really like them. But kudos to our grandson Liam who makes a perfect golden marshmallow, every single time. Never burnt, never uncooked in the middle. He's the master.

By this time the two little girls have snuggled up onto my lap. The sad truth is that they're not so little anymore. They're eight and nine years old. They're going to be taller than me in a couple of years. I squeeze them tight and it's love at its best. Bria, Jason's youngest, whispers in my ear,

"Grandma, when can we come and stay with you at the cabin?"

Tenley, Emily's daughter, hears that and whispers also, "Yeah, without our parents."

I bring up the subject to everyone around the campfire. Naturally, our adult kids are all in. A weekend without their kids? That's a no-brainer.

I tell them, "Let me talk to Ellie, and we'll come up with a weekend. I promise."

The kids are pretty excited and start making plans.

Finally the adults decide it's time to call it a night. This process begins around 10:30, but by the time everyone says their goodbyes and they're actually driving off, it's closer to 11:30. Mike and I continue to sit by the fire and watch it slowly die down. Peaceful. There's something so mesmerizing about watching a fire and listening to the noise in the woods behind us. Another part of summer at its best.

The next morning I'm awakened by Mike's alarm clock. It's 6:15 AM but he has to be at the fire station by 7:00. It's been really handy that the station he works at is less than a mile from our house. He could walk to work, but no, he'll get plenty of exercise once he gets there. He'll also get plenty of food.

Those guys know how to cook! The majority of Mike's really outstanding meals happen at the fire station, not at home. Not that it can't happen here, but the odds aren't as good.

The firefighters' favorite motto is "Eat until you're sleepy and sleep until you're hungry." Our tax dollars at work.

I wake up around ten and can see through the blinds that it appears to be sunny outside. Hallelujah! I give Ellie a call.

"What do you think? Time to head back to the lake?"

Since Abby has the day off, she and Ellie have decided to go shopping and do lunch before we head back.

"Call Emily, see if she's available, and we'll meet you at the mall."

I call Emily, hop in the shower, and in about thirty minutes' time, we're there. It's a little quiet, but with just enough foot traffic to make it not seem weird.

I'm starting to mourn the death of one of the greatest inventions ever—the mall. So many cities are closing their malls and building a lot of outdoor shopping centers. When you live in South Dakota, for at least seven months out of the year, the last thing you want to do while shopping is to go outside. It gets extremely cold here, folks! Who wants to deal with winter coats, hats, gloves, boots, every cold weather gear you could possibly think of, just to go shopping? Certainly not me. If you do find something you'd like to try on, it's an Olympic event to get out of all of that stuff, try something on, and put all of your winter gear back on. By that time you're a sweating pig and can't get anything to slide on or off. Quite the ordeal. Not my idea of a good time. In the summertime some of that outdoor shopping does work, but we have to look at the big picture here.

The good news is—our mall is not dying. Probably for the very reasons I just listed. We South Dakotans may be perceived as a little backwards sometimes, but we definitely are not dumb. And even though we're not known as the haute couture capital of the world, we have some great stores with some nice fashion sense.

We meet up with Ellie and Abby at the food court. And no, we won't be eating there—we'll find a restaurant with a nice wine list. After looking around a bit, we all decide we're not into it. We all love seeing summer clothes appear in the stores in February, but we're kind of depressed to see fall and winter clothes appear in the stores in July. Just let us pretend that summer's not over yet.

The four of us have a great lunch. Salads all around, because we're all on a diet. By the time the meats, cheeses, croutons, sunflower seeds, and dressings are all added to the salads, we could've just as well gotten a burger and fries. But we feel so much better about our choice. Aren't we just the healthiest women ever?

I bring up the subject from last night. "Our grandkids want to come to the cabin for a weekend without their parents. What do you think?"

Ellie is fine with that, and Abby is ecstatic. She and Emily start making plans about what they could do together as couples that weekend, without their kids. I don't blame them, but they sure jumped on the bandwagon mighty quickly. I just hope Ellie is up for entertaining our seven grandkids, along with her two. That's a lot of kids.

CHAPTER 24

ELLIE

Grace is driving, while I snooze just a little. A full stomach and a glass of wine make for a nice little nap. We come driving down the driveway, and see Lucas floating on an air mattress in the water, reading a book. He gives a big wave. Did he miss us? Or me?

We decide to quickly join him, and the three of us paddle around the docks. Now this is why we're here. He asks about our overnight adventure. Not so much an adventure, but a nice getaway, even though it was back to reality. But the truth is, it's a really nice reality. I just wish that winter didn't have to go along with it for much of the year. But spending time in Sioux Falls has gotten me to thinking.

Why am I living in small-town Iowa? None of my kids live there. Bethany and Sean and their families live miles away. Abby and Greg, Mike and Grace and their kids, and even

Mom, all live in Sioux Falls. What am I hanging on to? Not my job—I hardly ever work. Not my friends—they're all couples and I always feel like the fifth wheel. Memories of my life with Will? That's just it—they're memories, and I can take them with me wherever I go.

Lucas looks at me and says, "Wow, it seems like the wheels are really turning. What are you thinking about?"

"My life, and what I should do with it."

Lucas and Grace look at me with eyebrows raised. They must think this sounds a little too serious for the occasion, because Lucas comes bounding towards me and turns my air mattress over. I come up sputtering, and then a full-blown water fight is on. We splash and dunk each other until we're tired out, and decide a drink on the lawn chairs is in order. Grace offers to get us something, and comes out a few minutes later with a bottle of pinot grigio and three glasses. We relax in the sun, doze off a little, and I'm sure we're all thinking, "This is the life."

As the sun is setting, I run into the cabin to find something that could pass as dinner. Meats, cheese, salad, chips—good enough, right? We sit out on the porch in some incredibly comfortable chairs and decide that this is more than enough. We have a small propane-lit fire table and turn that on for ambience. We don't need it for the heat. It's still in the upper 80's. Perfect.

Even though it's not terribly late, and none of us have done anything today to warrant any tiredness due to physical labor, we're all lethargic and decide to call it a night. Good night, all!

The next morning I get a text from Abby.

"Emily and I came up with a date for the kids' weekend. How about this coming weekend?"

Yikes. Today is Thursday. I text back.

"Do you mean tomorrow?"

"Yep."

I go upstairs to find Grace.

"Abby and Emily say that this weekend would work for them."

"You mean tomorrow?"

"I guess."

"Mike's four days off do happen to fall this weekend. I'll check with him to make sure he doesn't have any other plans."

Grace calls Mike—he's fine with it. More phone calls are made to figure out the logistics. This is too complicated for texting. I can talk much faster than I can type. We decide that Mike will bring some of the kids with him on Friday, and Jason will bring the rest, because who has a vehicle big enough for nine kids? Emily and Abby will come and pick them up on Monday.

We need to get in high gear to get this all arranged. That means a huge grocery store shopping extravaganza. Sorry to say, (or maybe not so sorry), Ellie and I are the "spoil them rotten" type of grandmas. So quite a few treats make their way into our cart. At some point during the weekend we'll be dealing with a few sugar highs. Oh well, we can handle that. We're grandmas, and this is what grandmas do.

After we finish with our marathon at the grocery store, we decide to be bums on the beach for the rest of the day. We've earned it.

Friday morning. Are we ready for this? Mike drives up right at noon with four of the kids, and Jason pulls up right behind him with the other five. These kids range in age from 8-18. Pretty easy ages. About the time I'm starting to pull food out of the fridge for lunch, wonderful Mike and Jason inform me that they just went out for fast food and the kids are all full. Those two guys are the sweetest, most thoughtful people ever. Jason has to head back to Sioux Falls. He takes one look at the chaos that is already starting and just laughs.

"Good luck with this. You guys are crazy!"

Probably.

The kids proceed to haul all of their bags and stuff—oh, loads of stuff—up to the bunk room. A couple of the older kids claim some of the open bedrooms on the second floor. They're getting too old for the bunkroom stuff. Or so they say. I can guarantee you that tonight they'll all be up in the bunkroom together, playing games and having fun just hanging out together. And none of us cares how late they stay up. Because that means they'll sleep in a little later in the morning.

In no time at all the kids come running down the stairs, dressed for swimming. They go tearing out of the cabin, across the lawn, running and splashing into the water. They horse around for quite a while, throwing frisbees and footballs, jumping off the dock, dunking each other. Grace's oldest granddaughter, Rayna, is no longer a kid—she's a young lady—and she soon tires of the splashing around. She grabs a lawn chair to lay out by us, puts her earbuds in, and picks up her phone. This is where we'll find her all afternoon. Who can blame her?

Soon enough the kids are starving, so we haul snacks, soda and water to the picnic table. The kids are in their glory, busy planning all of the things they're going to do this weekend. Quite the list. We adults will be dead by Monday.

Lucas walks on over. I'm sure he heard the commotion. I re-introduce him to all of the kids. He remembers some of their names from being with them on the Fourth of July. He probably thinks we're bat-crazy for having all of these kids here for the whole weekend.

He makes a little small talk, while Grace's older grandkids seem to be assessing the situation. I can see the wheels turning and the looks they're giving each other. They're probably grossed out by the fact that two old people could have something going on. Teenagers are too smart nowadays.

After the snacks are done, the kids go running back to the water. Mike and Lucas don't actually run, but they do follow them and throw the football around with them for a bit while Grace and I clean up the mess. Actually, not such a mess. I guess we've taught them all well.

Even Grace and I go back and forth from our lawn chairs to cooling off in the water—it's another hot day. We'll take that any day over clouds and rain.

Big surprise—the kids are hungry again. I guess it is time for dinner. I was kind of enjoying the relaxing thing. The kids ask what's on the menu. I don't know why they're asking, because there's only one thing they want to do. Make pizza pies. I'm not talking about pizzas that you put in the oven. That would be far too easy.

What they're talking about is making their own individual pizzas over a bonfire. We have these cast iron pie makers. You put buttered bread in them, add whatever toppings you like, and you have your own made-to-order pizza. Except they're a lot of work. And we have to light a fire, in this heat. And you have to make sure no one burns themselves on the irons. A great activity for kids, don't you think?

Time to haul out all of the ingredients. Why we bought all of this stuff I'll never know. Some of them won't even use pizza sauce. Most of them will only use cheese. A few of the older ones might get a little adventuresome and add some meat, but there will be no mushrooms, black olives, green peppers or onions going in any of their pies. Grace's fault, for sure.

Lucas and Mike start building the fire. It has to be a roaring one for a bit, because the flames need to die down a little and produce some hot coals to cook the pizza pies over. Once the fire gets to that point, we four adults help the youngest ones make their pizzas, and then we proceed to cook them for them. Man, it's hot! But it is fun—one of our family traditions every year. I look over at Lucas, and I'm really happy to see that he seems to be having fun. He passed this test.

CHAPTER 25

GRACE

What a fun day. Which I knew it would be. Dinner is done, the stuff is put away. I think the kids are full (we'll see how long that lasts). What's next on the agenda? The decision is made–a kids' bean bag tournament. Some people call it cornhole, but our kids kind of snicker at that. They think it sounds a little dirty, in some crazy way. The names are in the hat to draw the teams. Oops, you need an even number.

Rayna volunteers to sit out, not in an "I'm too old for this way," but in a "I'm mature enough to be gracious about this" way. The first-born in her family, our oldest granddaughter. She is wise beyond her years, and always has been. Off to college soon. How did that happen so fast?

The teams are drawn. To be honest with you, it was rigged. We paired an older child with a younger child so the teams would be even. Our older grandkids know this and play along. Let the games begin! We get halfway through the double elimination tournament, when we have to call it quits due to darkness. What, you don't think it's smart to have kids throwing weighted beanbags at each other in the dark?

We set up our chairs around the bonfire that Mike kept feeding throughout the evening. Lucas hangs around. Good deal. Our kids are talkative; Ellie's two seem a little overwhelmed by the older cousins. They'll hit their stride before the evening's over.

Caleb, Liam and Keegan decide to tell jokes. Most of them we've heard before; some are really funny, some are just stupid. Keegan is 12, that junior high age that likes to tell jokes that are just a little on the naughty side. So does Grandpa Mike. I glare at Mike a few times to tell him that this is not an adult audience. He looks at me with a shrug that says it all—oh come on, lighten up, it's all in good fun. He's right.

Somehow the mood turns a little more serious. I don't know exactly how we got on this topic, but one of the kids says something about how they'd remember us when we're gone.

So I ask the question, "How will you kids remember me?"

Kayla and Bria both say, "That you like wine and you're a party girl."

What? Where did that come from? Not sure what they mean (well, I get the wine part), but I'm a little shocked. Caleb and Liam both say that I'm the wildest jet-skier ever.

I look at them and say, "That's what you're going to remember me by?"

I should back up a little. Ever since the kids were born, Mike and I babysat them and had them overnight a lot. I always thought it was my grandmotherly duty to entertain them from the second they got to our house until the second they left. That meant playing lots of games and watching lots of movies. I played more games of "Go Fish" than any adult should ever have to play. I watched so much Barney that I have some of those videos memorized. I always let the kids sleep in our bed with me (Mike would hightail it to the guest room). One summer we put a queen-sized mattress in our room next to our king-sized bed so we could have wall-to-wall beds. This is not an exaggeration—that summer I had all seven kids in bed with me on many occasions.

Besides that, I have had lots of one-on-one time with each grandchild. I started doing overnights with each of them separately, because sometimes dealing with seven kids at once is too much. The day and night were theirs to choose. Should we go shopping (even the boys liked that if grandma was buying), should we go to a movie, should we go to an arcade, where do you want to eat lunch, where do you want to eat dinner, what games should we play, what movies should we watch, how late do you want to stay up? I loved every minute of it, and I know the kids did too. Once, when Liam was about ten, after I had brought him home in the afternoon the next day, he called me about an hour later.

"Grandma, I'm so homesick for you. Can I come back?" Melts my heart.

So this is what I thought the kids would say when I asked them how they would remember me. Not so.

"You're going to remember me for my jet-skiing?"

I was a little taken aback, I have to admit.

Caleb, our 17-year-old, soon to be a man, said, "Grandma, everyone has grandparents that do stuff with them, like playing games, watching movies, baking cookies—oh wait, we never did that. Do you know what my friends think when I tell them I have a grandma that slalom skis and jet-skis like a maniac? They think I have the most awesome grandma ever, and they're jealous of me. There is no one that I know that can brag about that."

Liam (our 16-year-old) chimes in. "Grandma, all of that stuff we've done together is great, but I agree, it's the jet-skiing that wins hands-down every time."

That makes me smile. Okay, I'm good with that.

CHAPTER 26

ELLIE

I'm sitting out on the porch, drinking my coffee, waiting for the kids to wake up. I see Lucas out on his deck and wave him on over. About that same time, Mike walks out with his coffee. I'm sure it'll be a little while before the kids wake up. I heard them up late last night. I'm also sure I heard Grace laughing upstairs with them. She won't be laughing this morning when she has to get up earlier than she usually does.

The three of us just sit and talk, enjoying another sunny morning. Once again I'll say it–it's just so comfortable. Lucas and Mike act as if they've been best friends forever. As for me, I'm loving it. How nice to be in the company of a man again. Other than my male relatives.

Time to make plans for the day. Lucas has a great idea. There are thirteen of us–too many for our boat.

"How about we rent a pontoon for the day and just hang out on that?"

Mike responds, "That's a great idea. I'll call the marina to make the arrangements and we'll be all set once we get this whole crew moving.

"Thanks, Lucas," I tell him, "that was really a great idea."

I'm glad we'll be together for the day. He just smiles.

Breakfast is a fiasco—everyone wants something different. My grandkids, Colton and Brooke, are having the time of their lives with these cousins. The younger girls have had lots of overnights and plenty of time together. Colton, not as much. He's in awe of these older boys that he gets to hang with.

Grace and I pack a lunch (boat buns) with lots of chips, snacks, and plenty of drinks in a cooler. Boat buns—just hamburger buns with lots of ham, butter, mayo, some with cheese, some with pickles. It doesn't sound great, but when you haul them out of the cooler while you're sitting on a boat, for some reason, they're extra delicious.

Lucas and Mike take turns navigating the pontoon, sometimes driving up the river, sometimes anchoring out in the middle. We hauled the humongous floating water mat along. The kids can't get enough of it. They spend hours jumping off the boat into the water, climbing up on the mat, trying to push the adults off the mat—truly a perfect afternoon for all ages. By the time we bring the boat back to the marina, everyone has had enough sun.

Oh great, now it's time for dinner. Something easy—hot dogs it is. The kids finish up their beanbag tournament while the adults slump in their chairs. A winner is declared, and the kids all head up to bed. So do Mike and Grace. That leaves Lucas and me.

I grab a bottle of wine and some glasses. Lucas and I sink side-by-side onto the sofa on the porch. We both yawn—how old are we?

"Lucas, you were so good with the kids today. I really appreciate it—it was an excellent idea that made for a wonderful day."

We sit there drinking our Cabernet, a good one from Sonoma. Who's going to make the first move? He does, thank goodness. He tips my head toward his, and it's the first kiss I've had in years. All in all, an awesome day.

CHAPTER 27

GRACE

Sunday. Another day that dawns bright and clear. South Dakota weather can be a little iffy at times. Honestly, that's a bit of an understatement. It's not unusual to have a week of cool, cloudy and rainy weather for a week or so in the middle of summer. But not this year. This has been one hot and sunny summer. I feel sorry for the farmers, and that's the truth. But yeah for us! We picked the best summer in years to be at a cabin by a lake.

The kids are slowly getting up (man, we've trained them well). Normally we're a church-going bunch, but there's no way we're hauling nine kids to church. We decide to have our own service. A devotion read by Brooke, and a prayer read by Tenley and Bria. Those girls do us proud. I ask if anyone wants to sing a hymn. Big thumbs down on that idea.

On to the next thing--Sunday brunch. The sky's the limit today, as long as Ellie and Mike are doing the cooking. Lucas is here also, and we find out he makes a mean omelet. It seems he made quite an early morning appearance today. Lots of meaningful glances between Ellie and him. Or maybe just my imagination in overdrive.

The kids are bringing their plates with them around the island. Eggs cooked to order, omelets made to order, pancakes in their favorite shapes; bacon, both squiggly and crispy; sausages, fruit, cinnamon rolls. Caleb, Liam and Keegan go crazy. They're growing boys and they know how to put the food away. An easy way to make them happy and create a good memory.

But now we're at the point where I say, "I hate big breakfasts."

Because along with big breakfasts come big messes. But my older grandkids all step up to the plate and help clean up everything. They are good kids.

So now, time for fun in the sun!

ELLIE

The kids are all outside on the lawn in their swimwear long before we adults have had time to finish cleaning up the kitchen and get our own swimsuits on. But hey, we're here now, so what's the plan?

Mike and Lucas decide to take the boys on the boat first. Caleb and Liam start hauling equipment from the shed—skis, a wakeboard, and the all-important tube. The tube that we have is called "The Big Daddy." The kids think this is hilarious, since Mike is a bigger guy, and they all start calling him "The Big Daddy." Once that joke gets old, they throw everything in the boat, along with towels, life jackets, sunscreen, and any other paraphernalia that they deem necessary. We send a cooler of water along, since it'll be a bit before they're docking again. Four boys and two men can do a lot of water sports before they call it quits. But they'll be riding by often, where we'll have to wave at each one of them, like they're doing something that's never been done before. We'll also take some pictures, which will basically be worthless because they'll be too far away to even figure out who's doing what.

In the meantime, Grace is getting everything ready to take off on the jet skis with the girls. She'll be busy with those five girls for a good long time. Fortunately Rayna and Kayla are old enough to drive one by themselves. Grace will be on the other one, letting the younger girls take turns driving, while she has to hang on for dear life riding behind them. Grace might not like making breakfast and doing dishes, but she's a rock star for the amount of time she has spent with kids on a jet-ski. And me, I'll just be here on shore, watching the fun happen. My time to relax.

The boatload of rowdy boys finally returns. Time for snacks and drinks. And then the switch is made—boys on the jet skis and girls on the boat. I don't think Lucas is aware of how different this will be. Those girls can scream. Loudly! And often!

Caleb and Liam are old enough to drive the jet skis by themselves. They put on quite a show for us. Racing, doing 360's, jumping wakes, and sending up as much spray as they possibly can. They've been taught by the master—that would be

Grace. She then proceeds to get on one of the jet skis and shows them up. Take that, boys! Then it's Keegan's and Colton's turns with Grace encouraging their every move. For junior high boys, they'll be a force to reckon with when they're old enough to drive on their own.

Finally the boat comes back. Lucas and Mike look exhausted and dehydrated. Grace and I feel sorry for them. Unless you've done it yourself, you don't realize how much work it is to drive a boat pulling skiers and tubers. And then you add being out in the sun and heat with no shade—exhaustion for sure. I run to get them a beer, and bring Grace a wine spritzer. She's earned it also.

From there, we go into "relaxation mode" on the lawn chairs, making small talk and watching the kids swim. Maybe we're in more than "relaxation mode." I think we've made it into "dozing mode."

Brooke wakes me up. "Grandma, do you know where Colton is?"

I instantly sit up. "What do you mean?"

"Well, he was jumping off the dock, and now I can't find him."

Instant panic and high alert! What? I start screaming, "Colton! Colton!"

I'm a crazy woman, rushing into the water. Everyone starts yelling Colton's name.

Mike takes charge immediately. "Okay, everyone. We're going to make a line across on both sides of the dock."

Grace and Mike rush to one side of the dock and gather up some of the kids. Lucas and I run to the other side and grab up the remaining kids. We hold hands in a line and start walking from the shore. This is way too slow, but I know it's the best way. Colton could be anywhere. I keep hurrying the line. Faster, faster! We're all screaming Colton's name. We're crying, shrieking and freaking out. Mike and Lucas try to keep us calm with encouragement.

"We'll find him—he's got to be right here."

I can't begin to concentrate on their soothing words or calm demeanor, while I'm living the worst nightmare ever.

We keep moving deeper. The little girls are sobbing and don't want to keep going. None of us do, knowing what we might find. But maybe it hasn't been too long. There's still hope, right? The line continues. Nothing! How can this be? These kids are all good swimmers. We've taught them the buddy system. We should've been watching them closer! Oh God, have you taken this sweet little boy to heaven? How can we ever tell Abby and Greg? How can I ever bear another loss? How did we let this happen on our watch? The thoughts keep screaming through my head in fast-forward motion as we keep searching.

"Please God, please God," I keep saying, over and over.

All of a sudden Brooke says, "Oh, there he is!"

She's smiling. And she's not looking at the water; she's looking at the cabin as Colton comes walking down the steps and across the lawn. We all just scream and come rushing toward him. I make it there first. I grab him in a huge bear hug. My body is shuddering with the weight of my sobs. By then everyone is crowding around us in a giant group hug. It's mass chaos as we all are crying, but now at least some of those tears are tears of joy. Poor Colton in the middle starts crying as well—he's overwhelmed, even though he doesn't know what's going on.

"Colton! What in the world? Where were you? We were so scared! What were you thinking? We thought you had drowned!"

Colton just looks at us with tears running down his face. He shrugs. "I had to pee."

I could've slapped that kid—he had no idea the catastrophe, terror and heartache he had caused. But of course I would never do that. Not now, and not ever. Because one of the most precious gifts that I had ever been given, was given back to me. And that doesn't always happen.

CHAPTER 28

GRACE

What a horrible day. A day that started out with so much potential turned into such a disaster. Grandparenting is supposed to be so much fun. But can you imagine the flipside of that? Having to tell your daughter that her son died on your watch? I can't imagine anything worse. Ellie is a wreck, understandably.

Mike and I order some pizza for the kids, which will be delivered soon. Can't say that anyone is that hungry. The older kids are feeling like we are—horrified, relieved, thankful—yet in a deep funk. The younger kids are so resilient and have bounced back into "fun mode."

Poor Colton. He's only ten years old, and doesn't realize the trauma that he caused today. Especially to his grandma. And we're never going to dump that on him, because he's just a kid. A kid that had to pee. Didn't anyone ever teach him how to pee in a lake? He should've told someone that he was going to the cabin, but like I said, he's just a kid. Someday maybe we'll talk about it, but today is not that day. My guess is that day will be many years away.

Mike and I get the kids fed. Ellie is around physically, but mentally she's miles away. Can you blame her?

Once dinner is done, the kids start to get a little restless.

Tenley asks us, "Could we go to that go-cart park? The one we saw on our way here?"

Mike and I just look at each other. We're done-in. Nothing sounds better than to sink into a sofa and veg out in front of the TV. The last thing we feel like doing is taking nine kids out on an excursion. But it's the best thing to do. We don't want to end this fabulous weekend on a horribly bad note, and Ellie could probably use a little time to herself.

"Great idea, Tenley!"

And we're off.

ELLIE

I just can't stop crying. I can't stop re-living the horror of thinking my oldest grandson was gone. The terror, the helpless feeling, the panic, the screaming. Those pictures and those emotions just keep playing back, over and over, in my mind.

The weird thing is—I once had a nightmare about this. Colton was really little, too little to swim. He was standing on the end of a dock, and accidently fell in. I jumped in after him, but couldn't find him. "How can this be? He was right here." I swam and swam, but couldn't find him. I jumped awake, gasping for air with my heart beating out of my chest. I sat there, alone, in bed, trying to get my heartbeat back to normal and slowing my breathing. This nightmare happened years ago, but I think about it often, as if I dreamed it last night. Do dreams mean anything? I don't think so, but it does give me an eerie feeling that one of my worst nightmares almost happened today.

As I'm crying, I'm praying. "Oh God, thank you, thank you, thank you."

I need to get a grip here. It was a horrible experience, but I just need to think about the outcome, not about the experience. A comedy of errors, if you will. No, I can't make light of it. This is going to stick with me for a while. But I know, with God's grace and peace, that this too shall pass.

There's a knock at the door. Lucas. He stands there and then wraps me in a hug. We stand that way for a long time. And I have to say, it is comforting. To feel a man's arms around you, when that hasn't happened in years, is a good feeling. I ask him to come in.

"Maybe for a little while," is his response.

He seems really quiet and a little withdrawn. Who am I to analyze behavior and emotions, today of all days?

There we sit. Me, emotionally spent, and him—I'm not sure what?

"Ellie, are you okay? Are you going to be okay?"

I give him a sad smile.

"Yes, I'll be okay. Maybe not tonight, maybe not tomorrow, but I know in my heart that I'll be okay."

He gives me a sad smile back. He's happy to hear that. But something is wrong here. It's as if I have to try and comfort him.

A really weird vibe. I ask him what's going on. He looks at me with tears in his eyes.

"I just have to say, I've got some issues, and I'm really struggling here. I'm sorry I led you on, and I shouldn't have gotten so emotionally involved. To be honest with you, I'm a loner, and it's always going to be that way. I'm so sorry, Ellie. Truly I am."

With that, he walks out. If I thought I was having a bad day before, this has just gone from bad to worse. I pour myself a glass of wine and head up to bed. I can't face anyone right now.

CHAPTER 29

GRACE

"Morning, everyone!" I say with a big smile on my face.

The kids are talking about their night at the go-carts. Who drove the fastest, who bumped each other the most, who ended up spinning out. Even though Mike and I were beyond tired, it was fun watching them in action. All of them were old enough to drive their own car, which was pretty liberating for the younger ones. After that it was a round of miniature golf. But 18 holes is too long, and we were finally just throwing the ball in the hole to get the game over with. Then, on to the Ice Cream Shack. Do you know how long it takes for nine kids to pick out their favorite flavor of ice cream? And do I want a cone, or a sundae, or a malt?

When we got back, things were pretty dark and quiet.

"Is Grandma Ellie going to play games with us tonight?"

"Probably not," I tell them.

Mike and I are groaning inwardly. After the events of today, we are beyond tired, and now we have to play games?

Rayna and Caleb are so sensitive. They take one look at us and say to the rest of the kids, "Why don't we just go up and play games in the bunkroom?"

Bless you two—you're the best.

But now it's morning. It's sunny and a new day. We're all here, and life is good. Grandpa Mike is in great form; cooking eggs and bacon. I make another batch of cinnamon rolls. The frozen kind, nothing from scratch. I did have to put a little work into it—setting them out the night before to thaw and rise.

Halfway through breakfast, Ellie puts in an appearance. Oh my goodness, she looks awful. But she does put on a good show. She gives her grandkids a hug, pours herself a cup of coffee, and sits down and chats with the kids. She even eats a cinnamon roll.

"I'm so sad you kids have to leave today. This has been the best ever!"

Just a tad bit of an exaggeration, but the younger kids don't realize it.

"May we go swimming for a little while until our moms get here?"

Mike volunteers to watch them and they're outdoors in an instant. I look at Ellie.

"Don't even ask," she tells me.

I shrug and then say, "What are we going to tell Abby and Emily?"

"I don't know. Nothing?"

"That's not going to work. You know the kids are going to tell them. It's better they hear it from us versus from the kids."

We agree on that.

"Ellie, you just have to get past it. It was the most traumatic thing ever, but you need to dwell on the outcome, not the event. Think about the rest of the weekend. How much fun we had, how much fun the kids had. We're all here today—safe and sound. I know it was terrible, but as you know, we've always tried to accentuate the positive, right?"

She nods her head in agreement. The tears start forming in her eyes when she tells me, "Not only was the whole thing with Colton a tragedy, but Lucas came over last night. He says he should've never gotten involved with me, with you and Mike, with the kids. He's a loner and he's going to stay that way. How could have we been so wrong?"

I'm stunned. I never saw that one coming. I am devastated—think how Ellie must feel. Did I push for something that wasn't there? Did we come on too strong? How could we all have been such a poor judge of character? But I don't think we were. He was friendly, he was fun, he was great with the kids—just a wonderful guy that we felt so close to. And darn it, we built that shack on his property! What were we thinking?

"Oh, Ellie, there are no words."

No truer words have ever been spoken, while we sit there crying together. Eventually, we're cried out. We proceed to clean up the breakfast mess, knowing that Emily and Abby will be here soon.

—————————

ELLIE

And just as we're thinking that, Emily and Abby come driving up. In two separate vehicles, of course, since they have to drive nine kids home. Oh, for the days of the big old station wagon. No seatbelts, pack in as many people as you possibly can. It's amazing that any of us lived to adulthood.

There are moans and groans outside. Grace and I just smile because we know what's going on.

As we walk outside, we hear the kids yelling, "Why are you here already?"

"We want to stay longer!"

"Do we have to go home?"

Emily says, "Wow–feel the love!"

It's a joke because this has been happening for years. These kids are not pining for their moms when they're with their grandparents. Kudos to us, I guess.

Mike keeps horsing around with the kids in the water. He's a saint. He knows we'll need a little time to talk to the girls.

Abby gives us a zinger. "I have to say, you two look terrible. Rough weekend?"

We sit down on the porch. How do we start? We start by telling them all of the great stuff we did and the fun times that we had.

"We made great breakfasts. We rented a pontoon. We did pizza pies over the fire. We boated and jet-skied. We did a bean-bag tournament. We played games. We stayed up late. We even did church!"

A pretty impressive list, I'm thinking. The girls aren't buying it.

Abby finally asks, "Is there something wrong?"

Where do I start? I start by bursting into tears.

GRACE

"Okay, girls, the good news is that everything is okay. It turns out, we got worked up over nothing."

I try to minimize the damage before we get off to a bad start.

"Abby, this is going to be hard for you to hear."

I then go on to tell them the whole story. How we were relaxing on shore, we'd had a big day on the lake, the kids were swimming. All was well, right?

Then I get to the hard part.

"Brooke told us that she couldn't find Colton. We freaked out. Understandably. We started looking immediately, but couldn't find him. It was so very hard. Hard on the kids, hard on us."

Abby has tears. So does Emily, and grabs Abby's hand.

"But it turns out, he was in the cabin the whole time. He had to go to the bathroom."

Abby asks for details—we give them. Then we all sit in silence. For what seems like a long time.

Ellie is sobbing, I'm crying softly, trying to get through this. This is an ordeal we'll never forget. The girls just look at us, while we're wondering what their first thoughts, and words, are going to be.

Abby crosses over to Ellie and embraces her in a big hug.

"Oh mom, I'm so sorry you had to go through that."

This is the daughter that Ellie has raised. Thoughtful, kind, loving—more concerned about her mom than she is about herself.

"Colton can be so thoughtless at times. Why didn't he tell anyone that he was going inside? I can't believe how awful that was for all of you. I am so, so sorry that your weekend was spoiled."

Abby isn't being crass or unloving towards her son. And yes, she wasn't actually there for the whole ordeal, so she truly doesn't know how awful it was. Tonight she'll go home, tell Greg about it, and cry her eyes out. She'll think about it for months to come. But she knows what her mom has been through, and she's giving her the best grace possible.

The four of us are in a puddle of tears. But we know we'll get through this. We're strong women.

ELLIE

"Mom, are you going to be okay? I'm really concerned about you."

This is Abby's question to me as we're gathering Colton and Brooke's belongings. I don't know—am I? But I do know in my heart the answer to that question is yes. There are many joys and many sorrows thrown in our way in our lifetimes. Are you going to be strong? Or are you going to cave? We all know people who have caved, and I have always vowed that I am not going to be one of them. I'll get through this.

GRACE

I get a chance to grab Abby alone during all of the commotion of the kids packing up.

"Abby, are you really okay?"

She tells me that she is just so glad she wasn't here. I agree with her.

Then she looks me in the eye and says, "Grace, I'm so thankful that you're here with mom. You're exactly what she needs."

I give her another tidbit. "She's really going to need me the rest of the summer. For some reason, Lucas has checked out."

Abby is devastated.

"I really thought he was the one for mom. What happened?"

"After the catastrophe, he came over and told your mom that he just can't do it. No reason, no details, just an 'I'm sorry.'"

"Keep working on him, okay? I still believe that he's the one."

The kids are loading up in the vehicles. Massive hugs, along with "I love you." "Can we stay longer?" "Can we come back soon?" "Thanks, Grandpa and Grandma!"

We could do this forever. They really did have a great time. For the younger ones, I think the trauma is totally forgotten and they'll only remember the wonderful memories that were made at the cabin. For the older ones, they'll remember the incident, but they're still teenagers, and I think that they'll also look back fondly on this time together. I will too, but it will always be tinged with the feeling of somehow failing our kids.

CHAPTER 30

ELLIE

We're back to the two of us. Grace and I. That was our original plan, right? Yes, it was, but somehow it changed over the course of a month. For a month, there was fun, there was excitement, but most of all, there was hope. Is that hope gone? For now, yes. And maybe forever. Was I a stupid, middle-older-aged woman that should've never thought that things would go any further? Probably. But yet, if there's never any hope in your life, does that mean that life is over? Do we just give in to drudgery and day-to-day existence, waiting for our day to die? And does that mean that life is only about having a loving relationship with another man? What does that mean for people who are single all of their lives? That sounds horrible, as if their lives aren't fulfilling. I don't mean that at all. I know many single people that have lived very meaningful, fulfilling lives, and wouldn't have it any other way. But if you have lived in a loving relationship and have negotiated the years as a couple, the loneliness after a death can be overwhelming. Maybe people are wired differently.

I was never a "woman's-libber." I'll be honest. I loved having Will open the door for me, haul my luggage in an airport, mow the lawn, take care of small repairs in the house. And it definitely worked both ways. I took care of him whenever he was sick (he was a typical man if he wasn't feeling well—pathetic). I made the meals because I loved it, I liked cleaning the house; I didn't even mind taking out the garbage. We didn't fight over little jobs because we both found our niche—things that we didn't mind doing, along with things that we loved to do. When that symbiosis is taken away, the adjustment is huge, and can be very difficult to overcome. I thought I had done that. Maybe not as much as I thought. And is that wrong?

Grace and I start out the day with the original plan. Sleeping in, no breakfast, laying out in the sun. How many days in our lives have we spent like this? Too many to count. But that's okay, because that what makes us the sisters we are. Thank goodness it's a hot, sunny day. I don't think I could've stood a dreary day. We both take a glance now and then at Lucas' cabin. It is quiet there and his pickup is gone. Probably working on a "handy-man" job.

We're doing our usual—reading our books, enjoying our books, when all of a sudden it hits me.

"Oh my gosh, Grace, it's your birthday this Saturday!"

Her response, "Yeah, I know, no big deal."

Well, we know that's not true. Just as much as Emily's birthday on the 4th of July is a big deal, Grace's August 1 birthday has always been a big deal, because it's in the summer, right? I'll be giving Mike a call to make plans.

MIKE

August 1, 1973–Grace's 17th birthday (I came to find that out much later). The day my life changed in the most dramatic way possible. This day made the difference between living the rest of my life in construction, marrying a local girl, and staying in this neighborhood the rest of my life (not that it was a bad thing–I would've been perfectly content with that). Or, meeting a new girl, one who was adventurous, had moved around a bit, who thought that there was a whole new world out there, and who thought I was destined for greater things.

Grace and her family moved in across the street from us on that day. We had heard that there was a new family moving in. One who had four daughters and a son. (I came to find out later that the oldest daughter had gotten married the week before). Oh well, down to three. Still interesting.

It was the summer before my senior year of high school. I was a late bloomer, but it happened fast. I shot up from five-foot-something to six-foot-five in less than a year. To be honest with you, I was also a late bloomer in the fact that I wasn't really into dating until that summer. Through the local realtor, we found out that one of those daughters was my age, and would be in my grade in high school.

I told my mom, "When that new family moves in, I'm going to ask that girl out on a date."

My mom looked at me like I was someone she had never known.

"Are you kidding me? You've never been on a date in your life. Why do you think you're going to ask out a girl you've never even met?"

"I don't know. I just have this feeling."

When I got home from work that day, I sat out on the front lawn and watched the "ins-and-outs" across the street. Lots of them. A middle-aged couple. A few girls and a younger boy hauling stuff in and empty boxes out. I scoped it all out. Two tall girls and a short one. One of the two taller girls must be the one my age. The short one looked way too young.

A few days went by as I kept watch across the street. Which girl was the 17-year-old? I couldn't tell. A few weeks later, once I met the family, I came to find out that I thought Ellie was the right one. But that wasn't the case.

I played softball a lot during that summer. I was the first baseman for our church's team. When you're 6'5", you have a long reach. My brother was the second baseman, one of my cousins was the third baseman, and another cousin was the shortstop. A family affair. We were pretty good.

After one of our games, I was introduced to one of the "girls across the street" by a friend of mine.

She told me, "This is Grace. She just moved to town."

The short one? I didn't see that coming. I had been watching that house for eleven days and wouldn't have guessed that.

My response was, "Hi." What a smooth talker.

She was a little more fluent. "Nice to meet you. By the way, are you the guy that lives across the street from us? I've seen you outside."

Four days later I asked her out on a date, to a drive-in movie. I think it was "Live and Let Die." We rode in my '70

Ford Maverick. It went pretty well, except I wasn't good at small talk. But she was.

Grace has always been a talker, and I've gotten so much better at it over the years. But it's amazing to me that she stuck with me after those first dates. I was really quiet back then, and very awkward and had never dated before. Finally, on our fifth date, when I was saying goodnight to her on her back porch, she just looked at me and asked me if I was finally going to kiss her. Enough already! That's all it took. We were a couple from then on.

We loved each other's families. I was the oldest in my family—two boys and two girls. This was a new experience for them. Grace captured their hearts immediately. And she instantly loved them as if they had been her family their whole lives.

My family had lived a sheltered, hard-working life. My dad built houses, and never took time off from work. We had never been on vacation our entire life. Grace's parents went on vacation every summer, and started inviting my parents and family along. We went to pro baseball games, amusement parks, and cabins at a Minnesota lake. My mom was a nervous wreck—she had never packed for vacation before, but it's a time in our lives that we look back on with lots of great memories.

We got married (my parents thought we were way too young). And then Jason was born. The first grandchild for both sets of grandparents. Was there ever a child that was more loved? Except he had one annoying habit. About five o'clock in the evening he'd start crying. And keep on crying. And on and on it went. My mom worked the evening shift at the local hospital. My dad was bored, or so he said. I doubt that was the case, after working hard at construction all day. But every evening he would come over and walk with that kid. The only way Jason would stop crying was if someone was walking while holding him, especially under a bright light. Dad did that night after night when Grace and I were too tired to do it anymore. The bond was formed. When Jason got married 22 years later, he asked his grandpa to be one of his groomsmen. Makes me cry to this day.

Anyway, I'm reminiscing way too long. Grace and I—we've been blessed. She gave me two beautiful kids. She encouraged me to go to paramedic school when the construction business took a downturn, which involved a move to Michigan. She went to college to get a nursing degree while she was in her thirties, to help out financially. She was there for me when my dad died of cancer at the age of 71. She was there for me when my mom was fighting sepsis after a knee surgery. She, Jason and Emily knew how serious it was, and supported us all when we knew that we had to turn off Mom's life support, also at the age of 71. I know how hard it can sometimes be for a daughter-in-law to get along with her husband's parents, but that was never the case with Grace. She loved them unconditionally. She can't stand "mother-in-law" jokes, because she's always said that she had the best mother-in-law ever.

So yes, we're going to celebrate her birthday.

CHAPTER 31

GRACE

"Oh Ellie, I know you're not in the mood. We don't have to do anything special. I'm sure Mike will come up for the weekend, and that'll be good enough."

"No way. Just because I'm having a crappy week doesn't mean we can't celebrate. Who do you want to invite?"

"Let me talk to Mike. We'll decide."

I give Mike a call and fill him in on the fact that we haven't seen Lucas all day. Mike is questioning everything as much as we women are. He has talked to Jason and Emily. Since we just saw them this past weekend, they're going to wish me the best and we'll have a big family celebration when I get home. Understandable. I'm totally fine with that.

"What do you want to do, hon? Who do you want to invite? No one, lots of people, a few people? I'll arrange anything you want."

"Let's just go with our closest friends and keep it small. Evan and Ruth, Scott and Carma. That's all I really want."

Evan and Ruth have been our dear friends for over thirty years. Their kids were the same age as ours, so we ended up at a lot of the same sporting events, and we go to the same church. We've taken lots of fun vacations together, Cancun, Puerto Vallarta, Jamaica. Many great memories.

Scott and Carma are a few years younger than us. And yes, she's the same Carma that was in chemistry class with Ellie years ago. She's been a friend of our family since she was born. She and Scott moved to Sioux Falls when they got married, and the four of us really like hanging out together.

I don't need a huge group of friends at my birthday party—I just want my best friends.

"Okay, hon, I'll take care of it. The food, inviting the friends, whatever you want."

That's why I love this guy.

We end up spending the next few days pretty much like we spent Monday—doing nothing. Lucas is definitely MIA. We haven't seen him all week. He must've left town for a while. This is how little we know about him--neither one of us have a clue where he's gone. I finally Googled him. I wasn't going to, but my curiosity got the better of me. He's not on any social media, and the only thing that popped up was his connection with the car dealership. Boring and not very enlightening.

Ellie and I go into town a few times to shop, just to waste some time. We pick up a few groceries now and then, go to a movie on the one cloudy day that we have, and read a lot of books. Very relaxing, definitely. But also a little depressing, I must admit.

Jan Dirksen

This is what we wanted for the summer—the original plan. But you can lie around for only so many hours each day. I think we would've been very content with that if Lucas hadn't appeared on the scene. We both got caught up in the possibility of something exciting for Ellie, a new dream. No one ever wants to see a loved one being lonely, so when Ellie had this chance, Mike and I wanted it almost as much as she did.

CHAPTER 32

ELLIE

Here's the truth. I am a great cook. And I love doing it. But I must say, it was a whole lot more fun cooking for Lucas, Mike and Grace than it is cooking for just Grace and me. And it's not her fault. She'll try anything I put in front of her, and will be very complimentary, but I know she's just not into the experience. Food truly doesn't matter to her. There are a few things she likes, and she enjoys going out to eat, but she ends up taking most of her meal home with her. It'll last her at least two more meals. On the nights that Mike works, she'll usually end up eating one of her leftovers from a previous night out, a bowl of cereal, or a piece of peanut butter toast. I don't really get it, but in a way, I do. Because eating by yourself is no fun, and why would you bother to actually cook something for an audience of one?

So one of the things on my list of "fun things to do" isn't that fun right now. No one's fault, just a fact. But it sounds like

I'll get my fun back this weekend, because friends are coming. They're not just Mike and Grace's friends; they're my friends too. And yes, once again I'll be the fifth wheel, but I guess I'm used to that. Or I really should be by now.

"Grace, what do you want for dinner on Friday night? It'll be the beginning of your birthday weekend. It sounds like everyone will be here by five, so we have to plan all of the food for the evening."

"I thought Mike said he was taking care of all the food."

"Yeah, well, Mike's plan of taking care of the food was putting me in charge."

Go figure—no big surprise there. Actually, Mike would've taken care of it, but he knows it wouldn't have been nearly as good. I don't resent it for a minute, because it gives me a focus, something to do. Grace and I talk and decide on doing the shrimp boil. Her favorite food is shrimp, the pot will have all kinds of food that everyone loves, and it's something social to do when everybody is hanging out tomorrow evening. Not that we'll need anything to do—the conversation will be enough. I'll also make some appetizers, we'll have great wine, and I'll come up with something for dessert. Something chocolate. As far as Grace is concerned, if it's not chocolate, it's not worth the calories and really shouldn't be considered dessert.

Friday morning I'm headed to the grocery store with a really long list. This will take a little time, and a little money. No worries there—Mike's paying.

Grace tells me she'll come along to help me out, but I tell her, "No way. This is your birthday weekend. You're the princess and my royal duty is to make your life totally enjoyable."

All of this is being said while I give her a curtsy and a bow. Total crap, but it makes us both laugh. We've taken turns trying to make each other's lives wonderful. Sometimes it doesn't work, but most of the time, it does.

A couple of hours later, I'm driving down our driveway when I notice that Lucas's pickup is back in front of his cabin. Hmm, interesting. I wonder where he's been. No time to go and talk to him, I'm thinking, as I start unloading groceries. Grace runs out to help me.

"How many people are we feeding, and is it for the entire month?" is her question as she helps me haul the bags in.

I then proceed to shoo her out of the kitchen.

"Go and lay out. Take a jet-ski ride. Take a nap. Do whatever you have to do to stay out of my way in the kitchen for the next few hours."

I don't have to tell her twice. I know she feels a little guilty for not helping me, but I remind her it's her birthday weekend and it only comes once a year. Enjoy!

————————

GRACE

Mike comes driving up around two in the afternoon. He sees me laying out on the beach. He's going to give me a hug when he notices that I'm all greased up. He skips that and gives me a kiss instead.

"It's your almost-birthday! Are you excited for the weekend?"

Of course I am. But in a way it's a little weird. To have all of that attention directed at you almost seems a bit much. Oh well, I guess it's not every day that someone turns 65 and becomes an official senior citizen. Medicare and all of that. It's still unbelievable to me that I'm this old and yet feel this good. I should be thankful, and I am, but I just wish it didn't sound so ancient.

Mike and I walk up to the cabin. He and Ellie go over the food details while I go up to shower. Our friends will be here in a few hours. Let the party begin. When I come back downstairs, Mike and Ellie seem to be in a serious conversation. One guess, and I'm right, they're talking about Lucas. Mike asks Ellie if she'd like for him to go over and talk to Lucas to find out what's going on.

"Absolutely not. If anything's going to come of this, and now I really doubt it, we'll take care of it ourselves."

She's right—this isn't junior high. But Mike and I are "fix it right now" kind of people. And if we could fix it, we'd be marching over there in a heartbeat. The sad thing is that everything was going so well, and boom—it's over. We're all in the dark, and I hope that eventually Lucas will be able to tell Ellie what's going on. We all want to know.

But it's my birthday weekend, and Ellie says that we're going to have fun. After all she's been through, I don't doubt for a minute that she can pull it off.

CHAPTER 33

ELLIE

The three of us go out to the porch to start happy hour early. Lucas' cabin is right in my line of view. I just want to glare at that stupid cabin and will him to come out and talk to me. It definitely hasn't happened so far, and probably never will. I just don't get it.

One of these days I'm going to get up the nerve to stomp on over there, knock on his door until he opens it, and say to him, "Tell me what's going on or I'm never speaking to you again."

Maybe that's not much of a threat, seeing as he hasn't wanted to talk to me this whole week.

But I'm putting that out of my mind for the weekend. Time for some new topics of conversation, and that'll certainly happen once our friends put in their appearance. And as I'm thinking that, they come driving down the gravel driveway. You can't mistake that sound, or the cloud of dust that happens whenever someone drives down.

We come down the stairs to greet them. Hugs and "hi's" all around. What a great group—this is going to be fun! We help them haul their bags in as they "ooh and aah" about the cabin. They've been here before, but it was many years ago, back in the "we're roughing it at the cabin" days. Mike and Grace take them all upstairs and they pick out their rooms, impressed with the new beds and comfy mattresses. Grace gives them the grand tour while I haul out the drinks and glasses for happy hour. Lots of compliments from them all on the redecorating. Yeah, like we had a choice.

Everyone grabs their drinks and some of the many appetizers I've prepared, stylishly arranged on a charcuterie board. Oh, I know, that sounds really stuffy. And pretentious. But hey, it's the thing right now, right? Once everyone is loaded up on their first round of drinks and plates full of food, the next decision has to be made. Should we sit out on the beach, the grass, or the porch? Since the porch has the most comfortable furniture by far, that's the choice that gets the most votes. I can tell, we're going to be a bunch of bums this weekend. Who's to complain?

It's fun to see these friends again. They all live in Sioux Falls, so I don't get to see them as much as Grace and Mike do. Most of us go back a long way. Except for Mike and Scott, the rest of us lived in the same town when we were little kids. Small town South Dakota. Really, really small. A place with a few paved roads and lots of gravel roads and tumbleweeds. Picture the old wild west in your mind. Except it wasn't wild (the church was the central attraction), and South Dakota is considered a "plains state," not west. We went to the local school together for a few years, until our family moved to Michigan.

And no, it wasn't a one-room schoolhouse. It was a four-room schoolhouse, first grade through eighth. Two grades for each teacher. No kindergarten then—I guess we were too smart and went right to first grade. It sounds a little backwards, but I really don't think it was. It was just a tiny town where we were allowed to run wild, with our parents never worrying about us or wondering where we were. We came home to eat, and spent the rest of our time playing games, spending our nickels at the grocery store, occasionally getting a bottle of soda pop from the gas station, and throwing firecrackers at each other. We came home when it got dark. Winter wasn't quite as much fun, but we did build some awesome snow forts and caves. Our family looks back fondly on those days with no cares or worries. I should clarify that. We as kids had no worries and loved our carefree days there. Our parents had lots of worries—money was extremely tight—thus the move to Michigan.

The seven of us sit there together, reminiscing. For a while. A long while actually. It's time to start cooking dinner or we're all going to be sleeping in our chairs. Evan and Ruth are the "early to bed, early to rise" type people. So not Grace and Mike's style, but their friendship has survived this glitch. Love overcomes all, right?

The guys go outside to get the water in the pot boiling. We women go in the kitchen to prepare all of the food. Oh yeah, that's right—I prepared all of the food. Which amounted to cutting up some potatoes, slicing the sausage, cutting the ears of corn in thirds—yeah, that's about it. Impressive, huh?

We put our chairs in a circle around the pot. Mike throws things in the pot on my direction with my expert timing.

Whatever. No expert timing involved. We just thrown in stuff when I feel like it. Potatoes and Cajun spice in first while we sit and talk, onions in next while we sit and drink, corn in next while I refill the drinks, then the crab and shrimp. Throw it on the table, drizzle butter, salt and other seasonings on it–it's a meal. Pretty easy but somehow impressive for those who have never had it before. All of this thanks to Lucas. Wish he was here.

Mike builds one of his trademark, huge bonfires as we sit around it, talk, and tell stories. He then hauls out some cigars for the guys. Oh please, Grace and I have horrible memories of cigars.

For some strange reason, whenever we went on a trip in our super cool station wagon, our dad decided he was on vacation, and this was his time to smoke a cigar. Grace has a queasy stomach and got extremely carsick if we drove for more than an hour. Naturally, she always had to sit in the front seat, between Mom and Dad, because this was supposed to help. Out would come the cigar. We would all moan, but Dad thought everything was okay, because he held the cigar out the half-opened window. No air-conditioning in those days. And never mind where he was blowing the smoke–it didn't help. We could all time it to the millisecond.

At 65 minutes, 30 seconds, Grace would be yelling, "We gotta stop. I have to puke."

Dad would pull over, Grace would jump out over mom, and retch by the side of the road. It never failed.

And Dad would always say to Mom, "You have to give that girl more Dramamine."

Grace and I crab at Mike about the cigars, and the guys move down-wind from us. It helps, but it's not perfect. I give my brother-in-law a hard time.

"This is Grace's weekend. Please put them out."

Carma joins the men because she likes the smell. She's always been a bit of a wild breed, but in a really fun way. The guys puff extra-fast, while I'm hoping they get sick. It's all in good fun, and Grace and I are good sports about it. This too shall pass.

We are turning into old people. It's only ten o-clock, and half of us are yawning and struggling to stay awake. We women had talked about sleeping in the bunkroom together so we could stay up late—a good old-fashioned slumber party—but I can see that that's not going to happen.

"Let's pack it up. We have a big day of celebrating tomorrow."

The whole group agrees, even Grace. Amazing that she gave up so easily. Maybe she is getting old!

CHAPTER 34

GRACE

I wake up slowly, as I always do. All of a sudden it hits me—it's my birthday! The first thing I do is look out the window. Oh, thank goodness, the sun is shining. I've had a few birthdays where it's been cloudy. It spoils the whole mood of the day. It could just as well not be summer if it's going to be cloudy. So this is a good start. I look at my phone for the time. 9:45. I don't feel guilty. Our friends have probably been up for hours, but they know this is my "modus operandi." They won't be mad. I see that I have some texts from the kids and some of the grandkids. I scroll through these with a smile.

I come down the stairs greeted with a chorus of "happy birthday" from everyone. I was right, they're all up and have been for a while. Their problem, not mine. Most of them have been drinking coffee (not Ruth—she hates it as much as I do).

Ellie declares, "It's mimosa time! Or should we just have champagne?"

We decide on mimosas. Not that it makes much difference (the orange juice is negligible), but it makes us all feel like we're not actually drinking this early in the morning.

Mike and Ellie start making their famous big breakfasts. This is not for me, and we all know it. But I go along with it, because it makes everyone else so happy. Mike goes all-out and makes me a Belgian waffle with strawberries and whipped cream. Now this I could get used to! Then things get a little crazy with everyone shooting whipped cream into their mouths. They go beyond crazy when we start shooting it across the island at each other. Laughs all around. Except when we have to clean it up.

It's a lazy morning as we sit around the island, eating until everyone has had more than enough, along with numerous cups of coffee and glasses of mimosas. Ugh—now it finally is clean-up time. But yay me! I'm the birthday girl! I get shooed out of the kitchen. August 1 is looking to be a good day.

Now it's time for "a plan." Different options: boating, jet-skiing, lying on the beach, swimming. Boating it is. While everyone goes upstairs to change into their suits and get their towels and sunscreen, Ellie and I pack a cooler. Make that two. One for water and other various beverages, and the other for food. We make our famous boat buns, and pack them along with veggies and fruit (we'll pretend we're healthy), and chips, crackers, and peanuts. More than enough to tide us over after our big breakfast.

We load everyone and everything and take off. Our boat is good-sized, but with seven people and all of the stuff we brought along, it's full enough. We start out driving east, along the south bluffs. We make our way along the dam, and then start heading west along the north shore. There are a lot of boats out on the lake. Not at all unusual for a hot summer Saturday. Everyone is friendly and we all wave at other boaters as we drive by. Some people are trying to ski. Definitely amateurs. Either that, or gluttons for punishment. There are so many waves and boat wakes that your chance of being successful at it are slim to none. Better off tubing or wakeboarding on a busy Saturday.

Mike keeps driving along, but all of a sudden it hits us—we're extremely hot. Even the breeze isn't enough to cool us off. I look at my watch—90 degrees. No wonder we're baking in this boat. I ask Mike to anchor it. Time to jump in the water. We pull up into a nice cove and Mike drops the anchor. The waves aren't too bad here, so at least I won't end up getting seasick. News flash here—it's actually motion sickness. Cars, airplanes, boats, they all make a motion that makes me extremely nauseous. I'm just on the edge—we'll be in the water soon and all will be well.

We all jump in, and it feels so good. Oh wait—not all of us. Poor Evan and Ruth never learned how to swim, so they won't be jumping in. Mike goes back in the boat and finds a life jacket for Evan, so now he's game and jumps in with the rest of us. Ruth put her life jacket on the second we boarded the boat. She's deathly afraid of water. She does make it a few steps down the back ladder and sits there with the lower half of her body in the water. She'll do fine there and manages to cool off that way.

Ellie and I are fortunate in that respect. Mom was a farm kid and never had the chance to learn how to swim. She was petrified at the thought of going in a lake or pool. She was adamant that all of us kids would learn to swim. Even though we knew she didn't have the time, she religiously took all of us to swimming lessons, year after year. We never appreciated it at the time, because many times it was early June and the water was freezing, but it's a gift that was truly sacrificial on her part, and means the world to all of us as adults.

We putter around in the water for a long time, just laughing and talking. This is what summer is meant to be!

Believe it or not, it doesn't take long for Mike to ask, "What did you bring along to eat?"

I know swimming makes you hungry, but you can't really say that treading water for as long as we did is going to make you ravenous. But then there's Mike. I love him, but his stomach is a bottomless pit.

We climb back into the boat. Ellie and I open up the coolers. Water, pop, beer, wine in one; buns, veggies, and other snacks in the other. Okay, I just have to say it—no matter how healthy we try to be, the water and veggies are the last to go. What's that ancient proverb? You can lead a horse to water, but you can't make him drink? I don't know if this really applies to this situation, but you catch my drift.

We spend the whole afternoon doing this—boating along the shore, jumping into the water and cooling off, and then back in the boat.

Mike offers again. "Does anyone want to ski or tube?"

Wow, we are getting old. There are no takers. I finally make the call—it's time to quit. I want to get off this boat before I'm queasy and can't enjoy the evening. Everyone agrees; it's time to head to shore.

We head in and haul a ton of stuff off the boat and into the cabin. Why does it always seem that you don't bring that much stuff with you on a boating excursion, but when you get back, it seems like all of that stuff has multiplied? That's definitely the case here. But we're all able-bodied adults and everyone's willing to help.

I tell everyone, "Okay, here's the plan. We're going out for dinner tonight. There's no hurry—we have all night. Get cleaned up, take a nap if you'd like. We'll meet back downstairs here in an hour and a half. Sound good?"

This is met with overwhelming approval. I don't want these people falling asleep at eight o'clock on my birthday!

I take a quick shower and towel dry my hair. It gets curly when it's hot and humid. I fluff it up—so easy—and decide to take a quick nap. I'm the world's best day-time sleeper. But also the world's worst night-time sleeper. I guess we all have our crosses to bear. I hear Mike in the shower as I doze. I know he won't sleep in the afternoon. I tune him out and zonk out for an hour.

I wake up a little groggy. I hear voices downstairs and I think, "I can't sleep my birthday away!"

I put on a cute little summer dress—spaghetti straps, flippy skirt. So glad I can still wear this at the age of 65. Not a hot 30-year-old, but nothing to complain about either. I match it with some strappy sandals. A few years ago I would've put on high heels, but it seems like a little much, and they're not as much in style as they used to be. I take some time on my makeup. The older you get, the longer it takes to apply makeup artistically. Especially in the morning. If you have to be somewhere on time, you have to get up an hour earlier just to let the sleep wrinkles relax before you can be seen out in public.

"Okay, Grace, where are we going for dinner?"

I've picked out a place with a beautiful patio and a great view of the river. We get into two vehicles and drive into

Yankton. We reach the restaurant, and we're seated out on the patio with the best view, because Mike called days ago for reservations.

What fun! My beloved husband, my wonderful sister, and the best friends ever. My kids and grandkids aren't here, but that's okay. We'll get to celebrate my birthday all over again when we're together.

Time to order. This place is known for their steaks. And when you live in this part of the country, they're going to be good. Probably better than anyplace in the world. Mike tells the waiter that it's my birthday, and jokingly tells him that we expect great service because of it. The waiter is looking for a great tip, asks me how old I am, and fawns over me when I tell him I'm 65. Predictably, he tells me that I don't look a day over 40. Unrealistic, but nice. Just as expected.

The food arrives. I'm not a great eater, but besides shrimp, steak is my favorite (with some really great white bread on the side). We used to take our oldest grand-daughter to a local steak place when she was only three years old.

She always said, "Steak and buns, that's all I need."

And that was truly the case. She could eat a whole steak and stuff a bunch of those warm, gooey white rolls in her mouth all night long. Well, she takes after her grandma in that respect.

My thoughts exactly. Skip the vegetables, even skip the potato. Give me a decent steak with some warm, gooey white bread with cinnamon butter, and that's all I need. As the steak is placed before me, there's always the anticipation of that first cut. I cut into the middle of my ribeye. That first cut is going to make or break my evening. I hold my breath. It's perfect! Extremely rare, probably not even warm in the middle. Just the way I ordered it. Everyone around the table is grossed out, but none of them is surprised. They've known me long enough.

We have great conversation over great food. We're sitting out on a gorgeous patio with a tranquil view. Until the live music starts. I like music; all kinds of music. Oh wait, I really don't like country or jazz. I'm not crazy about rap either. Now that I think about it, I guess I don't like all kinds of music. I must admit, this guy who just started singing, accompanied by his guitar, is pretty good. But why do they always have to play so loudly? We're trying to eat and talk here. We had no intention of coming to a rock concert where we have to yell at each other to be heard. Thankfully we're all done eating and decide our next step for the evening.

Carma mentions that they went to a fun karaoke bar here in town earlier this summer. Sure, why not? She does inform us that this is not your typical karaoke bar, but we'll see for ourselves soon enough.

She's right. This isn't typical. When you think of karaoke, you picture a somewhat rowdy place, with people who have had too much to drink, getting up and making fools of themselves while no one is really listening to them. This is not that kind of place.

This would be called geriatric karaoke. It's located near a retirement community, and it looks like this is their primary clientele.

I give Carma a look. "What were you thinking? This is supposed to be fun?"

She laughs at me and says, "The most fun part is watching these people. They take their karaoke very seriously."

We find a table for the seven of us while everyone stares. It's like walking into a rough biker bar, wondering when we'll get chased out. Physically we won't be challenged, but we're not getting a lot of warm, fuzzy looks either.

And Carma is right. These people do take their karaoke very seriously. There is an elderly woman who's singing a 60's ballad. Her eyes are closed, she has some serious expression on her face, along with dramatic sweeping arm movements. You would think she's auditioning for American Idol. Good thing we're sitting way in the back, because we can hardly contain our laughter. This is going to be good!

The DJ is years younger than anyone else in the place, and you can tell this is not his greatest gig. But he puts on a smile and makes it as much fun as he possibly can. Along with the singing, there's a pretty good-sized dance floor with a number of couples slow-dancing. I'm not making fun of any of them, because Mike and I are terrible at slow-dancing together. Our height difference makes it nearly impossible. We took dance classes once and quit after the second session because we couldn't stop laughing hysterically. The DJ comes over during his break and sits down and chats with us.

"Do any of you sing?"

Ruth encourages Ellie and me to sing something together, but that's not going to happen. We ask him if he sings. If so, we'd love to hear him.

"What do you want to hear?"

"How about Uptown Funk, or any other song that has been recorded in this current century?"

He laughs. "I'll see what I can do."

And just like that, he's up there, and we hear the familiar opening beats of the song.

"Let's go dance!" I yell.

We go up to the dance floor and all start dancing. Ellie doesn't have a partner, but it doesn't matter, because we're just doing one big group dance. Scott is a tall, slim man who typically is a little on the quiet side. But he's had a few drinks and we egg him on, and out comes this person who can dance like Michael Jackson. It is so out of character, and we love it.

However, from the looks of the crowd, I don't think our antics are being appreciated. Who cares? The DJ is into it, as if this is the most fun he's had here in weeks. There are a few people who get up and join us. Maybe this'll be the most fun *they've* had in weeks. Possibly, or possibly not, but at least we shook things up for a little while.

We stay for another hour or so. We finally get to the point where we can't stand the song choices anymore (how many Elvis songs can you listen to?), and decide to head on out. The DJ waves at us. I think he's sorry to see us go.

CHAPTER 35

ELLIE

What a fun night. We're back at the cabin, sitting around the fire that Mike built. Evan is even worse than Mike is: he keeps throwing logs on the fire until the flames are almost reaching the tree branches above us. I go into hostess mode. Grace wants to help, but I tell her absolutely not. Ruth and Carma join me in the kitchen instead. We get drinks for everyone, and I bring out the birthday cake with candles lit. Not 65 of them—that would make a fire almost as big as the one we have in the fire pit. We sing the obligatory happy birthday song, and I dish out the molten lava cake. Deep, dark chocolate of course. No one's hungry, but it would be rude if anyone passed this up.

I glance over at Lucas' cabin. Lights on. Wouldn't it be fun if he would just come out and join us? It's been a long week of wondering what his problem is. I don't know how much more of this avoidance and tension I can take.

Mike looks at me. "Should I go over and see if Lucas wants to join us?"

I just shake my head no. He knows we're out here, and obviously has no intention of joining us. Disappointing. But life goes on, right? And right now we're celebrating Grace's life, and doing a darn good job of it.

Mike stands up and makes and makes a toast. "To my amazing Grace. Cheers!"

Lots of glasses clinking.

Carma, Ruth and Grace start in on some of their nurses' stories. I'm not a nurse, never wanted to be a nurse, and would've been terrible at it, but their stories do bring lots of laughs. Then Mike starts in on some of his firefighter and paramedic stories, which are even more hilarious. Evan, Scott and I don't have any fun work-related stories to share. I guess being a social worker, a prison counselor and a computer programmer aren't the types of professions that make you laugh until you cry.

As much fun as we're having, I can see some of the crowd starting to wilt. It's after midnight, the conversation is winding down, but it is a comfortable feeling just settling back in our chairs. The stars are shining brilliantly and it's a full moon.

Grace remarks, "I'm so glad that I'm not working tonight. It's always super busy and the craziest people put in an appearance on a full-moon night."

Carma has worked in the ER and she totally agrees—at all costs, try to avoid working during a full moon.

Evan and Ruth are nodding off in their chairs. They decide to call it a night.

Grace is a little disappointed.

"Seriously? This is it?"

Mike points out to her that technically this is no longer her birthday, and we start making our way inside, all agreeing that it was a great night. Grace is still smiling in her "post-birthday" bliss, and gives me a huge hug, thanking me for her best party ever. Strong praise—and I'll take it.

GRACE

Everyone is up and sitting around the kitchen island by the time I make my way downstairs.

"Happy day after your birthday," they all shout.

Obviously planned ahead of time. They are certainly more awake than I am. I'm sure they've already gone through numerous pots of coffee and Ruth is on her second Diet Coke. I wish I could do caffeine. I think it would make my mornings more pleasant and definitely more productive. I used to drink three Diet Cokes a day, but once, when I had the flu, I didn't drink any caffeine for almost a week, and now I can't do it. My hands start shaking, I'm jittery all over, and I get heart palpitations. I feel like I could crawl out of my skin. It's a horrible feeling. I suppose I could try and wean myself back onto it, but what's the point? Besides being a "more awake, more fun" version of morning Grace, I really don't think it's worth it at this stage of my life.

Time for a scaled-down version of a big breakfast. Ellie's delicious English muffin breakfast sandwich. I can handle this.

An added plus is that the clean-up is relatively easy. We take our paper plates outside and eat out on the beach. Another gorgeous, sunny day. Ellie absolutely could not have picked a better summer to be here. We make our plans for the day. Great idea–how about a repeat of yesterday? Boating, swimming, eating, drinking. What's not to like? Everyone moves a little slower today, but we finally get everything organized and we're off.

Another fun day, but you can tell the group is seriously lacking in the energy department. The sun really does take it out of you, or else we're just old. A combination of the two, perhaps. We grill some hamburgers for supper, and then we start with the goodbyes. Not sad, because we'll all see each other soon, but a little bit emotional, because we had so much fun. This "65" thing? So far, so good.

ELLIE

"Well, Grace, how was turning 65?"

Grace, Mike and I are sitting on the porch with glasses of wine, basking in the post birthday-bash euphoria. We got to see another beautiful sunset, and now we're just sitting in the dark, watching the fireflies twinkle on and off.

"It absolutely could not have been any better. Between the sunshine, the food, the friends, the karaoke–the whole weekend was perfect. Thank you both so much! I couldn't love either one of you more–you know that, right?"

All of a sudden it hits me. We forgot to give Grace her presents! I run in the cabin and come back carrying a small gift bag. She reaches in and pulls out an envelope. Inside it says, "Good for a one-hour massage and a pedicure." She tries to look excited but she's not really pulling it off. I start laughing and tell her I'm just joking. Grace is so incredibly ticklish that she hates massages with a passion and pedicures are even worse. She's had only one or two in her entire life and she spent the entire session literally praying for it to be over. She's incredibly relieved that it's only a prank and that she won't have to live through that ordeal.

She just glares at me and says, "I thought you knew me better than that! I was beginning to wonder if you'd totally forgotten what I like and dislike."

I tell her to dig a little deeper. She pulls out another envelope. This one is a legitimate gift card to her favorite boutique in downtown Sioux Falls. Gift cards may seem impersonal to some people, but we both love them. We're at an age where we shouldn't have to fake that we like something, so just let us pick out our own stuff.

Mike pulls a box out of his back pocket and hands it to Grace. She's usually not excited about surprises or gifts that she hasn't specifically asked for, but she looks pretty animated when she opens the box. A spectacular diamond tennis bracelet.

"Oh, Mike, I love it!"

Mike comments, "I know you don't play tennis anymore, and I really don't get what a bracelet has to do with tennis, but I thought you'd like it."

We laugh and Grace proceeds to try it on. A perfect fit, which truly is a miracle. And here's why. We have the hereditary trait of having freakishly small wrists. Our mom and some of the other women in our family tree have wrists the size of a child. Do you know how hard it is to find watches or bracelets that fit? Grace once picked out a beautiful watch and the jeweler said it was no problem, he could make any watch fit any wrist. After he had taken off more than half of the band, he informed her, "Yeah, this is a problem." Back to a leather strap where she could cut off most of it and poke a new hole where she needed it.

"Mike, how did you find a bracelet to fit me?"

"Special order, a few months ago. It appears that really wealthy people sometimes buy these bracelets for their young daughters. Lucky you," he says with a smile.

Lucky Grace, exactly. To have a guy that takes the time to come up with the perfect birthday gift—well, what a blessing. And I truly am happy for her. But I can't help but remember when I had a husband like that and felt as fortunate as Grace feels right now. And when, just a few short weeks ago, I felt that this good fortune was going to happen to me again. Instead, I'm sitting here, watching the lights on in Lucas' cabin, with him nowhere in sight. But I'm not going to turn into a bitter, jealous old woman. I'm better than that, and I've proven it time after time. God has blessed me over and over, and for now, it's enough.

CHAPTER 36

GRACE

Mike is ready for bed. He has to head back to Sioux Falls tomorrow and has a big week ahead of him. Actually, Ellie and I are more than ready for bed also. Being in the sun and on the water really does tire you out.

As we're picking up our drinks and my gifts, we see something we haven't seen in over five years. Lights on in the cabin next door. No, not Lucas' cabin; the cabin on the other side of us.

A couple about our parents' age have owned that cabin as long as we've owned ours. Years ago Dad and Mom would hang out with them some evenings. Their last name was Jansen, I think. It's been a while. The Jansens didn't have any children, and since we haven't seen them in so many years, we lost touch. I don't even know if they're still living. But even though we haven't seen any life at that cabin in years, it's always been kept up immaculately. The Jansens must be paying big bucks to some cleaning company to keep it looking that nice.

It's definitely weird to see lights on there. I ask Mike if we should go over and check it out.

"None of our business," is his reply. Besides, he knows that Ellie and I will go over and check it out tomorrow, because we're just that concerned (or nosy).

We go upstairs, brush our teeth, and fall into bed. I guess I'm sleeping on the left side tonight. Neither of us care what side of the bed we sleep on. I usually like to sleep on the side that has the clock, but that's not written in stone. I like to think that it means we're not a couple of old people too set in their ways.

The other interesting fact about our sleeping arrangements as a married couple: due to our occupations, we've probably slept apart as much as we've slept together. Between my work as a nurse, working mostly nights, and Mike's work as a firefighter, working 24-hour shifts, we both have slept alone—a lot. I look at this as possibly a plus. Maybe God's preparing us for the day when one of us is gone. At least sleeping alone won't be the biggest adjustment one of us will have to make.

Mike wakes me up in the morning. "I have to head out. Love you."

"Love you too. Drive safely. And hon, thanks for the present and the wonderful weekend. It couldn't have been better. And by the way, happy 48th anniversary of the day I first saw you."

He smiles and gives me a long good-bye kiss. I smile. This guy is the best thing that could've ever happened in my life. I fall back asleep with that smile still on my face.

I wake up later to the sound of music. Ellie is busy cleaning in the kitchen with her favorite playlist on. Early 70's to mid-80's. Who doesn't like that era in music (if you bypass some of the disco stuff)? Music is so incredible in that it conjures up all sorts of memories—high school dances, hanging with friends, making out in a car, even jobs that we had at the time. You can easily picture yourself in a specific situation when you hear a particular song. Our minds are amazing!

Ellie and I dance in the kitchen a little, but then I tell her, "Enough of this cleaning! You worked hard this weekend and today is just going to be a lounging day. Go get your swimsuit on."

I don't need to tell her twice. I already have mine on because this was my plan for the day—relaxing without any work. I'm still in my post-birthday euphoria. Or depression. I haven't figured out yet which one it is.

We're dozing on the beach when we hear someone approach us.

"Hi gals. I just thought I'd come over and introduce myself!"

Ellie and I sit up and gawk at this person who's standing over us. She's tall and thin with bleached blond hair pulled up in a fashionably messy ponytail. She has more makeup on than should ever be allowed on a beach. She's dressed in a minuscule hot pink bikini. She looks pretty good in it, but the longer I stare my first thought is "This woman has had lots of work done." Not very charitable on my part, but really?

Close up she looks to be in her fifties, give or take a few years. Her face is pulled back really tight, her lips are huge, so is her chest. Her stomach is sporting a six-pack. Okay, I have to give her credit, that did take some work on her part, probably after the tummy tuck she had done. She appears to have had a Brazilian butt-lift done also. I also have to give her credit for her legs—toned and muscular.

"Hi, I'm Cyndi. That's Cyndi with an 'i.' Actually, it's first a 'y' after the 'C,' and then an 'i' at the end. Just a little different!" She giggles.

I can't say as I really care because I don't plan on putting her name in writing anytime soon. But now that I look at her closely, she looks exactly like a Cyndi with a "y" and then an "i." Kind of like a hooker or stripper name? Okay, that thought was really harsh. I'm kinder than that and I need to give her a chance. Maybe?

"May I join you? There's nothing better than lying on a beach, chatting it up with your girlfriends!"

Your girlfriends? Us? We were just relaxing, reading and sleeping, perfectly content. And now we're your girlfriends? Chatting it up?

I can almost hear Ellie sigh in the same way that I'm sighing in my mind. It was so peaceful. But we were taught to always be friendly by our super-friendly parents, so our trained response kicks in.

We make small talk and of course ask the question, "Are you staying at the cabin next door?"

Quite the deductive reasoning on our part. She proceeds to tell us that she's renting it for the month of August (a whole month? There goes our peace and quiet). Supposedly the Jansens are both still alive and kicking but live down in Florida. She then goes on to tell us this extremely complicated story about how she knows them—something about an ex-father-in-law and some second cousin once removed. Our eyes are glazing over as she prattles on about every branch on her family tree. Why do people always think we care about their relatives that we've never heard of or have never met? After she goes through this whole long, convoluted story, it turns out she lives in Florida right next door to the Jansens. Incredible. Incredibly boring, if I'm being honest.

The saga continues. We pick up on the key points. Twice divorced, one adult son, no grandchildren. Enough. Ellie and I pick up our books and point out that we just love reading on the beach, since it's so relaxing. She doesn't catch the hint. She probably hasn't picked up a book since junior high. The good news is that she has lots of friends in town and will probably be partying with them every night. What a relief!

We hear the slap of Lucas' screen door. Wow—a Lucas sighting—it's been a while. He walks out on the dock to his boat and takes off with a wave.

"Who is that and what's his story?" asks Cyndi. "Is he single? Is he involved with anyone? Does he live here year-round? Does he have any kids? Oh, I hope not, because that just makes things messy. I'll have to introduce myself to him when he comes back. Come on, ladies, give me some details!"

Ellie rolls her eyes and ignores all the questions.

I respond, "His name is Lucas, he's single, and that's about all we know."

Evidently, that's all Cyndi needs to know too. She's up and running, talking about how it's hot, she's sweaty, she needs to shower, she needs to change into something nice, until she's finally out of view and out of vocal range. This last month here could prove to be exhausting.

CHAPTER 37

ELLIE

"What just happened? I feel like we've been hit by a tornado."

"Yep. A blond one named Cyndi," Grace smirks.

I know that Grace has the same feeling that I do. We truly are kind people, and are friendly to everyone that we meet, but do we really have to spend the last month of our summer with someone who could have the word "bimbo" tattooed across her chest? Okay, maybe that's a little extreme, but it's not too far off the mark. Heaven help us!

Lucas comes back from his boat ride, gives us another wave, and heads back into his cabin. And then it hits me. Maybe we've been dragging him down this summer, the way Cyndi has immediately dragged us down. He's probably been perfectly content to have this beautiful cove all to himself for years. And then we came in, monopolized his time and space, forced him to build a shack that he probably never wanted, and never gave him a moment's peace. I feel sick about it. I mention this to Grace.

"You know, maybe there's a bit of truth to that. We definitely invaded his space. But he came along, hook, line and sinker. He was friendly from the start, and he definitely was into you. Remember, he asked you out; you didn't ask him. And the way that the four of us got along so well—he wasn't faking that. I truly believe he was having a great time. So yeah, maybe we did upset his world a little, but I got the feeling that he was ready for it."

"Maybe so. No—no maybe about it. He was into it! I really believe that. And that's why I can't make any sense of what's going on now."

"Ellie, you really need to talk to him. Make him open up. Maybe it won't be pleasant, but it's better than living life in limbo. You deserve more from him than the fact that he's just ignoring you and shutting you out."

I agree with her assessment, because it's the same thing that I've been thinking for days. Maybe I'll walk over to his place this evening and see what he has to say. Grace agrees with that thought and pushes me to make the effort.

We go in, shower, and take our glasses of wine out on the porch. Dinner tonight will be leftovers from the weekend. Actually, our dinners for the next few nights will be leftovers. Certainly easy, but it might get a little sickening. Grace will be fine with that, since that's usually what she does most nights that Mike is working.

"So are you getting up the nerve to go over to Lucas's place? What are you going to say? How are you going to get him to open up? Should we role-play? Tell me what you're going to say and I'll pretend I'm Lucas."

"Absolutely not. That's stupid and it's totally meaningless because neither one of us know what he's going to say. We're shooting blind here."

And that's the truth. How a relationship could go from fun to done in the short time that it happened is beyond anything I've ever experienced.

We heat up some leftovers in the microwave and bring our plates back to the porch, along with refilled glasses of wine. I've switched to red but Grace will drink white all evening. She has a limited nose for good wines. Now that I think about it, she once told me she has a limited nose, period. Supposedly if you can smell things more with your right nostril than your left, it's a sign you're going to get Alzheimer's Disease. Who knows? But I know that she's not wasting any time worrying about it.

We're just finishing up our meal while I'm getting up the nerve to head over to talk to Lucas. A vision of pink shows up on our lawn.

"Yoo-hoo, gals, I'm just heading over to introduce myself to Lucas. Hope it's okay that I'm walking across your lawn. See you later!"

I'm seething! After all of the thought and the nerve that I was going to put into this evening! Seriously! The guts of that woman. I've known her for less than a day and she's as annoying as fingernails on a chalkboard. Grace is as ticked off as I am. We sit there fuming about this foiled attempt–how dare she?

Of course, we watch the scene play out. Cyndi knocks on Lucas' door. He comes to the door. Darn it, we can't hear the conversation, but we see the body language. There's lots of it going on. She's flashing a huge smile, fluffing her hair, jutting out one hip, leaning forward so he can see down her low-cut dress—all the tricks of the trade. Oh wait—we don't know she's a professional—but she's definitely done this routine before. We watch the conversation go on. Then all of a sudden Lucas goes back inside while she's standing there. We want to laugh. She got shot down. But wait! Out comes Lucas, holding two beers. Are you kidding me? How shallow is that?

They go and sit on the barstools by the shack. The walk isn't exactly pretty, because she has on 5-inch stilettos that sink into the grass with every step she takes. We do have a little laugh at her expense as we watch that take place. But watching them sit at the bar of the shack doesn't make us happy. This is the shack that was our idea. We helped build it. And we decorated it personally, and with our own money. Whose stupid idea was that? Oh yeah, Grace's. I'm not taking responsibility for that.

Who needs binoculars when the drama is unfolding right before your eyes? A gorgeous sunset takes place. Naturally. And they're watching it together. And we're watching them watch it. Painful. Cyndi is pulling out all the stops. Caressing his arm, moving in closely, laughing at his every word. Lucas seems interested, but not all-in. His body language tells me that he's holding back a little. Thank goodness. At least I don't think I'll have to watch a full-on make-out session.

About the time that I think "He's really not that into her," they stand up, she grabs his hand, and they head inside. I didn't see that one coming. And then there's nothing more to see. They're inside his cabin, and I refuse to sit out here and wait to see when she comes strolling home, if that even happens tonight. I've had it.

GRACE

Sitting on the porch like peeping-toms isn't my idea of a good time. This has been a long day and an even longer evening. I feel sorry for Ellie. On the day that Lucas checked out so abruptly, we all got the feeling that he didn't want to be involved with anyone, not just Ellie. Tonight gave a different vibe to that whole theory. Is he that shallow that he could be taken in by someone like Cyndi? Is he just another idiot guy that falls for the whole "looks" package? Don't get me wrong. Ellie is a beautiful 62-year-old woman, but she's not a made-over Barbie doll.

Maybe our warm-fuzzy feelings about Lucas were wrong from the start. But the guy seemed so sincere, so invested in our family, so much fun, and so perfect, that it's hard to alter our feelings for him. But there has always been one red flag--the fact that he never wanted to share his past. Yes, we know the basics about his family and his teenage and college years, but that's where his information ends. There's a huge gap that we know nothing about, and that is concerning. If there is going to be any closure here, Ellie is going to have dig a little deeper for the truth.

ELLIE

What do I do with this? About the time that I think I'm going to make a huge all-in effort with Lucas, Cyndi shows up. If this is what Lucas is after, I am so not that girl. And if this is what he wants, I am out of here. I'm looking for a meaningful relationship, not a roll in the hay. To be honest, I never got the feeling from him that that is what he was looking for either. I'm sitting up in bed with my head spinning. Tonight was the night I was going to get some answers. Or at least I hoped I was. Why did I think tonight was going to be any different, when I've questioned him before and have gotten nothing? He seems to be such a wonderful guy—everything I'm looking for. Or so I thought.

For some reason, the day of the "near-drowning" did him in. The day that he told me that he couldn't get close to me, the kids, and the grandkids. Relationship issues? Something that happened in his past? Something freaky with kids? Pedophile issues? No, can't be.

Okay, this is just crazy. I don't believe any of this for a minute. But when it's 1:00 AM and you can't sleep, your mind takes you to weird places. I go to Grace's room. No surprise—she's still awake.

"May I take one of your sleeping pills?"

Sleep does come after that. But it's filled with wild dreams. Dreams of Will, dreams of grandchildren drowning, dreams of falling off cliffs, dreams of Dad dying. Not a restful night. Pretty much a disaster. I wake up to a beautiful day, but it takes me a while to put all of those nightmares out of my mind. I say a prayer in which I ask God to bless us with another day filled with love. It gives me peace.

The next few days are a repeat of yesterday. Sunny skies, a light breakfast, lying out on the beach with Grace, reading, Cyndi joining us for most of the afternoon, cleaning up, drinking wine on the porch, dinner. And the worst part of each day, watching Cyndi prance over to Lucas' place in the evening. Torture. With each day that passes, I feel like I know Lucas less and less. Seeing him with someone like Cyndi is nothing I could've ever envisioned.

I just want to scream at him, "What are you thinking?"

I am in a place of deep disillusionment right now. Grace knows it and tries to entertain me. One evening we go out to eat. Another evening she suggests a movie. We even go miniature golfing one evening. How desperate are we?

It's Friday and Mike shows up for the weekend. Good deal–it's time for some new conversation. We tell him all about Cyndi. About this time the woman in our conversation shows up to introduce herself to Mike. Can she just smell when a new man is around? Mike asks her if she'd like to join us for a glass of wine. Really, Mike? Are you taken in by her too, or are you just being friendly?

The four of us are sitting out on the lawn, enjoying happy hour. Or some of us are. Surprise, surprise. Who should come walking over but Lucas? He and Mike are happy to see each other and they catch up on their latest projects. Now this is the old Lucas. Or the "we knew him for six weeks" Lucas. Cyndi is desperately trying to get Lucas' attention but he and Mike are deep in conversation.

Cyndi pouts and finally says to Lucas, "I'm going out tonight with friends. You're welcome to come along."

Lucas declines, to our surprise. Cyndi flounces off and it's back to the four of us.

“I’ve got some steaks marinating and a Caesar salad ready to go. Do you want to stay for dinner, Lucas?”

He hesitates for just a minute and then agrees. He thinks it would be fun to eat at the shack, like old times. Old times? It’s only been a few weeks since we sat there together.

It is like old times—and very good times, at that. Probably the best times I’ve had in years. This is the way it should be. But not quite the way it should be, because I still have questions, and there’s a conversation that needs to take place. I know it, and Lucas knows it. And obviously Grace and Mike know it too, because once we’re done eating, they escape to their bedroom.

“Lucas, we really need to talk.”

“I know.”

CHAPTER 38

LUCAS

"I know I've hurt you," is my opening line. Ellie and I walk over to my cabin, and then I pour each of us a glass of red wine. We decide to go inside. Who knows what time Cyndi will get home and come trotting over?

I tell her that I'm really sorry I've been so closed off and basically have disappeared from her life. Ellie sits there with no comment, arms crossed and staring straight ahead. She's a strong person and is trying to steel herself for what I'm going to say. Wise, on her part.

"Ellie, first let me say this: I love spending time with you, I love spending time with your family. There's nothing wrong with any of you, especially you—you're perfect."

Ellie gives me a sweet but sad smile.

"What I'm going to tell you is a painful story—a story that I feel totally responsible for."

Ellie looks up at me with sad, searching eyes. She knows this is not going to be easy, but in that moment, I can also tell that she wants to be there for me—supportive and understanding. She's been through a lot also, and people who've been hurt and have survived are the most sympathetic people in the world.

Where to start? I'm not sure. I take a deep breath and just go for it.

"I've told you about some of my past. Being a farm boy, working at the car dealership, going to college, and then eventually owning the dealership. Obviously I've left out any part of a love-life that I might've had.

I dated girls off and on, but there was never anyone that was special. It would last for a while and then we'd just drift apart because it wasn't meant to be. I was in my late twenties by now, and was starting to buy the dealership. I put in long hours and didn't really have lots of time for a relationship. But I was lonely and bored. I started going to different bars in the evening just for something to do. Alcohol was not the problem. I could nurse one beer for an entire evening. I just wanted some conversation and interaction with people. Working long hours wasn't enough for me.

One night I went to one of the Mexican restaurants for dinner. I sat at the bar, because there's nothing more pitiful than seeing a person eating alone at a restaurant. The bartender and I started talking. She was beautiful. Her family owned the restaurant. They were originally from Puerto Vallarta. I asked her why anyone would move from Puerto Vallarta, Mexico, to Yankton, South Dakota, and she just laughed. Better opportunities, better income, and lots of family. Her name was Lola. And I'm not kidding, Lola was beautiful. I was instantly smitten. Is that a word that's even used in today's society? But it applied to me. Let's just say that I ate Mexican food and drank Coronas for two weeks straight, before I finally got up the nerve to ask her out.

And that's how it started. I was busy at the dealership during the day, and she was busy at the restaurant in the evenings, but somehow we managed to find time together. Her family was very welcoming and would let her off work early just so we could go out. I think they were looking at a new car in their future.

Things progressed, and we decided to get married. My family liked her, but had some reservations. People from this area are accepting of other nationalities to a point, but my parents didn't know if they wanted to make Lola a part of our family. But they went through the whole ordeal with smiles on their faces and made the best of it. Besides, they were getting anxious for grandchildren, so if this is what it took, so be it.

The first year of our marriage was pretty normal, I guess. Some adapting, some growing pains, but all in all, I can't complain. She continued to work at the restaurant, while I was putting in way too many hours at work. I could tell she was starting to get bored. On the evenings that I wasn't working, we'd go out to eat or to a movie, but what she really wanted to do was go to different bars and dance.

And wow, that woman could dance! She would have everyone watching her every move. Initially I would dance with her, but I was usually tired, so when other men cut in on me, I'd say go for it. I knew I couldn't keep up with her. It all started out innocently enough, but as months of this went on, it didn't always seem so innocent.

Then one night I came home from work to hear her crying in the bathroom.

"Lola, are you okay?" I asked.

I walked into the bathroom to see her sitting on the toilet, staring at a pregnancy test. She held it out to me—it was positive. I was excited. I was almost 30 years old and more than ready for children. But her look told me the exact opposite.

"Lola, aren't you happy? We've talked about a baby for a while."

She just shook her head. A feeling hit me in the pit of my stomach.

"It's mine, right?"

"Of course, it's yours. How could you even ask me that?"

As much as she loved dancing with other men, she vowed she'd never been with anyone else but me. She begged me to believe her. And I did, rightfully so.

The next months passed in a blur. First came the months of morning sickness, then a lull where she felt pretty good, and then the last few months of pure torture when she was uncomfortable and just wanted all of this to be over. My parents (and hers also) were ecstatic to be grandparents for the first time. We painted the nursery in neutral colors and put together the crib and changing table. Lola was getting into it and started getting excited about seeing our baby. We had decided against finding out if it was a boy or a girl, so that added to the excitement.

The big day arrived when she went into labor and we went to the hospital. It was a long, torturous labor. Her epidural didn't work and towards the end I thought I was going to go deaf from her screams. But with that one final push, my life changed forever. The moment that I heard our daughter cry for the first time sent me into overwhelming tears of joy. That was the moment that Lola and I felt the closest we've ever been. We sobbed together, we laughed together, we changed the first diaper together. We named her Lily, because of course she had to have an "L" name like we did.

Lily had beautiful dark skin, with the biggest headful of black, curly hair you have ever seen on a baby. Has anyone ever been more in love with their baby? Absolutely not. Lily was perfect; life was perfect.

For Lily's first year of life, everything was as it should be. Lola was a doting mother, I couldn't wait to get home from work to hold her, and the grandparents were over the moon. There was never a little girl that was more loved and adored. Her first birthday party consisted of a cake with a big number "1" candle that she tore into with her fingers, lots of singing, about 100 pictures, and too many presents.

"Thank you, God," I just kept saying over and over. I could hardly believe that I was this blessed. In my mind I was thinking, I wonder when we'll start trying for a little brother or sister. I was smart enough that I didn't bring that up to Lola yet because I knew she wasn't anywhere close to wanting to get pregnant again. But it was a wonderful day celebrating this beautiful angel that we'd been given.

The next year was a little different. Lola was starting to get a little restless. She was no longer working at the restaurant because her parents wanted her to stay home full-time with Lily. Lola would take Lily to play-dates with other parents and kids, but to be honest, they bored her. At home, Lily was walking, digging into everything, and needed constant attention. Lola was sick of that also. I would come home in the evening and she'd practically throw Lily at me.

"Here, you can watch her!"

After a few more months, when I'd come home, Lily would tell me that she had "cabin-fever" and just had to get out of the house. Would I mind if she went to her parents' restaurant for the evening?

This went on for months. Spring was here. That's when I came up with a great idea.

"Should we build a pool? We can afford it, and that way you could get some sun, and invite friends over in the afternoon so you'd have something to do. What do you think?"

She instantly warmed to the idea. Finally, some fun and something to do. Lily loved the water, and at the age of two, loved paddling around in any water with a life jacket on. I got the contractors lined up, and by the time June rolled around, we had a beautiful in-ground pool, with lawn chairs, umbrellas and a tiki bar surrounding it. We invited our families over the first night that it was ready, and Lily, and even Lola, were in their glory.

It definitely gave some relief from Lola's nagging about boredom, and Lily slept well at night after swimming all day. But it started happening day after day that I'd come home from work with Lily napping in Lola's lap. Sounds great, right? But Lola would also be pretty drowsy from the glasses of tequila that were setting on her pool-side table. I talked to her about that.

"Lola, you can't be drinking if you're at the pool with Lily. You have to watch her!"

I was adamant about that and pretty ticked off about the whole deal.

"I mean it! Watch your daughter, and no more drinking by the pool!"

Lola was very apologetic and understood my anger. Contrite, would be the word, I guess. Thankfully, things improved for the rest of the summer.

Until August 28. The worst day of my life. It was a typical day. I was getting home a little later than I would've liked to—about 6:30. That seems to have been the story of my life that summer. And to be honest with you—it's been that way ever since I took over the dealership. You try to provide a good life for your family and you always end up concentrating more on your work than on your loved ones.

I walked out to the backyard, expecting to see Lola in her lawn chair and Lily playing with toys beside it. When you see something so totally unexpected, it takes a few seconds for your mind to really register it. I stood there like a statue, trying to take it all in. And then I dove into action, literally dove. Because what I saw was Lily lying in the bottom of the pool, the deep end, with no movement whatsoever. At the same time I also saw Lola lying close by in the water, but my mind only concentrated on one thing.

"Get Lily, get Lily, get Lily."

I grabbed her, flung her and myself onto the concrete, and started CPR like a wild man. Somehow in the midst of this madness I managed to call 911, while sobbing uncontrollably and beating that poor little girl's chest and blowing air into her with so much force; way too much force, I knew. The mantra of please God, please God, please God, kept going through my mind as tears were streaming down my face.

I heard sirens and then people running into the backyard. The paramedics wanted to take over for me, but I wouldn't let them. Two cops pulled Lola out of the water and started CPR on her. It seemed to go on forever, but in reality, it was over way too soon. The paramedics put their hands on my shoulders and told me to stop. To stop? How can you stop when you're trying to give life back to your daughter? Eventually they pulled me back and then gently lifted Lily and placed her on their stretcher. She looked way too small and still. Her black curls were matted around her face and I couldn't help but think of how she looked when she was born, with those very same curls. The screams that came out of my mouth were blood-curdling, and everyone looked away in horror.

I then looked around me and saw that Lola was being placed on a stretcher also, with nothing being done to her except a paramedic pulling a sheet up over her face. Oh my God, the worst nightmare ever. In that instant I was so angry with her that I wanted to go over and strangle her myself. But there was no use. She was already gone.

And now my nightmare was just beginning. Because a police officer was walking towards me saying, "What exactly happened here?"

————————

ELLIE

I just sit there trying to take it all in. I'm crying, Lucas is crying, and I say the exact same words he said to me when I told him about Will.

"I'm sorry, I'm so, so sorry."

There are times when words are truly meaningless, and this is one of them. I move to put my arm around him, but he pulls me into his arms instead. We sit there for a bit, both silently sobbing.

"Tell me what happened next."

LUCAS

I just looked at this cop that I knew—his name was Jim—and stared at him as the tears kept pouring down my face. I told him the story—how I came home from work, saw both Lily and Lola face down in the pool, and how I dove in to get Lily.

"Is there any reason why you chose to get her first?" Jim asked.

"She's my baby, my little girl! I just had to save her!"

"And you didn't want to save your wife?"

What is this? Sophie's choice? I had a split second to decide. Of course I'm going to try and save a two-year-old, my only child. No thought went into it—just a parent's instinct.

"We're going to need witnesses—where you were this afternoon, the timeline of your whole day. We're probably also going to have to get DNA results on the little girl. There were rumors, you know."

"You don't mean it! You're serious? Really? Jim, you've known me your whole life. I sold you your last four cars. And this is how you're going to treat me?"

I went ballistic. I wanted to punch that guy out, but by this time others were around and held me back. I managed to calm down but just stared at Jim in the face.

His face finally fell and said, "We could be looking at a double homicide here. I don't want there to be any impropriety and any accusations of me not doing my due diligence. You understand."

I still wanted to yell all of those nasty four-letter words that we all know but usually don't say. But amazingly I held back.

"I was at the car dealership since 7 AM. Ask any of my coworkers. They'll also tell you what time I left."

And I walked away. Let them put me in handcuffs—my life is basically over. But no one followed me into the house.

The next few days passed in a blur. Family and friends made a parade of casseroles and desserts in and out of the kitchen. People offered me their condolences. The grand-parents were just as inconsolable as I was.

Fortunately for everyone involved, Jim hadn't put in an appearance. That almost made it worse. Was I looking at charges? Even though the timetable and my alibi made that impossible, you hear of weirder things happening. I imagined people looking at me weirdly. Did he do it? Is he responsible? Was Lily even his? The stress and tension were more than I could bear. Alcohol and sleeping pills became my only friends, and even their effect was negligible.

Finally, on the morning of the funeral, Jim showed up at my front door.

"Lucas, we just got forensic results back. I came immediately. I know the timing isn't great, but I wanted you to know."

I found myself holding my breath as he pulled out an official-looking envelope.

"You can look this over yourself, but here's the gist of it. As we all figured, Lily's manner of death was drowning. According to the estimated time of death, she had been gone for 2-3 hours before you found her. Lola's time of death was estimated at 1-2 hours before you found her. And this might not be a surprise to you, but her blood alcohol was high. Point 18. More than twice the legal limit. We'll never know for sure what happened, but our scenario suggests that Lola was drunk and sleeping, Lily fell in the pool, Lola woke up and tried to get to her, and died trying. This is only conjecture. But it's definitely more than enough to wrap up this investigation and declare you totally innocent. I'm sorry I had to pursue this, but from now on there won't be any questions about what happened. You are a wonderful man that had the world's most unfortunate incident happen to him. You have my deepest sympathy."

And with that, he turned and walked away. I didn't know whether to be relieved that the investigation was concluded or angry that there had ever been any question at all. When he was opening his car door he looked at me.

"By the way, according to the DNA test, Lily was your daughter. Sorry to have raised that question, but hopefully this gives you some peace."

Some peace? Something I had never doubted for a minute had been raised into question. But it hit me then even harder. My beautiful little girl, my flesh and blood, was lying in a little white casket and I had to bury her that afternoon. I also had to bury Lola, but for now, those emotions were so mixed that I couldn't even think about that.

So, Ellie, that's my sad story. A tragedy in my life that I just can't seem to get past. I thought I was getting past it with you and your family. And then, that day that we thought Colton had drowned, I just knew I couldn't do it. I can't bear another tragedy—there's no way I can live through another ordeal like that. And when you allow yourself to love people, bad things can happen. And I don't think I can survive another tragedy.

I picture Emily and Abby in my mind, and think, Lily would've been almost that same age. She would be a beautiful young woman, possibly with a husband and children. I could've been a grandpa! I would've been a darn good one, I think. And when I look at you, and see that you've gone through tragedy and have come out on the other side, I think—good for you! I think that's awesome, and deeply admirable.

But I've never quite made it there. I just keep holding back. I know I have issues about Lola that I've never resolved, and that's part of the problem, but I just can't imagine ever loving a child again, only to have them taken away from me. And that includes your kids and grandkids. I fell in love with all of them in a heartbeat. But I can't take that chance. It hurt me so deeply that I guess I'm broken. I'll just watch from a distance.

ELLIE

I'm speechless. Where do we go from here? I get what he's saying, but it's been 30 years. Can't he move on from this? Did he ever get any counseling? I give him a big hug and there are many tears involved. I've been through a loss also, and I know he understands this, but does he realize that he needs to move on from his loss also? We sit there a little while. I try to gather my thoughts, and finally speak.

"You never knew my dad. He was a deeply religious man. And he was always right, or at least, that's what he thought. Actually, it wasn't far from the truth. If he was here right now, he'd stand up tall (all 5 foot, 8 inches of him), point his index finger at you, shake it, and say 'Lucas, enough! You have two things to do here. Number 1: You have to forgive yourself. What happened to you wasn't your fault. Number 2: You have to forgive Lola. What happened *was* her fault. She was drinking, and she let your child die. That's horrible. That never should've happened. But it did. And it's worse than anything you could've imagined. But God wants us to forgive. Even in the worst circumstances. Seventy times seven is what God commanded us in the Bible. Impossible, we think. But possible, I know. I have seen people forgive other people for the most heinous of crimes. And their lives go on. Your life will be lived in stagnation until you can forgive yourself and forgive Lola. Please, for your own sake and for the sake of the people who love you, please forgive. It's the only way. Or your life from here on out will never have any meaning, or any love. It's the only way to have a future.'"

I feel like I was inspired by Dad, or God, or maybe both. Lucas just shakes his head.

"I'm not there yet."

I sob, give him a kiss, and tell him, "Let me know when you are."

I walk out the door.

CHAPTER 39

GRACE

I hear Ellie come in the door. Mike and I are watching TV in bed. A Netflix series that Mike is in love with. It's good, but more of a guy's show than a chick series. But that's okay, because that's what makes a good marriage. Any guy who is willing to watch some dating series or singing show with me weekly definitely deserves for his wife to watch his "man shows." The women at work are amazed at the shows that Mike and I watch together. They think it's amazing. I know of many couples who sit in separate rooms every night watching their own favorite shows without spending a single second together. How sad. Our "date nights" consist of us picking out our favorite shows that we've recorded. And we've picked these shows out together. I never realized how unusual that was until I talked to some of my coworkers and friends. Honestly, we love it. It's what we do.

It's a far cry from what went on as we were dating. Three channels. Watch the shows when they're on or you can only pray for reruns someday. And heaven forbid there would be some big storm coming through. The weathermen would continuously interrupt your show (no scrolling across the bottom back then), looking for their ten minutes of fame. No internet to tell you what you missed, no movie channels, no ESPN, just those three lousy channels. I poured over the TV Guide every night like it was the bible of our television viewing.

Here's another blast from the past. As Ellie and I've said before, we were a very religious family. One of the "Sunday rules" was no TV on Sunday. I look back at that now and just think it was one of the most archaic rules ever. When Mike and I started dating, he just couldn't believe it! What? No Sunday football? You're kidding me, right?

On Sunday evenings, my parents usually went over to other people's homes for "coffee time." It was a thing in the rural Midwest. Mike and I would sit home together, since no restaurants or movie theaters were open on Sunday. Even if they were, I never would've been allowed to go. So there we'd sit—with no TV.

One Sunday, early evening, Mike had had enough. (And to this day, I can't believe he had the guts to do this.) Before my parents left for the evening, Mike came up to my dad.

"Mr. Anderson, I understand your rules, and I don't mean to question them. But on these Sunday evenings, time gets a little long. Would you rather I make out with Grace all night, or would you like us to watch TV?"

Dad looked at him for a second, and then squeaked out, "You may watch TV."

Kudos to Mike. So we did both.

Our show is almost done, and I whisper to Mike, "I'm going to go and check on Ellie."

He's all for it. He's as curious about the Ellie-Lucas story as I am. I hear Ellie in her room and knock on her door. I hear a faint "come in."

What I see is as sad as it gets. She's sitting up in bed, dabbing tissues to her red, swollen eyes. Pathetic, for sure.

"What is going on?" I ask.

I crawl into bed with her. We slept together throughout our whole childhood, so this is nothing new. She then proceeds to tell me the sad, sad story. We knew something was very wrong, but how do you predict this? But yet, for the split second that we were wondering if he was a pedophile, isn't this much better? Can't he get past it?

"I don't know if he can," is Ellie's response. "This happened more than thirty years ago, and it seems as if he hasn't moved on in any respect. He's stuck in the past and can't let go of it."

"Has he had any counseling? Any reaching out to family and friends? Any anti-depressants? Any sharing of his story to co-workers, his parents, or Lola's parent's? Anything?"

"It doesn't sound like it. He made it sound like he's been going on his own since the day it happened. I don't think he's reached out to anyone or has made any headway in his mind since that August day many years ago."

"That's a long time to be stuck in one place."

Ellie and I continue to commiserate over his story. One thing about it, we're both eternal optimists. We'd both like to go marching over there right now and fix it. Fix whatever he can't get past, and fix his overwhelmingly negative outlook on life. We talk about the fact that if we lived our lives never getting too close to anyone, well, you might as well just give up and die on the spot.

I ask Ellie if Lucas had anything to say about Cyndi.

"No, but now that I know what's going on with him, it kind of makes sense. I don't think she's the type that's looking for a long-term commitment, or her 'forever love.' He probably just likes to have someone to hang out with that just wants to have fun. Maybe kind of like Lola?"

I agree, but look how that turned out.

Ellie says, "I shouldn't have come on so strong. I threw my whole family at him within a couple weeks of meeting him. I feel so stupid."

"Don't be silly. The great thing about it was that it felt so natural, and fun. But even if you would've waited months or years to introduce him to your family, the result would've been the same. If you commit to someone, it's a package deal. It's not just the two of you on an island. Especially in our family. Ellie, the day that you meet the man you're supposed to marry, and I *know* it will happen again for you, well, he has to want to be part of your whole family too. Because if he can't commit to that, then he's not the right man for you."

We continue talking well into the night. Lots of tears are shed, but yet, some questions have been answered, so maybe Ellie can move on from here. She snuggles down in bed and finally closes her eyes. I wait until she's asleep—that doesn't take long. The poor woman is emotionally exhausted. Quietly, I slip out of bed and go across the hall, and just as quietly slip back into my own bed. Mike is sleeping soundly. I cuddle up to him and say a prayer for Ellie, for Lucas, and then thank God for the umpteenth time that he has blessed me with such a wonderful husband.

CHAPTER 40

ELLIE

"Did I hear Mike take off early this morning?"

"If you did, then that's more than I heard. I was zonked."

We hear a lawnmower start up. I take my cup of coffee, Grace grabs a glass of lemonade, and we make our way to the porch. There's Lucas, making his way across all three lawns, one long strip at a time. Grace looks at me, and we're thinking the same thing. How much has happened since that day we first got here.

"I'd like a do-over with Lucas. Do you think anything could turn out differently?"

"No, because it's Lucas that has to change, not you."

"How can I get him to change his mind? Do I beg him, ignore him, pretend I don't like him, or turn him over to someone like Cyndi?"

The words are no sooner out of my mouth than we see Cyndi come running out of her cabin. She goes over to Lucas and offers him a bottle of water, and tries to make conversation with him, which is pretty near impossible over the noise of the lawnmower. He mouths the word "thanks" to her but keeps on mowing. She looks a little dejected and starts walking away, but then notices us sitting on the porch.

She comes bounding up the steps and says, "Hi, girls! May I join you?"

Sure, just what we need at ten a.m. A fake conversation with a chatty airhead that can't seem to find enough clothes to cover her body. Sorry, I guess I'm not in the most charitable mood this morning.

But if nothing else, she is amusing. I truly don't hold any ill-will towards her. In fact, she's one of those girls that you almost feel sorry for. It appears she doesn't have a lot going for her—no career, family, social graces—except I will give her this—she has one hot body for a fifty-some-year-old. And good for her. Maybe some of it cost her tens of thousands of dollars or more, but she's also put in a lot of work. Who are we to say what's important and what's not?

Okay, enough of this moping around. I'm sick of it! Instead of gracious Grace, I'm in the mood to be gracious Ellie.

"Well, girls, it's time for some fun. Enough of this beach, we have other beaches to explore! Let's pack up the coolers, load up the boat, and make it a lake day."

Grace raises her eyebrow at me in surprise, but jumps on the idea. Cyndi is excited.

"What do I bring? What do I wear? How long will we be gone?"

One question after another. The "what do I wear" question kind of surprises me. Let's just hope that it's a little more than a few strings with triangles, and that it involves a top.

I tell her, "Just bring a beach bag with the usual stuff and we'll take care of the rest. Meet us out on the dock in a half-hour."

Grace and I walk in the cabin and she gives me a "what the heck" look. I shrug my shoulders.

"This is what we came for, and even though she drives us nuts, I just had this feeling that we should include her."

In less than an hour we're in the boat, loaded and ready to go. I take the wheel as we back out of the dock and wave to Lucas, who is still mowing. Poor guy. He looks a little surprised, and jealous. He probably thought I was going to be moping about all day, replaying his sad story in my mind. Well, I am, but he doesn't need to know that.

Cyndi has a huge hat on, and I warn her, "You better hold on to that, because we're going cruising!"

I gun the boat and we take off with the bow in the air. It's exhilarating to feel that power, along with the beauty of the lake and the sun in the sky. I take off to the west, because there's always less boat traffic in that direction and the water is calmer. We drive for a while, just watching the scenery and enjoying the day. The sandstone bluffs are beautiful. Golden yellow with pine trees on top—they're basically cliffs on both sides of the lake. Mike hates it when Grace and I call it a lake.

"It's a river," he says.

And he's right. It's the Missouri river that they dammed up to make a lake. So we're all right, as far as I'm concerned. Who cares? It's water and it's pretty, and we've had a lot of fun on this river/lake over the years.

We pull into a nice cove, cut the motor, and throw in the anchor. We all throw our towels on the lay-out deck on the rear of the boat, and then proceed to relax. Or at least Grace and I do. Cyndi is busy talking a mile a minute. For someone who talks so much, it seems like we still really don't know much about her.

Grace finally has the guts to say, "Shh, Cyndi, this is the part where we veg out."

Cyndi takes the hint (or more of a direct order, I guess) and lies back. Good for her—she's teachable. And it's not like we don't like talking; it's the incessant chatter that drives us crazy. Eventually we do start talking.

Cyndi asks us about our background, and tells us, "I can't believe you're sisters. You look nothing alike!"

Wish we had a buck for every time someone told us that. She shares a little of her story with us. Military family, divorced parents, not a lot of stability as she was growing up. Stuff that Grace and I could've easily guessed. Once she got past her giddy, "I'm trying to impress you" persona that she had when she first met us, she is gradually starting to grow on us.

But by now we're starving so we throw open the cooler. Naturally we made the traditional boat buns, and brought along some chips and other snacks.

Cyndi comments, "I haven't seen this many carbs in one meal in a long time!"

We just laugh and tell her to enjoy it for one day in her life. And she does. We share a bottle of wine amongst the three of us and then go back to lying on the deck. No snoring, because we're dignified women, but there's definitely some napping that's taking place. We all wake up hot and sweaty, and decide to take a flying leap off the back of the boat. It feels so good!

We paddle around until we're totally cooled off, and then try to haul our lazy butts out of the water, up the ladder, and into the boat.

"Does anyone want to ski?" Grace asks.

I tell her that I will, since it's one of those rare days where the water is like glass. I am most definitely a fair-weather skier. If it's rough or windy, I won't even waste my time. We haul the ski up out of the storage area. I jump into the water and get my ski on while Grace gets the rope ready. She throws it out to me in a perfect arc (we've done this a few times). She then goes to the wheel, turns the motor over and hits the throttle. Everything sounds perfect but we don't go anywhere. Oh wait, we forgot to pull up the anchor! We're all dying of laughter and decide we're not telling anyone that this happened. Okay, let's try again. I'm up and it feels so good. There are only a few perfect skiing days and this is one of them. Jumping the wake gives you a little bit of an adrenalin rush, and it's fun to see your girlfriends cheering you on from the boat. It ends sooner than I'd like, not because I fall, but because I'm out of shape and my hands and thighs are killing me.

"Okay, Cyndi, how about you?"

She looks a little embarrassed.

"I haven't done it in a while, and I have to ski on two. I don't even know if I'll be able to get up."

We encourage her and throw out the other ski. First try, a flop. Second try, she's up! A little wobbly, but she's skiing.

Grace yells at me, "I hope she doesn't lose her bikini!"

We give her a thumbs up when she tries to go out of the wake. She makes it! But comes down hard when she tries to go back in.

"Do you want to try again?"

She does, and pops right up out of the water. This time she manages to go in and out of the wake a couple of times. We're surprised at how long she skies. But finally she gives the "cut it" sign and lets go of the rope. As she's pulling herself up into the boat she's back to her chatty self.

"That was so much fun! I haven't done that in years! I didn't know I could still do it! Thank you so much!"

As she pulls off her life jacket Grace is making a motion towards her. Cyndi doesn't catch it.

Grace says, "Check your top!"

"Oops!" Oh well, just women here.

Cyndi says to Grace, "It's your turn now!"

Grace smiles but her face has fallen.

"What? Don't you ski?"

"Yeah, I did, but those days are over."

"Really? What happened? You look like you're still in good enough shape to ski."

I don't know if that's a compliment or not, but I guess I'll take it as one.

"I have some problems with my eyes. My retinas keep detaching. Sorry to say, I'm legally blind in my right eye, so I really have to protect my left. When you're getting up on a slalom ski, it creates too much pressure in your eyes, so I've had to give it up. I really miss it, but it's not worth going blind over. My grandkids love to proudly say that their grandmother was an awesome slalom skier into her 60's. But that's as far as it goes."

Cyndi feels terrible. "I'm so sorry, I had no idea. And when anyone looks into your eyes, which are the most beautiful turquoise, by the way, they would have no clue that anything is wrong."

Grace says, "And for that, I'm thankful. My eyes aren't distorted, externally. And I'm just vain enough that that means a lot to me. Who knows what the future holds, but for now, I can see and I can function. But since I have no depth perception, I've turned into a terrible driver!" She smiles with that remark. "Poor Mike has had to become quite the chauffeur."

Cyndi continues to apologize. Grace blows her off.

"Don't feel bad, and don't be sad for me. Everyone has something to deal with. Some things are more visible than others, but as far as I'm concerned, everyone is 'walking wounded.' Ellie lost a husband, Lucas has losses, our kids have concerns that we probably don't even know about. And I'm sure you've had your share of issues. Everyone has something. It's how you deal with it that makes you the person you are."

I want to shout, "Amen, Grace."

It's what I'm thinking, but I don't say it out loud. But I can sense that the wheels are turning in Cyndi's head. She just looks at us and says, "May I give you guys a hug?"

We all laugh and join in a group hug. This day has been therapeutic for all of us.

CHAPTER 41

GRACE

What a fun day. Why aren't we doing this every day? Laziness, I suppose. Who wants to haul the boat out when we can just lie on the beach? But I will tell you this, we made Cyndi's day. She thanked us, and thanked us, and thanked us over and over again, until we finally made her stop. I don't know if this woman has had any true female friends in years, or ever. And to be honest with you, Ellie and I were very judgmental when we first met her. I'm embarrassed about our response to her. Like they say, a person is like an onion. You have to keep peeling away the layers to get at the good stuff. Who says that? I don't know, but I know I've heard it somewhere, so it must be true. Like everything on the Internet, right?

Ellie and I get cleaned up and now we're sitting on the porch with our evening wine. And leftover boat buns. They just keep getting better as the day goes on. Cyndi walks on over to thank us again for the great day. She has spruced up a little better than Ellie and I have. A gorgeous dress, full-blown hair, make-up with fake eyelashes. We look a little dreary in contrast to her. We showered, we put on sun-dresses, but that's as far as it went.

We offer her a glass of wine, which she gladly accepts. She seems to have toned-down a bit. No more screeching conversation, no more boisterous laughing. We are having a normal conversation amongst three women friends. Nice.

And then she says, "Well, I suppose I should get going. Lucas and I are going out tonight."

Nothing like dropping a bomb on a party. Ellie and I just look at each other and then wish her well. She goes prancing over to Lucas' while we sit and stare. So much for that.

"Oh Ellie, I feel so bad for you."

And that's the truth. She's been through the wringer. Even though she now knows what's involved, and the obstacles that lie before her, to see Cyndi going out with Lucas has to be a punch in the gut.

Ellie is fuming. "The nerve of that woman. And we were so nice to her today."

"Okay, we're going in. What movies haven't we watched since we got here?"

"I don't know if I'm in the movie mood. I am in the process of reading a good book. Should we just go inside, watch some TV, and read at the same time?"

I'm up for that. We stop by the fridge to refill our wine glasses and settle in on the sofas. Comfortable. And quiet. Until my phone rings. It's Mike.

"Grace, I just want to tell you that everything's okay."

It sounds more like a foreboding of something not okay, but we'll see.

"We just got a call to your mom's retirement building. To be honest, her apartment."

I put my phone on speaker so Ellie can hear this too. My hands are shaking and my heart is beating a mile a minute.

"Your mom fell. We're loading her into the ambulance as we speak. Not sure what's going on. She seems a little out of it. We're taking her to the hospital to find out what's wrong. I'll ride with her. You should really come."

At this point the sound of sirens overtakes our conversation and Mike hangs up.

Ellie and I stare at each other for a split-second, and then Ellie jumps into action. She runs to her room to pack an over-night bag. I basically do next to nothing while I wait for her to come running down the stairs. I don't have to pack since Mom will be in a Sioux Falls hospital and I have everything I need at home.

We run to the car.

"Can you drive?" I ask.

That's a given, since I no longer drive at night. Ellie jumps into the driver's seat and we take off. With wheels spinning up the gravel, I yell at her, "Slow down! This trip is going to take us 90 minutes, whether or not you drive like a maniac!"

We fly through town and finally hit the interstate. The speed limit on South Dakota interstates is 80 miles per hour. Plenty fast, I think. Ellie pushes it by a few miles. I can live with that.

We drive up to the ED parking lot at the hospital and run in the front doors. Mike is there waiting for us. I run to him and he swallows me up in his arms. He also manages to enfold Ellie. He's a big guy.

"Here's what we know so far. Your mom fell in her apartment. As soon as we got here to the hospital they immediately brought her to CT. They wanted to check to see if she'd had a stroke, so they could give her the 'clot-busting' med if that was the case. Good news—she didn't have a stroke. Right now they're drawing some blood and doing an EKG to see if she's had a heart attack.

"After that they're going to do an MRI to see if there's anything else going on. They'll also be taking a look at all of her bones to check for any fractures. Who knows how brittle her bones are at her age? Of course, one of the big questions is, why did she fall? I asked her a few times but she seemed a little confused and couldn't really remember the fall. All of this takes time, so just take a deep breath and we'll just have to be patient and see what we find out."

The three of us sit in the waiting room. Numerous people keep parading in and out. Every time a nurse comes through the double doors, we hope she's going to call our name. But it doesn't happen, for a long, long time.

Emily and her husband come running in. Mike had called both of our kids as soon as he got to the hospital. This is the hospital that both Emily and I work in. It's nice to have connections. This will come in handy down the road, whatever road that might be. Our son Jason comes in next. Even though he doesn't work here, he's a sports medicine doctor and has lots of connections.

Sorry to say, none of those connections have made a difference because we're still sitting here an hour and a half later with no news. Ellie called her kids and Abby is here now also. None of us are any good at playing the waiting game.

Emily goes up to the desk. “May we go in to see Mrs. Anderson? How’s she doing?”

Not much of a response. But Mike has a way. Since he was one of the paramedics that brought her in, he basically tells the person at the front desk that he’s going to check on his patient. He walks right in. I’m thrilled that maybe he’ll be able to get some answers soon. I follow the sight of his back until the double doors swing shut, blocking him from my view.

It’s not long before he returns with a thumbs up.

“Oh, thank you, God,” is my first thought.

“We can go on back now,” is his response.

We all follow him back to an ED room with curtains drawn around it. We hesitatingly go in. What are we going to see?

Our mother, 88 years old, sitting up, with a black eye and a smile on her face. What? I didn’t know what to expect, but I must say, this wasn’t it.

“Mike, what’s the deal?”

“The doctor will be in shortly, but I must say, everything sounds really good.”

Ellie and I go up and give Mom a gentle hug, not wanting to hurt her.

Her first words are, “Oh girls, you didn’t have to drive up from Yankton to see me.”

So typical. Never thinking about herself; always thinking about us. The kids all walk over to her and give her a big hug also. Jason instantly turns into doctor mode, asking all kinds of questions.

Mom answers, “I’m not sure of all that’s going on. Maybe your dad can tell you.”

About this time, the doctor and nurse practitioner walk in. The doctor is going to begin telling us his diagnosis, when he recognizes a few of us.

"Hi, Jason. How're you doing? Is your football team staying healthy? And, Emily, you're here too? It's been awhile since I've been up to ICU. Keeping busy there? And, Grace, you're here too? How's L & D? Luckily I don't get there too often. I have to tell you, I'm not very fond of taking care of pregnant patients. Wow, I didn't put that together that you guys are all related."

Can we get to the point? We all want to scream, but this is part of hospital etiquette. And as belaboring as it is, this is what will get Mom the best care possible. If you know someone who knows someone, you have to use it to your advantage, because it does make a difference.

The doctor finally gets to the point. "Your mom and grandma is a very lucky woman. Whenever an elderly patient falls, you have to rule out many things. First of all, the question, why did she fall? A stroke, a heart attack, a fainting episode? So that's what we concentrated on first. I am very happy to tell you that all of those things have been ruled out. She does not have a brain bleed or a clot, her cardiac enzymes are normal, and her blood pressure and heart rate are normal also. That is very good news indeed. So now we look at the effects of that fall. We've done a CT scan, an MRI, and X-rays, and I am very happy to tell you that she absolutely doesn't have any broken bones. Not a one. Her eye is a little bruised, and her left wrist is sprained, but other than that, she is one healthy woman! You may take her home shortly. By the way, does she have any throw rugs in her apartment?"

We murmur affirmatively.

"Throw them away, immediately. It's the number one cause of falls in an elderly person's home. It's been nice seeing you all, and by the way, you have an amazing mother."

No news to us, but always nice to hear.

Once he leaves, that's when the tears start flowing. Tears of joy. We all take turns giving Mom a hug. This could've been so much worse. I walk up to Mike as he holds out his arms for me.

"It must've been so awful for you, to hear her apartment number come up on your call list."

And then Mike breaks down, finally.

"Babes, it was the worst. To go on a call when you know the person. And then to think that it's your mom, our mom, well, it was truly terrifying. I prayed the whole way here."

We stand that way for a while, giving each other the comfort we both need. And then, he finally says the words that we both know are true.

"We dodged a bullet this time, but she's 88. She's not going to live forever."

"I know, and that's why we just need to take advantage of every minute we have with her."

CHAPTER 42

ELLIE

"Do we have everything signed? May we break free of this place?"

The nurse just brought Mom her splint. She shows her how to use it, and when she can take it off. It's just a short one, below the elbow. Mom will get along just fine.

I offer to take Mom home and spend the night with her. Grace protests and says that she can stay with her.

I tell her, "That's ridiculous and you know it. Go home with Mike and we'll see you in the morning."

I bring Mom home. By now it's after midnight and we're both exhausted. I give Mom a Tylenol PM and we get ready for bed. Mom has a queen-sized bed—big enough for the two of us.

I give Mom a hug and I tell her, "I'm so glad you're okay."

Thoughts swirl through my head. This day could've turned out so differently. The fall wasn't the big thing. So many other things were. She could've had a stroke and be lying comatose right now. Or have had a heart attack, and have coded and be gone by the time we got there. Life is short. Even 88 years is too short. Because if we would've lost Mom today, I would've lost the dearest person I know.

The sun is peaking through the blinds when I hear Grace using her key to let herself in, bright and early in the morning. Amazing! Grace can get up before 8 AM! Mom is still sleeping so I tiptoe out of the bedroom and talk with Grace in the living room. We talk about how different this might've been and how thankful we are that it turned out so well.

Mike shows up a few minutes later with some caramel pecan rolls—Mom's favorite. I put the coffee pot on, and about this time Mom comes walking out of the bedroom.

"My, this looks like a party. What are you all doing here?"

We all give her a big hug. And then Mike, being Mike, gets entirely emotional and has tears rolling down his cheeks.

"Mom, we're just so glad you're okay."

And that's when it hits me. Mike calls our mom, Mom, as if she were his mom. That used to be typical, back in the day. When you got married, you immediately began calling your parents-in-law Dad and Mom. Or at least that's what happened in the Midwest. That doesn't happen anymore. Not that it really bothers me, but I think we've lost something here.

But when I hear Mike call our mother, Mom, he means it from the bottom of his heart. He lost his mom before he should have, but he loves our mom as if she was his own. And that's the way it should be.

GRACE

Ellie and I decide to go and stock up on some groceries for Mom. She doesn't need much. She eats a huge meal at noon in the dining room at her retirement center, and brings home enough left-overs to tide her over through the evening. But she likes some snacks, and something for breakfast, and likes to have some candy around if the grandkids stop over.

Ellie informs her that she's staying over again tonight.

I tell her, "No, it's my turn. Just go back to Yankton."

Ellie says, "No way–I'm winning this argument. You stay here with Mike and I'll stay with Mom. No arguing, that's just the way it is."

Then Mom steps in.

"This is all ridiculous! I sprained my arm. My left one, at that. No one needs to stay. You girls go back to Yankton and enjoy the rest of your summer."

The conversation is interrupted by the phone ringing. It's our sister, Ann, wondering how Mom is getting along. We had kept Ann, Katie and Dan all updated during the emergency room visit. They were as relieved as we were when things turned out so well.

Ann asks, "How is Mom doing? I must say, I didn't sleep that well, thinking about her."

"Things are going great. As you know, we have one tough mom."

"That is wonderful to hear. I've decided I'm driving up today. I haven't seen Mom for a couple of months and I have nothing pressing for the next week. And don't try and talk me out of it and tell me that's not necessary. It's my turn to spend some time with her and take care of anything that she needs."

"I would never keep you from coming, but Ellie and I do have it covered if it really doesn't work for you."

"No problem at all. I'll be in Sioux Falls later this afternoon."

"Great! Plan on dinner at our house."

Ellie and I plan a grilled meal out on the back deck at Mike and my house. We go grocery shopping again for the evening menu. Steaks, grilled potatoes and onions, sweet corn, French bread. Should be good. Ann shows up at Mom's around 4:30 p.m., and drives Mom the five blocks over to our house. To be honest with you, we haven't seen Ann in a few months, so this is a blessing in disguise.

To think of the uncertainty, grief and fear of last evening that has given way to the spontaneity and joy of tonight is definitely a juxtaposition of emotions. The five of us are sitting out on the back deck: Ann, Ellie, Mom, Mike and I. The bugs are a little annoying, but other than that, it's a perfect evening. We decide to Facetime with Dan and Katie, just to let them see how well Mom is doing. The call is made, and we're all connected. To be honest with you, Katie and Dan (and his wife Linda) are a little disconcerted to see Mom's black eye, but we quickly assure them that it's worse than it looks. We talk for more than an hour. It's all good and very necessary, but those of us who are actually sitting next to Mom can see that she's wiped out.

We turn off the call and Ann says, "I'm taking Mom home to bed." Good call.

Ellie asks if she can stay here overnight, and definitely the answer is yes. We make up the guestroom. We're all shot—we call it a night. But a good night—much better than we could've imagined just 24 hours ago.

I hear Mike getting up and getting ready for work. We have the perfect set-up. When we remodeled our master suite a few years ago, I put a lot of thought into it. One thing for sure on the list: separate walk-in closets for each of us. My closet is directly off the bedroom, and might be just a little bit bigger than Mike's. His closet is off the bathroom. That way, when he gets up in the morning, he goes directly into the bathroom and can get entirely ready there. A master plan, alright, meaning that he won't be waking me up by turning lights off and on and walking in and out of the bedroom to his closet. Pretty brilliant on my part, I think.

But this morning I do get up and go in the bathroom to give him a hug.

"I hope this shift goes better than your last one did."

"I agree. I'll be more than happy to help people that I don't know."

I kiss him goodbye and crawl back in bed.

Two hours later I wake up to the sound of Ellie making coffee in the kitchen. We sit by the table and watch the morning news, and then decide to walk over to Mom's. I can't say as I'm accustomed to taking a walk at nine in the morning, but it's certainly a good idea. We're both anxious to see how Mom is doing.

We come walking up to Mom's apartment building and see her and Ann sitting out on the patio, enjoying their morning coffee. I really wish I liked coffee–it seems like such a social, cozy thing to do. But think of all the money I've saved by drinking my morning tap water instead.

Have you ever had a bruise that seems to get worse before it gets better? Mom certainly has that going on–what a shiner!

Her eye is swollen almost shut, and she has all of the colors of the rainbow going on there, predominantly dark purple.

"Oh Mom, you look terrible!"

We both give her a hug.

"Good morning girls! You two are just full of compliments this morning," she jokes with a smile.

"Sorry, Mom. But have you looked at yourself in the mirror? That's quite an impressive shiner."

She thinks for a minute and then says, "You know what? I think this is the first black eye I've ever had in my life. That's quite something, isn't it?"

We all agree and tease her that this is one more thing that she can cross off her bucket list. I ask Mom if she remembers what caused the fall. She doesn't. She remembers standing by the counter and then she doesn't remember a thing until Mike showed up. There is definitely a window of time that is unaccounted for, but the doctor told us this is pretty normal since she must've hit her head while she was going down. We're not going to dwell on it since all of her test results came back negative. Ann tells us that she did throw out the kitchen rug last night. Mom is a little disgusted with that.

"That was an expensive rug!"

"So, Ann, what are your plans?" I ask.

"I plan on staying until tomorrow, or I could stay longer if Mom needs me to."

Ellie and I start making plans for which one of us should stay with Mom after that.

Mom puts a quick stop to that.

"Just stop this nonsense right now! I had a minor fall and now you're all treating me like an invalid. I have a black eye and a sprained wrist. That does not put me into the 'assisted living' category. Ann, I'm so glad you're here just because it's nice to see you. And Ellie and Grace, you can just pack up your bags again and go back to Yankton. I am not going to be the cause of ruining the last weeks of your summer vacation."

Naturally we all put up our arguments, but we also know it's a lost cause. Mom will win this battle.

CHAPTER 43

ELLIE

Grace and I discuss what we should do for the day. We decide to stay in Sioux Falls for another day, mainly so that we can spend some time with Ann. We haven't seen her for a few months, so we have to take advantage of the situation. It's around noon and Mom's going to head to the dining room for lunch.

"You know girls, when I get done with lunch, I think I'm going to take a nap. Last night was a late night and I didn't sleep that well."

We totally get it. Ann, Grace and I decide where to go for lunch, and we promise Mom that we'll be back around four.

Ann asks us, "Are any of your kids or grandkids available today? I'd love to see some of them."

Grace and I start texting. Emily and Abby are available for lunch, and so are their kids. All of them. Next Grace texts her daughter-in-law, Michelle. She's not available, but her kids are. Now to make the big decision—where should we eat? Chinese, pizza, barbecue, burgers? Barbecue it is, so we head to the best barbecue place in town. It's on the opposite side of town, but who cares? Sioux Falls has a population of about 200,000 people, so it doesn't take too long to get to wherever you want to go.

We pile out of our car about the same time some of the grandkids come driving up. Do you know that it's legal for 14-year-olds to drive during daytime hours in South Dakota? An old rule that makes life easier on the farms and ranches in the rural parts of the state, but probably not the best idea for kids in the city. We chat a bit and then walk in to order. Five adults and nine kids—we'll be dropping a couple hundred bucks. We decide to eat outside. The patio is decorated nicely, but beyond that, we're basically looking at a parking lot. Oh well, in just a few months we'll be wishing that we could be sitting outside anywhere at all, even if it's only next to a parking lot.

Abby and Emily are busy talking with Ann, catching up on the latest news of her kids and grandkids. Meanwhile, the grandkids are begging us if we can also do supper together at Mike and Grace's.

"We want to see Grandma Anderson." They know it won't take much for them to wear us down.

I guess it's time to plan another menu and get some more groceries. This one will be easy—hotdogs and brats over the fire, chips, maybe a salad and fruit, and the dreaded s'mores for dessert. The kids are ecstatic and we're happy too—both Grace and I have been missing these kids. The kids and Grace head off to her house while Ann and I get the groceries. By the time we get to her house, everyone is involved in a game of some sort: dominoes, Wahoo, poker and blackjack. The last two games are compliments of Grandpa Mike. He believes in teaching children life-long lessons. Not sure gambling should be on that list but there's no real money involved. There are no computer games going on and no phones allowed. When you're playing games at Grandma Grace's, it's serious business. And that's why I can see Grace getting annoyed when Kayla is on her phone.

Grace warns her, "Kayla, put your phone down. We're playing a game here."

Kayla's response is, "Just a second. I'm texting my friend."

Grace is not happy.

"Kayla, put that phone down right now, or I'm taking it away from you."

Kayla laughingly says, "There's no way you would do that."

Not the thing to say. Grace is definitely at the "ticked-off" stage. To be honest, I think all of the kids are in a state of shock because Grace never gets angry with any of her grandkids. And this is not an exaggeration. She has patience galore when it comes to those kids.

Grace grabs the phone and informs her, "You'll get it back when the games are done."

The kids are really quiet, because they've never seen Grace in action like this. Kayla wisely decides to let it go. After the game she apologizes.

"Grandma, I'm sorry about the phone. But I really didn't think you'd take it away from me. I think that's the first time I've ever seen you mad at me, and I didn't like the feeling. Are we okay?"

Grace gives her a big hug, which is unusual, because even I know that Kayla is not a big hugger. But she accepts this one and knows that all is forgiven.

Ann and I put the groceries away and then join in the games. Suddenly Ann glances at her watch.

"Oh crap, it's after four. I have to go and get Mom!"

She takes off out the door.

Grace has a great playlist going and the kids are all singing along, but we turn it off because Mom won't be able to hear a thing once she gets here. The noise of this many people will make it hard enough.

Ann and Mom return soon enough, and the kids don't know what to say about Grandma. Finally one of them starts laughing and tells Grandma she looks a little rough.

Mom laughs too and tells the kids, "You should see the other guy."

She proceeds to take Grace's place at the dominoes table and warns them, "Don't mess with this tough lady!"

She's so competitive, all 125 pounds of her. None of this "letting one of the little kids win because I feel sorry for them." That's never going to happen. But you know what is going to happen? Keegan, Grace's 12-year-old grandson, is going to make sure that Grandma Anderson wins. That kid has the kindest heart. He was letting other people win "Go Fish" at the age of three because he didn't want anyone to feel bad. What a sweetheart.

Ann and I bow out of the game too so we can help Grace haul everything out to the backyard for supper. I guess it'll be a women's night. Mike is working, and Emily and Abby's husbands have to work late also. We can handle it.

GRACE

The house is getting a little noisy with nine kids and five chatty women that never shut up. That doesn't include Mom. She gets pretty quiet when there's too much going on. But she has a smile on her face and takes it all in.

We move out onto the back deck. I put Caleb and Liam in charge of the firepit. They've done this often enough to know what to do. They've learned from Grandpa Mike that the secret to a successful fire is starting small. Paper, kindling, and a little construction wood, then some small logs, and finally you start throwing the big logs on. The other kids position their favorite chairs around the fire before it's time to start roasting hot dogs and brats. The paper plates and food are all set up on the tiki bar, and drinks are in the outdoor refrigerator. It's time to start roasting. Except the three youngest girls don't like any black on their hot dogs.

"How about I throw them in the microwave instead?" I ask them.

Big-time affirmative. Easy enough. Caleb, Liam, Keegan and Colton are the men of the evening, of which they're all quite proud. They take over the roasting forks and proceed to overcook, and then undercook, most everything we give them. But we cheer them on and they're proud of their efforts. Everyone will be able to find something that's edible.

Dinner's over and everyone loved it. We women are cleaning up when we can tell that the kids are up to something.

They're whispering amongst themselves and glancing our way every so often.

"Okay, out with it!" I tell them.

They're all poking each other and urging someone to talk. Finally it's Bria, my youngest, who can never hold back.

"Grandma, can all of us kids come to the cabin again?"

The other kids chime in. "Yeah, before school starts." "Without our parents?"

Emily stands up to that one. "Whoa, whoa, whoa. You kids had that vacation already. This time, you're going to have to put up with us too."

The kids all groan, but Emily and Abby aren't letting these kids push them around.

"Emily is right. You kids can come, but this time your parents get to come along."

The argument goes on, while Ellie, Ann and I look at each other.

Ann tells us, "We're out. Football practice starts pretty soon." Her husband and sons are all high school teachers and coaches. Sports definitely takes precedence at their house.

Ellie and I look at Mom and she just shrugs her shoulders. "This is your choice. I might come along, but that's the extent of my decision."

The kids know they have this in the bag. My oldest granddaughter, Rayna, comes up to me and says, "This would be a great send-off for college, you know. Our whole family together."

Ellie and I give a small nod to each other and I tell Emily and Abby to find a weekend that will work for everyone. That'll be no small feat in itself. The kids are all cheering and making plans. They've learned it from the best.

CHAPTER 44

ELLIE

I slept really well. Even though it wasn't my own bed, being at Mike and Grace's is as close to being at home as it can possibly be. I've been up for an hour or so when I hear Mike coming home, so I go up and join him in the kitchen for a cup of coffee. He also brought donuts. Can't say as I needed that, but how can I refuse such a kind gesture?

He asks me what our plans are for the day.

"I think Grace and I are planning on going back to Yankton. Haven't you talked to her?"

He just smiles. "Well, let's just say things have been a little hectic here the past few days. Not a lot of talking going on."

I get it. Between his work shifts and the whole family taking over his house, it has been a little hectic.

"Well, I for sure will be out of your hair. But you better talk to Grace to find out what her plans are for sure."

As we're talking, the subject of our conversation comes walking down the stairs. Hair a tangled mess, black under her eyes from not taking the time to wash her face last night—a typical morning-Grace look.

"Hey, sis, how're you doing?"

"To be honest, I'm kind of shot. We've had some really big days. Emotional, too. I think that's what tired me out the most."

"I agree. Are you ready to head back to the cabin? We'll stop and say goodbye to Mom and Ann, and then take off. Or do you have to ask your husband for permission first?"

Mike laughs and says, "Why would she start now?"

Grace laughs too. "You know that whole 'should I ask for permission or ask for forgiveness' thing? Well, let's just say in the 45 years we've been married I've had to ask for a lot of forgiveness!"

Grace and I get ready to head out. Mike gives her a big hug.

Grace asks, "When are you coming down again?"

"Not sure. I think I'll stick around here for a few days to make sure your mom does okay."

Grace married a saint.

We both give Mike a wave as we drive away. Next stop—Mom's. Her eye is adding a few more shades of green and yellow besides the predominant purple. I guess she's on the mend. Ann is packing up also. We brought Mike's left-over donuts so they dig into them. We sit and chat a little, and then it's time to say goodbye. We thank Ann for coming, and Mom thanks all of us, over and over, for all that we did for her. Believe me, it was nothing. But she appreciates every little thing as if we were waiting on her, hand and foot. She'll be fine. She lives in a great facility with someone checking on her every day. But the thought of what happened and what might have been is in the back of everyone's mind. So we hug and kiss and say our goodbyes with a few tears.

"See you soon, Mom!"

We get to the cabin around noon. We bring our things in and then start poking around in the fridge. Plenty of things to scrounge up for lunch. Plus we're not even hungry after those donuts.

Next stop—the beach. We've missed this for the past few days. We set up our chairs and put on our sunscreen. Oh wait, that's not the full truth. The only place Grace and I are really concerned about sunscreen is on our lips. We break out in huge cold sores if our lips get fried. Painful and very unattractive. We do pay attention to our faces also—don't want any more lines than we have already. The rest of our bodies—let 'em fry. Our skin is tough as leather and we never burn. We constantly get "sun-screen" shamed by family, friends, doctors, you name it. But isn't everyone allowed at least one or two vices in their lives? We love the sun, we get tan. Sorry!

It's so warm and cozy—we're sleeping in minutes. And that's about all we get. Cyndi comes running down to the beach.

"I am so happy to see you guys! Where have you been? It has been so boring here—I was lost without you!"

She bends way over to give us big hugs as we're lounging on the chairs. Man, that's a lot of chest contact! But we all laugh because surprisingly enough, we did miss her and we're happy to see her. See, people can change in their old age.

"Okay, it's five o'clock somewhere, so I'm declaring it's margarita time," I announce.

I run into the cabin and fire up the blender. I come walking down the stairs, trying to balance three margarita glasses. Surprisingly, Lucas comes walking over.

"If you make one of those for me, I'll help you carry them."

"You're on."

I hand him two of the glasses, and then quickly make up another batch. The two of us come walking down to the beach and hand out the glasses.

"Cheers, everyone!"

Lucas seems pretty talkative—maybe he missed us too?

Now this is what you call a fun afternoon. Margaritas on the beach, along with a dear sister and good friends. And it feels pretty nice to have Lucas here with us. I'm not sure how comfortable either of us is feeling at the moment, but for now, it's enough. And to be honest with you, he's not paying Cyndi any more attention than he is me, which I think is a good omen.

The funny thing is, when I approached Grace with this idea at the beginning of the summer, I pictured day after day of lying on the beach, just the two of us. I never could've envisioned all of the parties, being the "hostess with the mostest," family fun times, and the new friendships that we've made. It's been a blessing.

"What's been going on here the past few days?"

Cyndi responds, "Absolutely nothing! It has been so boring. Where did you guys take off to? You just left us high and dry!"

Interesting, I think. It doesn't sound like she and Lucas have been having oodles of fun while we were gone.

I inform them, "Our mom took a fall in her home. Mike picked her up in the ambulance, we spent many hours in the hospital, and have been keeping an eye on her for the last few days. I guess that about sums it up."

Lucas and Cyndi both say all of the right things—that they hope she's okay, that they hope we're okay, etc. etc. We tell them about Mom's shiner—it's a beauty—and they laugh at that.

Lucas gets a little quiet and finally says, "Yeah, moms are important. Mine died a few weeks ago."

I shriek, "What? Why didn't you tell us? When was this?"

"That week I wasn't around much, remember?"

Well, I certainly do remember that week, but I thought he was gone because he didn't want to run into me.

"Oh Lucas, I am so sorry."

Funny how we keep saying those words to each other. Were there ever any two people who have led a sorrier life?

Grace chimes in, "Oh Lucas, you should've told us. If there was any way we could've been there for you, we would've done it, done anything for you. Was it sudden? Do you want to talk about it?"

Cyndi adds a few words of sympathy. Clearly she's out of her comfort zone. And it appears that this is the first that she's heard about any of this also.

Lucas clears his throat, trying to hold back the tears. I just want to go over and give him a big hug and hold his hand. But that's probably not my place at the moment, so I guess we'll just give him his space and let him talk if he wants to.

And he does. "Mom and Dad have been in a nursing home for a number of years. They were both failing—in their nineties. I visited them often, but it's never enough, you know?"

We commiserate with him on that score.

"Not that they were ungrateful. They were always so pleased to see any of us kids, and never put any pressure on us to visit them. But it just makes you so sad to see their world become so small. Most of their friends and relatives have already passed, and what is there to live for, day after day? I can't imagine it, but they were always upbeat and seemed to look at each new day as a blessing. And I think they meant it, but in doing so, they were blessing us kids, by not making us feel guilty that we didn't have enough time to spend with them every day.

"But then mom got sick, and she was gone in a week. And that's when you feel really guilty. I could've done more, spent more time with them. And my dad, my wonderful dad, said, 'She wanted nothing more than for you kids to live your lives. And that includes you Lucas. Live your life! Stop wasting it in mourning or guilt. Nothing would make your mom prouder or happier than if you would build a new life for yourself. Not as a loner, but with someone! That's all we wish for you.'"

Tears are running down Lucas' face as he's talking. No one knows what to do. If it was just the two of us together, I'd be hugging him tightly in an instant. But there sits Cyndi. She's totally at a loss for words, as is Grace, for a moment.

"Wow, I'm so sorry to lay all of that on you," Lucas apologizes.

Grace responds, "No way. We just wish you would've told us sooner. If you can't be honest with your friends, then we're not being the best friends we can be. Never be afraid to share anything with us."

Good old Grace, always coming up with the right words. And then she goes over to give him a big hug. I follow suit, and so does Cyndi. It's like our own little funeral procession.

Lucas feels bad that he brought us all down. We shrug that off as nonsense. I come up with a better idea.

"What did your mom like to drink?"

"She didn't drink much, but if there was one thing she liked, it was champagne," is his response.

"I'll be right back."

I run into the cabin and grab one of the champagne bottles that we have chilling in the fridge, along with four champagne flutes. I hand one to each of them, pour in some champagne, and say to Lucas, "We're toasting your mom. What's her name?"

"Gertrude."

We all choke a little and stifle back a laugh. Lucas smiles at that.

"She always hated her name."

"To Gertrude!" we all exclaim, and then ask Lucas to tell us more about her. He tells us stories, some funny, some sad, and we yell "cheers" after every one, and take a sip.

This goes on for hours. By this time we're all pretty giggly and feeling good. No more tears–just laughs and good times.

"My dad and sisters should be here. This is way more fun than the funeral and the wake."

We laugh, and then we all get somewhat meditative. The champagne has had its effect, and we all recline in the lounge chairs, thinking our own thoughts. We watch the sun set, while I have this amazing thought. Is this an odd set of people, or what? Yet, I can't imagine a group of four that I'd rather be with right at this moment. And instead of just thinking it, I say it out loud. Everyone says "cheers" to that, and there isn't a dry eye on the beach.

CHAPTER 45

GRACE

"Time for bed."

It's unusual for me to be the first one to make that announcement, but it's been an exhausting couple of days. Ellie and I spent the evening watching a light-hearted rom-com together, but the yawns were coming frequently towards the end of it. We have turned into a couple of summer sister deadheads. We're going to blame it on the emotions of mom's fall and Lucas's sad news. It has nothing to do with the fact that we're getting older or the other fact—that we've been really lazy this summer. Who cares? We're entitled.

The next few days pass in a blur of monotony—sun, boating, reading, wine, food, beach, sunsets, sleep. What's not to love? But it is a little embarrassing when you can't remember what day of the week it is. But then again, this was our goal, and there's no guilt involved. Actually, that's not true. On occasion we decide to get up and get moving—we go for a long walk in the morning, or swim and paddleboard in the afternoon. Ellie is even trying to get me into yoga. Can't say as I'm sold on that yet. We have our yoga mats (actually, just beach towels) out on the lawn, and Cyndi comes over and decides to join us. Not your typical yoga session—lots of talking, lots of laughing. Basically a waste of time as far as yoga goes, but a great time with someone we are starting to appreciate. Still loud, still a chatterbox, but a fun person who isn't as into herself as we first thought. First impressions aren't always accurate, or maybe the first impression she tried to give us isn't truly who she is.

"You know, Cyndi, that's asking a lot of a yoga outfit to hold in all that you've got going on," I laugh.

"You're right, but at least I'm not short and 65 years old," she shoots right back at me.

"Ouch! Cheap shot!" But well-deserved, I might add. My phone rings—it's Mike.

"Hey babes. Got off work this morning, and I'm heading your way."

"Perfect. How's Mom doing?"

"I checked in on her after I got off work. She's got some amazing shades of green and yellow going on around her eye, says she's pain-free with her wrist sprain, and gave me strict orders to take off and not worry about her. Feisty as ever."

What a relief. Even though Ellie and I have been calling her frequently, it's a relief to hear that she's doing well from someone who has actually laid eyes on her. Mom would say she's fine even if she was lying in bed unable to move.

Mike shows up a little before noon. We dig to see what we have in the fridge. Leftover chicken for one thing, which Ellie can whip up into a great chicken salad. Besides the chicken, she adds grapes and pecans, which give it just the right amount of sweetness and crunch. Put it on some grainy bread and you can't ask for a better lunch.

Mike walks over to Lucas' to see what he's up to. For two guys who used to be so busy with all of their handyman jobs, they both seem to have a lot of spare time lately. But I don't blame them, because it's been one of the hottest summers on record. Who wants to sweat on a project when you can cool off at the beach?

And that's how we spend the afternoon–on the beach. It's in the 90's today, so we're spending a lot more time in the water than we are on the sand. No surprise, but Cyndi and Lucas joined us the moment we came out here. We're lazing out on the air mattresses, sometimes talking, sometimes just quietly thinking to ourselves. Or sleeping. That becomes obvious when Mike starts snoring. Lucas puts his finger to his lips as he slowly slides off his mattress. He walks over in stealth mode to Mike, and suddenly flips him over. Mike comes up with a yell, and immediately goes over to Lucas and dunks him. The war is on. We women stay well out of the way, but that only lasts for so long. Pretty soon the guys are chasing us, dunking us, and tossing us over their shoulders. Even though there are only two of them and three of us, we come up as losers in this battle. Eventually it's time to call a truce and we all go sit on the lawn to dry off. I offer to run in and get everyone a drink, but Cyndi won't have it.

"I'll go get something. You guys have been feeding me and offering drinks since I got here. My turn."

She runs to her cabin–if it was in slow motion, it would be similar to that move by Bo Derek years ago. Except it's not in slow motion, because that's not a speed wired into her metabolism. I could use a little of her energy. Just a little–she's still way over the top.

It takes her a little while to come back. With a whole cooler on wheels! She has wine, she has beer, she has water, she has soda, she has rum.

"I wasn't sure what you all wanted."

"Cyndi, that's too much. But thanks!"

Our chorus of gratitude. As we're sitting there sipping our drinks, I can't help but think what an odd group we are. First of all, an uneven number is usually awkward. And then we have the make-up of our group: Mike and I, married forever; Ellie, my sister but yet by herself; Cyndi, a personality beyond explanation; and Lucas, who wants to be with us but yet doesn't want to be with us. It's kind of weird to think about the future. Will Mike, Ellie and I remember this summer as one where we met a couple of nice people that we never saw again? Or is this just the beginning of some forever friendships? The jury is out on that one.

Mike can only do so much lounging around. He suddenly jumps up and says, "Okay, people, how about we all go get cleaned up and take the boat to the marina for dinner? I haven't done enough of that this summer."

He's met with total agreement from the group. We don't agree on a specific time, because there's a big time differential in how long it takes each of us to get ready. Mike will be ready in 15 minutes, probably Lucas also; give Ellie 45 minutes, and I need an hour. I just hate to be rushed. And who knows how long it'll take Cyndi? That's anybody's guess. But no worries, because we're on lake time.

I come down the stairs and see that everyone is sitting out on the porch. Crap—it doesn't take Cyndi as long as me to try and make herself beautiful? I know exactly what Mike is going to say.

"Wow, you're ready already?"

This has been our standing joke for years whenever we're going to go out. Everybody laughs. Really people? It's not *that* funny.

We walk out on the dock and try to gracefully get in the boat. Hard to do when you're short and in a dress. But who cares? We're all friends here. Mike sits at the wheel and backs out of the slip. This is not going to be some crazy boat ride. It's a gorgeous evening, the water is relatively calm, and we're not in any hurry to get anywhere. We ride parallel to shore, and then along the dam, until we get to the marina. Mike and Lucas tie up at the dock, after which we make our way to the patio. I love this place. The colorful umbrellas, the patio lights, the sun reflecting off the water—what's not to love? It's close to evening now, so our waitress is appropriately dressed in a cute shirt and shorts, not a bikini like last time. She appears to be college-aged, and has the long blond hair and golden tan that anyone would envy. On top of that, she has personality, and we chat with her while she takes our drink order. If she doesn't totally goof things up, she'll be on the receiving end of a good tip at the end of the evening.

As we wait for our drinks, I remark, "Look at all of those boats. They're huge. And there are hundreds of them. But what makes me sad is that every time we come here, they're all in their slips. You hardly ever see them out on the lake. So these people who have big bucks that can afford these boats—they must not have the time, or make the time, to use them. What a waste."

Lucas has a smile on his face, but doesn't say anything. Finally Ellie looks at him and says, "Okay, out with it. Obviously you have something to say."

"Well, if that isn't the pot calling the kettle black!"

Ellie and I say in unison, "What?"

"You talk about all of those people not using their boats and how sad that is, but you have had access to a beautiful cabin that has not been used once in the five years that I've been around. So, touche'."

"Ooh, ouch, but you're right. Easy to see the faults in other peoples' lives, and not recognize the exact same fault in ours. As much as it pains me to say it, Lucas—you are absolutely right. We deserve that."

Mike says, "Okay, big mistake on our part, but that's done. From here on out we're going to make it the family-gathering place it was meant to be."

Nods from everyone at the table, even though two of the people aren't in our family.

The waitress walks up with our drinks. Rum and Coke for the guys, red wine for Ellie, white wine for Cyndi and me. We're so predictable. But when you get to our age, you order what you know you like. No use wasting the calories and alcohol content on experimenting with something you might not like.

She takes our dinner order. Actually, this isn't a dinner-type place. It's an appetizer and burger-type place, which we've always known and don't mind. We're in sundresses and shorts, not gowns and black-tie. That's okay on a rare occasion, but casual is more our style.

Mike looks at Cyndi. "I haven't gotten to spend a lot of time with you. What's your story? Where are you from, and any other details you might like to spill? How did you end up in Yankton, of all places, for vacation?"

Cyndi takes a deep breath. I can see the wheels turning—she's deciding how much to share. Should she go with surface chatter and laughter, or should she let us get to know her a little better? She decides on the latter.

"I think I told you this before, but I was an army brat. And when I say brat, I'm not kidding! We moved around a lot, not only in the States, but also in Europe and Asia. That was fine when I was little, but when I got to junior and senior high, the only way I thought I could fit in at each new place was to prove myself, which usually involved hanging out with the wrong kids. There was a lot of alcohol and some drug use involved. About this same time, my parents got a divorce. My mom met someone new and just took off. My dad was tired of dealing with me, and sent me to live with my grandma the last two years of high school. Guess where Grandma lived? Right here in Yankton."

Lucas raises an eyebrow. "Really? What was your grandma's name?"

"Eleanor Landon. Have you ever heard of her? She died shortly after I graduated high school."

"Did she work at the school? In the office?"

"Yep, that was her. A bit militant, perfect for a high school secretary, but with a great heart. I loved her, but did not make her life easy. I'm sure being in charge of a disrespectful, disobedient teenager wasn't her idea of what she wanted to do at that stage of her life, but she did her best. Which included grounding me, sending me to drug and alcohol treatment, and calling the cops when I didn't come home on occasion. I'm sure there were many times when she thought I made her life a living hell. But one thing I know for sure–she always loved me. I wish I could take back the things I did and the hateful things I said to her. And that's why I think it's so neat when you talk about your grandkids and the wonderful things you do for them. I just wish I would've responded in the right way."

We all commiserate with her and try to say the appropriate things. What else are you going to do? Cyndi bats away a few tears through her thick eyelashes and continues on.

"By the time I was done with high school, I had straightened out a bit. Grandma wanted me to go to college. I wasn't sure about that, but she was adamant. She pulled a few strings through her school connections and got me enrolled in a college in Omaha. I know everyone thinks I'm a dumb blond, but I do okay if I apply myself."

I ask her, "What'd you major in? And did you graduate?"

"You guys are going to laugh, but I majored in psychology. When I was going through treatment, I really appreciated my counselors. It got me interested in psych. You know, I think there are a lot of psych majors out there who have gone through counseling themselves and it makes them interested in the field. And yes, I did graduate. My biggest regret was that Grandma didn't live to see that day. But she had faith in me by that point and knew I was going to try and make her proud. Unfortunately, to do anything with a psych major, you have to go on to get your masters and probably a doctorate. By this time I had met a guy, and further schooling just wasn't in my future. And besides, could you imagine anyone coming to me for counseling? They wouldn't be able to get a word in edgewise!"

We all laugh at that, because that's the truth.

Our burgers, fries, and fish tacos arrive, so we all dig in. No counting calories tonight, because I don't think we can count that high. We order another round of drinks, and a chocolate brownie sundae to share. We ask Cyndi to continue on with her story.

"Oh, it's not great. I married that guy from college. We moved around a lot. He was a dreamer with lots of big ideas, none of which panned out. I worked as a waitress wherever we moved to, and about two years into the marriage, we had a baby—a boy.

"We hung onto the marriage for about ten years, probably nine years longer than we should have. But I did get my beautiful son Alex out of the whole deal. It's a typical dreary story. I was a single mom that tried my best and eked out a living for my son and me. He grew up, went to community college, and married his high school sweetheart.

In the meantime, I met an older guy at the restaurant where I was working at the time. He seemed to think he loved me, when in reality he was just looking for some eye candy. I married him because I wouldn't have to work so hard. He paid for numerous plastic surgeries, many of which I wasn't that thrilled about, but he was rich and made my life easier. Alex didn't approve, and we grew apart. He lives in Denver with his wife, and even though we're not really estranged, we don't have a lot of contact. Eventually my husband found someone younger and prettier, and I was out the door. But he did take good care of me financially, so that has made my life easier. Pretty much a story that you all could have predicted on the first day you met me."

What do you say to that? Because the truth is, that was the story that we all pretty much figured out the first moment we met her. So I feel it's my duty to speak the truth back to her.

"I'd like to deny that, but I can't, and I'm ashamed to admit it. I'm sorry we judged you—that was most certainly not very nice of us. But even though this is your story, you're so much more than that. Stop selling yourself short. You graduated college with a degree in psychology. You made it as a single mom. You kicked your addictions. And my goodness, you are a beautiful woman. Don't give us that 'dumb blond' persona. It took a little time, but we figured it out all on our own that you're way better than that. And we're glad you're here."

And that's when the tears come. All three of us women. The guys are uncomfortable and we try to keep the waterworks to a minimum, but it's obvious that Cyndi is touched. Of course the inevitable has to happen—hugs all around the table. And then the waitress comes out with perfect timing—our dessert with a candle burning on top.

She says, "It looks like you're celebrating a special occasion—the dessert is on the house." She'll get a good tip.

We head back to the boat and all climb in. Lucas offers to drive back. We can tell the days are getting shorter. Dusk has given way to darkness, but it's not total darkness because the "almost-full" moon is incredibly bright tonight. We cruise around for a bit, just relaxing and enjoying the beauty of the evening. Other boats are taking advantage of the same thing, and it's pretty to see the boat lights reflecting on the water. Mike and I cuddle up in the back of the boat.

He whispers to me, "I'm so happy we're here together. Is this a perfect night, or what?"

I whisper back, "Do you think Lucas offered to drive so he wouldn't have to pick sitting by Ellie or Cyndi?"

"Could be. This is something he's going to have to eventually figure out all on his own."

Mike is right, but I am such a fixer and I want things fixed right now. As much as I hate to admit it, I guess it's out of my control.

CHAPTER 46

ELLIE

Grace frowns a little as she comes walking down the stairs this morning. Mike is cooking bacon and eggs, but I don't think that's the reason for the frown.

She finally asks, "Have you heard from Abby at all? I haven't heard from either Emily or Jason. If they want to find a weekend for all of them to come to the cabin, we're getting a little scarce on weekends. This summer is flying by."

Grace and I both text our kids and tell them they better be working on finding a weekend to come because school is starting soon. Grace gets the first "ding." Emily is always really prompt in returning texts, unless she's sleeping after working a night shift.

"Working on it!" is her response. "Let u know soon. Won't be this weekend, but probably next."

Grace responds with a thumbs-up emoji.

That would be the weekend before Labor Day weekend. This gives us some idea of what to expect, at least. Or even, if it's going to happen at all. Because if it doesn't, there is going to be a bunch of very unhappy grandchildren.

"Well, guys, since it sounds like we have that semi-figured out, what are we going to do with the week we have left before that happens?" I ask.

Mike says, "I think you ladies should go back to Plan A. Sun, relaxation, wine, and anything else your heart desires. Next weekend will be a zoo, and the weekend after that is Labor Day. The unofficial end of summer. What a bummer that this has gone so fast. So I think you girls should just do whatever sounds good to you."

Grace and I nod in agreement. That didn't take much in the way of persuasion.

Mike continues, "But you know me, I can't sit around all day. And as you also know, I'm not a reader, so don't try and throw any 'most-awesome book ever' at me. We should go fishing today."

"Fishing?" we cry in unison. "You've never gone fishing."

"Gotcha," Mike laughs. "How about we go boating for the day? Maybe drive up the river, swim when we want, ski when we want, play it by ear?"

Grace and I are in. "Do we invite friends or just the three of us?"

"Friends, of course."

Grace runs over to Cyndi's while I run over to Lucas's. That takes all of three minutes. Everyone's in and everyone's going to get ready.

I'm thinking out loud, "We should really come up with a different menu than boat buns."

Grace's response, "Why argue with success?"

We do throw in some extra stuff—cheese and crackers, some sushi we bought yesterday, veggies and dip, and chocolate truffles for dessert.

"Should I bring the charcuterie board along so we can at least set out everything to make it look decent?"

Grace shoots me a look that can only be described as an "are you kidding me?" look.

"We are on a boat, and it's not a yacht by the way, with no one that we need to impress. Tell me you didn't just seriously ask that question!"

"Yeah, that was pretty stupid. Napkins and paper plates it is!"

Cyndi and Lucas arrive in our kitchen at about the same time, throwing their additions to the food and drink in the coolers. We could be gone for days with the amount of stuff that is in there. When we come home, we'll have to unpack and put away about two thirds of it. But it's fun to come well-prepared, because who knows what everyone will want over the next few hours? As Grace always says, "You've got to have options." That's her go-to line whenever she's going on vacation, lugging an overweight suitcase with umpteen pairs of shoes and more outfits than she could wear in a month. Mike just laughs and goes along with it. That guy has gotten really smart over the years.

The guys haul the coolers out to the boat while we women bring the beach bags and towels. We all pick our favorite spots while Mike backs out of the boat lift.

"Upriver or downriver?" he asks.

Upriver, we decide. We head west, driving close to the bluffs, studying the cabins that sit on top of the bluffs. Many of them are hard to see, buried in the trees. There are a number of them that are right on the edge of the bluffs, looking like they could fall off any minute. Big cedar cabins with green metal roofs that fit right in with the pine trees. They look more like mountain cabins than lake cabins. Not what a stranger to the area would predict to see on the shores of the Missouri River in South Dakota.

We drive past the marina on the Nebraska side—more boats not being used. Lucky for us. Fewer boats make for calmer water. We keep heading west. The bluffs start to flatten out a little.

Cyndi is facing the South Dakota side of the river and suddenly says, "Look you guys! Look at that humongous farm! What kind of a family owns a farm like that?"

Lucas laughs. "Not a family, a colony. A Hutterite colony."

"I have never heard of that. Kind of like Amish?"

"In a way, but a lot more modern. They dress somewhat like the Amish, but they use modern machinery and are very successful farmers and businessmen."

"Hmm, interesting."

We continue on past the colony. There isn't a boat out here, so we decide to anchor ours. Mike cuts the motor and there is total silence. We are out in the middle of nowhere.

I can't stand the total silence. Actually, I'm surprised there is total silence. That doesn't happen often when Cyndi's in the group.

"Mike, turn on the radio. We need some music."

There isn't much for radio reception out here, and the cell phone reception isn't any better, so we go back in time and throw in an old CD from the glove compartment. A playlist from the 80's. A lot of Foreigner, Journey, Survivor and REO. Immediately we're all singing along, until Mike interrupts and informs us,

"Ladies, it's time to break out the fine china. I'm starving."

Grace and I throw open the coolers, lay out a spread on the bench seat in the back, and tell everyone to just go for it. No one's shy, and soon we're all sitting back with plates full of sandwiches, cheese and crackers, grapes, nuts, and some chocolate to satisfy our sweet tooths. We pick out our favorite beverages, and everyone's happy.

Grace is good at making conversation, which we seem to be lacking today for some reason. She looks at Lucas and tells him, "I've only seen the inside of your cabin from the front door. Have you done a lot of work in there?"

Lucas looks a little embarrassed. "I'm so sorry. I should've had you guys over."

"Oh no, that wasn't what I was getting at all. I'm just curious."

"I did a total kitchen remodel. It was just a little galley kitchen. I knocked out a wall, put in new cabinets, countertops and appliances. Other than that, I haven't done a thing. After seeing what you guys did with your cabin, it's obvious that mine could use a little work. It just never seemed important. It's just me, and it's not like I do a lot of entertaining. But now that I take a good look at it, it seems a little tired. I guess you guys have inspired me. Or made me jealous, at least. Your place is gorgeous."

I give him a smile at tell him, "Well, if you ever need any ideas or help, Grace and I are at your service. It's one of our favorite things to do."

Lucas just smiles but makes no comment. I guess I overstepped with that offer.

We finish our lunch and the guys decide they're croaking hot. They both take flying leaps off the boat as they hoot and holler going in. Their goal was to get us wet with big splashes, and they accomplished that mission. We women scream, which is just what Mike and Lucas were hoping for. We pack the lunch away and then make our own little splashes as we go down the ladder and make our way into the water. The guys call us a bunch of pansies. They're not far from the truth. We paddle around to cool off, and then make our way back into the boat to dry off in the sun.

Cyndi is in her glory. Stretching out on her back in a white bikini, she is a sight to behold. I can only speak for myself, but I think Grace would agree that our animosity and jealousy towards her is gone. We all have our assets and talents, and with all that she's been through, kudos to her. She suddenly sits up.

"I never could've dreamed that when I decided to rent the cabin this summer that it would be this much fun. I thought I'd be lonely all day and spend the evening partying with some old friends in town. This is way better than that. You guys are the best! I could do this every day and never get sick of it. By the way, may we do this every day until I leave?"

We all laugh. But she's right–it doesn't get any better than this.

Mike says, "Enough of this lazing around. Who wants to ski?"

I go first because I want to ski in the calm water before we stir it up with too many boat wakes. Twice in one summer that I have the perfect skiing conditions–I couldn't ask for more. Cyndi is up next. We all cheer her on because we know she hasn't had a lot of experience. She's busy talking to herself while she's in the water waiting to be pulled up.

"I can do it. I'm not going to make a fool of myself. I'm with friends. They won't laugh at me. I can do it."

We just laugh because she can't keep her mouth from running when she's nervous. She's up and we all cheer.

Lucas drives while Mike goes next. He never got into the slalom thing. He can do it, but never enjoyed it because he said it's way too much work and he just wants to have fun. He pops right up on his old man skis—huge, wide things. He makes it look effortless as he goes in and out of the wake.

Lucas is next. "Even though it's been awhile, I'm going to try to slalom. It's the perfect water for it."

Mike guns it. Lucas drags for a bit and finally is up. He looks good out there, but doesn't ski for long before he lets go and sinks into the water. He looks a little pained as he climbs up the ladder and into the boat.

"Are you okay?" we all ask.

"Yeah, I'm fine. Just haven't done that in a while. A little out of practice, I guess."

There's just a moment of awkwardness as we realize that we all had our turn at skiing, except for Grace. We all look at her. The person who loved skiing the most.

"I'm fine. It was fun watching you all." And she means it.

Time to break out the drink cooler. We women share a bottle of wine, while Lucas drinks a beer and Mike picks out his favorite—a spiked strawberry lemonade. Mike is a sucker for sweet drinks. When he's at a bar, usually ordering a girly drink, he always tells the bartender to put it in a manly glass and hold the little umbrella. Our friends all know it and give him lots of grief, but he takes it like a man and doesn't apologize for his taste.

Cyndi chatters on, asking us for more details on our family, and trying to engage Lucas in conversation. He's not totally receptive. As I sit there watching him, I see him squirming in his seat, and grimacing as he tries to get into a comfortable position. I've seen that tell-tale sign before. Will used to have back problems that would flare up on occasion. Totally miserable.

"Mike, maybe we should head back. Lucas, are you doing okay?"

"Yeah, I'm fine. I think I did a number on my back while I was skiing. It's no big deal."

He's trying to minimize things, but I can tell he's hurting. Poor guy.

Mike maneuvers the boat slowly back home. We're all so bummed for Lucas, even though he doesn't want to admit how much pain he's in. We pull up by the dock, and we see the true picture when Lucas tries to pull himself up out of the boat. It's painful to watch. He wants to try and help us haul stuff up out of the boat, but we tell him to head on home, take some ibuprofen, and ice his back. He doesn't argue. Poor guy.

Cyndi yells, "I'll bring you some supper later. And I think I have some left-over pain pills. I'll bring them over too."

Don't know if feeding someone your left-over prescription drugs is the best idea, but when you're in pain, you'll take anything. Cyndi heads home, while the three of us go in and unpack the coolers. We were right—we're unpacking almost as much as we put in.

Mike remarks, "I feel so sorry for Lucas. I've been there, and it's totally miserable. He's going to be down for the count for a bit."

Grace and I both commiserate with him. Grace has seen Mike when his back has given out, and I saw Will in action. Supposedly they say that if you're really tall you have a bigger chance of having back problems. One downside to being a big, tall Dutchman, I guess.

We finish cleaning up, go upstairs to shower, and hunt in the fridge for leftovers for dinner. We decide to eat out on the porch so eventually we'll be able to watch the sunset. Cyndi comes walking, holding a picnic basket.

"Where did you find that relic?" I ask.

"It was in the pantry. It definitely took a little dusting off, but it works. I heated up a frozen lasagna to bring over to Lucas. A bottle of wine, a loaf of French bread, and pain pills. A dinner made in heaven, right?" she laughs.

We laugh with her, but the thought of them spending the evening together does spark that miserable feeling of jealousy in me. I don't fault Cyndi for doing a kind thing, but why does it seem like Lucas is willing to spend time with her but doesn't want to get involved with me? I guess he's just not that interested? Frustrating, for sure.

CHAPTER 47

GRACE

The next week passes in a blur. Not necessarily because the time seems to fly by quickly, but because each day is exactly the same. Mike is back in Sioux Falls. Ellie and I do our usual thing of taking a morning walk, lying out in the sun, hanging out with Cyndi, and bringing Lucas supper. I take one of the jet skis for a spin at least once a day, because they're sitting right there and they're so much fun. It's not Ellie's favorite thing to do, so I've gotten Cyndi to join me on occasion. She's starting to enjoy it a lot, and has gotten more daring as the summer has progressed.

Lucas's recuperation has been slow. He's been to a doctor, a chiropractor, and a physical therapist. They're all in agreement that it's more of a muscular inflammation thing than anything that would require surgery, so that's good news. Every day he's moving a little more freely and says the pain is definitely decreasing.

He also informed us, "No more skiing. I guess I'm way too old for that!"

I'm sure that's true for this summer, but there's always next year. I don't want to see him relegated to being an audience member like me.

Some evenings Ellie and I hang out with Lucas and Cyndi on our porch, some nights we build a fire, and some nights Cyndi goes over to Lucas' house. Ellie and I can't quite put a finger on their relationship. They seem comfortable with each other, but there is never any "public display of affection." Thank goodness—I think Ellie would come unglued if she had to watch that. The reality is—he treats all three of us women pretty much the same. Weird. He must be sticking with his vow to not get close to anyone again.

And now that this week has passed in a lull of summer haziness and laziness, it's time for the weekend. And this is not going to be relaxing in the least. This is the weekend that it works for all of the kids to come. Their "last hurrah" before school starts. Mike is coming this morning, bringing Mom with him. The kids will show up later this afternoon. Ellie and I have made the weekend menu, and have stocked up on loads of groceries. Tonight we're falling back on the meal that doesn't have much timing involved, and is a cinch to clean up—the shrimp boil. Of course, some of the kids don't like shrimp, so we've stocked up on the old grandkid standby—hot dogs for those who want them.

Mike and Mom show up just before lunch. The bruising around Mom's eye is totally gone and she looks like her wonderful self again.

"Are you up for this, Mom? It could get a little crazy here this weekend," I tell her.

"Of course. If all else fails, I can just sit in one of the recliners and let everyone run circles around me. I'll be fine."

Ellie goes over to her and gives her a hug. "Mom, I hope it's okay, but you're going to be sharing the master suite with me. That'll free up a bedroom."

Mom smiles, "That's fine with me. But only if you can stand having a roommate for a couple of nights, Ellie."

"Perfect. We can have girl-talk every night."

We all laugh because we know that the second Mom takes her hearing aids out to sleep, she won't hear a thing that Ellie has to say.

We hear the first car approaching around four o'clock. It's Chris and Emily and their four kids. The kids come flying out of the car, caught up in the excitement of the weekend. Mike and I look at each other. Are we ready for this? It'll be fun but it'll be wild. They go up to the bunkroom and claim their spots. Actually two of the beds are already claimed.

Tenley asks, "Who's sleeping in those two beds?"

Mike looks at her and says, "Guess. Guess who you're stuck sleeping with. And I'll give you a clue. It's someone who snores."

Tenley is confused, but her oldest brother Caleb guesses it instantly. "Grandpa? And Grandma? Why are you sleeping in the bunkroom?"

"Because Ellie and Grandma Anderson have one bedroom, and we wanted the three adult couples to each have their own room. So you're stuck with us. Suckers!"

I can tell Emily and Chris feel somewhat guilty about this arrangement, so of course we go through this little argument that they know they can't win. Mike will tolerate it just fine, because he's used to sleeping on a little twin bed at the fire station. And I think it'll be fun to hear the kids talking together into the wee hours of the morning. I just pray that they'll all sleep in late in the morning. Even if they don't, I can guarantee you that I will.

It's not long before Jason and Michelle and their girls come driving up, followed closely by Greg and Abby and their two. Oh my goodness, what were we thinking? But this is the stuff that memories are made of, right? Or maybe insanity. At this point it's a toss-up.

Dinner is a hit. The kids all love throwing things in the boiling pot. They turn up their noses a little at the onions, and also at the shrimp, but everything else is good to go in their book. We even end up throwing the hot dogs in the pot, instead of microwaving them. The little kids like seeing that their part of the meal is also a part of the grown-ups' meal. Thankfully the pot is huge, because we have a lot of people to feed. Everything gets thrown on the tablecloths, and everyone digs in. Lots of conversation, lots of food, and lots of fun.

After an evening campfire, it's time to turn in. Mike and I settle into our bunkbeds, just smiling as we listen to the conversations going on around us. It might not be our best night of sleep ever, but it will be one of our best nights ever.

ELLIE

Last night Emily, Abby and Michelle volunteered for breakfast duty. So very nice of them, but I have a hard time turning the kitchen over to them totally. Let's just say that I'm supervising. Grace thought this was the best news ever. I doubt if we'll see her until breakfast is long over. Do the concepts of not being a morning person and not liking breakfast always go together? Does one thing cause the other, or are they mutually exclusive? Someone should do a study on that.

Breakfast is served with kids coming down the stairs over a two-hour time period. The kids are having a great time, as are the adult kids. We raised some winners. Mom is just taking everything in and conversing with some of them one-on-one. She is still so interested in everyone's lives and the feeling is mutual. We all love her so much. Could anyone wish for a more loving, more gracious, more beautiful mom, grandma and great-grandma? We're so blessed to have her in our lives.

Now on to the crazy stuff. Boating and jet-skiing. We're all parked on the beach in our lawn chairs, watching the action and waiting for our turns. Lucas meanders over. He's moving better these days. Almost normal. I tell Mom about his back. He makes light of it but does tell us that he's almost 100%. Good for him. He proceeds to jump in the boat with Mike but makes it clear that he's only along for the ride–no skiing or tubing for him. Good choice.

A short time later Cyndi comes running over. She wants to be introduced to everyone and join in the fun. To be honest, Grace and I had warned the whole family about her. Our comments ran along the line of "she's a little over the top but is a really nice person once you get to know her."

Grace had also given Cyndi this word of caution, "You know, I have teenage grandsons. Umm, I don't know exactly how to put this, but do you have a swimsuit that covers a little more than usual? I guess I don't want them gawking at you. It's a tough age. You understand?"

Cyndi had just laughed and said, "I totally get it. I think I have something that might be a little more appropriate."

Well, let's just say that Cyndi is true to her word. And I don't think the suit she's wearing is some old relic that she just happened to dig out. This looks like an old lady's swimsuit that she bought recently at the oldest department store that Yankton has to offer. It's dark purple, has a neckline that actually goes up to her neck, and a "swim-skirt." I kid you not. Grace shoots me a look that has one eyebrow creeping up as high as it can go. We have a hard time not laughing out loud. But I also know that Grace is thinking the exact same thing that I am. What a great friend to make such a grand gesture. We are so proud of her.

The day goes on with the boat loading and unloading (courtesy of Mike and Lucas), Grace driving kids on the jet-skis, the older ones taking off on the jet-skis by themselves, Cyndi getting to know each family member, and food and drinks being carted down to the beach all day long. The thing that makes Grace and me beam with pride is the fact that the kids and grandkids are so helpful in the midst of their "fun in the sun." We (and their parents) have brought them up well. Mom is just enjoying the day with family, even though she has to get out of the sun for a while. She goes into the cabin to take a nap, and later comes out rejuvenated, ready to spend more time with all of us.

Finally it's time for dinner. Everyone has gotten cleaned up, and we set up all of the lawn chairs around the firepit. The guys are on drink duty—from the adults to the smallest child. We invite Cyndi and Lucas to join us—I think they are flattered by the invitation. Grace and I had decided on hamburgers for tonight, so Mike and Lucas fire up the grill. The kids are all sitting there with this glassy-eyed look on their faces. This was a day full of sun and lots of activity. Probably not enough sunscreen was used today because there are a lot of red cheeks around this circle.

Dinner is a hit because everyone is starving. We could've fed them cereal and they would've been grateful. We go back to our circle of chairs around the firepit. Mike and the grandsons build a fire that can be seen for miles. Mike won't have to get up again for the rest of the evening—Caleb, Liam and Keegan will fight over who gets to throw the next log in.

MIKE

What a day. I love my kids and grandkids, but I'm getting too old for this! To spend a whole day driving a boat, watching where you're going but also watching the skier or tuber behind you, well, it's a lot of head-turning and it's really hard on your neck. Especially when you slept in a bunkbed last night. But isn't that what you do for your grandkids? Crazy stuff that you never thought you'd do?

Finally, time to relax. I get the fire started with my grandsons. I don't have to do that—I've taught them all of the basics and they all have it covered. But I take joy in doing that simple task with them, and I think they feel the same way. Now that that's done, and they have it covered for the rest of the evening, I'm in relaxation mode, just watching the fire. I'm not a night owl like Grace, and who knows, I might be sleeping in my chair before long. Mom is sitting to my left, so I make small talk with her. Until Cyndi, to my right, starts talking. That's fun too. She always has lots to say and you don't have to put any effort into the conversation.

A few minutes later, Cyndi starts talking with Grace, to her right, while I hear Mom talking to Lucas, who is on her left. I'm enjoying just sitting there, watching the motion of the flames. The kids have been throwing in their "magic fire" color packets, so it's a gorgeous fire of reds, blues, greens and purples. Truly beautiful and mesmerizing.

I hear Mom saying, "Lucas, Ellie told me that you lost your mom recently. You have my sympathy. It's hard to lose a parent, no matter how old they are."

Lucas responds, "Yeah, it's been hard. Harder than I thought it would be."

"Lucas, I don't know you well. But Ellie has told me some of your history. You have been dealt some tragic blows. And I could cry just thinking about what you've gone through. Forgive me for saying this, and I know it's not my place, but here goes. You know that life has to go on, right? That you can't shut yourself off from other people and what life has to offer, right?"

"I know that's what my head is telling me, but I don't know if my heart is there yet."

"Just think of your mom. Sure, you're mourning her loss right now, but did it ever occur to you not to love her and have a relationship with her because you'd be sad when she died? No, that would be ridiculous.

"Yeah, you're right on that score."

"Lucas, in my mind's eye I see you as a young man, even though you're in your sixties. Hopefully you have many years ahead of you. But those years will be meaningless and empty unless you open your heart to love. We're not meant to live in a vacuum. I realize you open yourself to heartache when you choose to love someone, but the reward is so much greater than the risk. I'm not trying to tell you who to choose—Ellie or Cyndi—but please, choose someone. It'll make life worth living. Your life is so much richer when you share it with someone."

I look over at Mom, and her eyes are glistening. And then I look at Lucas, and his eyes are glistening too. I think she has reached him. Oh, I so hope she has reached him.

CHAPTER 48

GRACE

Lying in bed, talking with the grandkids—I love it. Mike is out for the count—no surprise there. The kids are still wired. Lots of conversations floating all around me. Someone asks me, "What's the funniest story you have about me?"

Here's the thing. If you're a grandparent, you think everything your grandchild says is the most profound thing ever said on earth. But here's the other thing: if you don't write it down, you forget. I wish that I had kept a notebook of every funny or amazing thing that my seven grandchildren have ever said. Because there were some good ones. And I'm not going to bore you with everything that I can remember. But here's a great one. Years ago, I was lying in bed with two of my granddaughters, who are sisters. The younger one, Kayla, was having a birthday the next day.

I said to her, "Kayla, you're going to be five tomorrow. Isn't that exciting?"

She agreed, but then shot right back with, "Grandma, how old are you?"

Feeling a little smug because I was a really young grandma, I said, "I'm 55."

Her response was, "Wow, you're going to be dead pretty soon."

Well, that took the air out of my balloon. But I died laughing. Because it was the last thing that I expected to hear and it was hilarious. I can't look at Kayla without thinking of that comment. And as much as that one comment rings in my mind, I could tell you a story about each of my grandkids that brings tears to my eyes. They are unique, and they are each so precious to me. They have no idea how much.

After what seems like a really short night of sleep, I see the sun peeking through the windows. I am so not ready for this. I look at Mike's bed–it's empty. He's "up and at'em." Good for him. This is what we do best. I stay up with the kids until after midnight, and he's up with them in the morning. Getting them breakfast and entertaining them until I get up. It's a good system, and it's worked for 19 years, since our first granddaughter was born.

I come down to a houseful of people. Mom, kids, grandkids. It's a great feeling, but please just give me an hour or two to adjust. Today will be a repeat of yesterday. Boating, jet-skiing, sunning, eating, drinking. Boring if we're telling about it, fun if you're doing it. And we're doing it!

After a full day of activities, and a dinner that's eaten in a few minutes by a hungry crew, the goodbyes start. Everyone is heading home. Mom is staying an extra day because Mike won't head home until tomorrow. But as the kids start loading up their vehicles, the tears start. The grandkids don't want to leave.

"Grandma, school doesn't start for a few more days. May we stay longer?"

"I miss you so much when you're gone."

"We'll be so good if you let us stay longer. We won't be any work."

Somehow all of these kids are focusing their appeals on me. Am I the "weakest link?"

Yes, I am, and they know it. I would say yes to any of them in a heartbeat. But their parents prevail and say it's time to get back to Sioux Falls. Mom just laughs and tells me that I'm the softest grandmother ever. Isn't that the truth.

Once everyone has left, we sit out on the porch with glasses of wine. Mike and his entourage of women: Mom, Ellie and I.

I look at Mom and say, "You must be bone-tired. But you did a great job of keeping up. The kids were happy to spend some time with you."

Mom agrees. "I'm beat, and I know it's a little early, but I'm heading to bed. But thanks so much for including me in this weekend. It was busy, but it was fun. Hope I didn't make any work for you girls."

We quickly put that notion out of her head. Mike offers to help her up the stairs. Normally she would refuse. The fact that she accepts that offer tells us how tired she really is.

Ellie and I sink back into our chairs and just relax. We listen to the cicadas making a racket, a sound which we both hate. It's a sign that fall is coming. So depressing. Mike comes back out to the porch, and like the gentleman that he is, refills our wine glasses.

He holds up his glass and says, "Cheers to you ladies for a successful weekend."

Ellie and I are almost too tired to clink our glasses with his, but we make the supreme effort. Mike tells us that he heard an interesting conversation last night at the campfire.

"Really? With whom?" I ask.

"Mom and Lucas. Mom was sympathizing with him in the loss of his mother, and he seemed to appreciate that a lot. And then she went on to tell him to not close himself off from love, because he'll be living a lonely and empty life."

Ellie asks, "Really? How did he respond to that?"

"He seemed to be taking it all in. You know, everyone always wants to hear what your mom has to say. She's the kindest woman, and she would never think this, but she's the smartest woman with a lot of common sense. How could anyone not take her advice to heart?"

"And do you think he'll put some thought into what she had to say?" Ellie wonders.

"Well, who knows," Mike answers, "but I don't think he'll take it lightly. He had tears in his eyes by the time Mom was done talking."

"Interesting," is Ellie's response. "Mom playing matchmaker at her age."

"I don't think I'd exactly call it playing matchmaker. She told Lucas that he could pick you or he could pick Cyndi—he just needs to pick someone."

Ellie shrieks "What? What was she thinking?"

Mike and I laugh at that one, and once Ellie calms down, she has to laugh too.

"My own mother, trying to talk a guy into getting involved, and not sticking up for her own daughter."

"Oh Ellie, that is too funny," I tell her. "But maybe she gave Lucas the nudge he needs. It will be interesting to see if anything changes."

It's getting late and we're almost too tired to crawl up the stairs to our rooms. No bunkbeds tonight, thankfully. Tomorrow the whole day will be spent cleaning bathrooms and washing more sheets than one family should own. But it was worth every minute.

————————

ELLIE

Mondays—ugh. Mike and Mom left after a late breakfast, and now we can't put off the inevitable any longer. The laundry pile is massive—sheets, towels, throw rugs full of sand. The bunkroom comes in so handy, but do you know how many toilets we have to clean today?

Grace and I are sitting by the kitchen island trying to get motivated when all of a sudden she decides, "Forget it. We're not doing it."

"What do you mean? Forget what?"

"The sun is shining, we're dead tired, and we deserve a day to ourselves. The forecast is calling for rain tomorrow. We'll clean this mess up then."

"Oh, you think? I'd just like to get this over with."

"Nope, not today. Today is going to be called our 'Grandma Needs to Relax' day. We're going to shut some doors so we can't see the mess, we're going to put on our suits, we're going to lie on our most comfortable chaise lounges, and we're going to invite Cyndi over to join us in our decadent laziness. Let the lounging begin!"

I laugh at Grace. For a woman who used to be driven with keeping the perfect house and perfect family, she has learned how to relax in her old age.

We head on out to the beach with our towels, sunglasses and book readers. I go over to Cyndi's to invite her to our afternoon of relaxation. She's on the phone but tells me she'll be right out. We're just getting settled when Cyndi comes running out of her cabin. She's back in bikini mode. I doubt if we'll ever see that matronly purple swimsuit again.

"Guess what? You'll never guess! I'm so excited! I was just on the phone with Alex. He called me! And you'll never guess! I'm going to be a *grandma*!"

Grace and I jump out of our chairs and we give her the biggest hug. The three of us are jumping around like a bunch of wild women. We whoop and holler and congratulate her and hug her over and over.

Lucas pokes his head out of his door and yells, "Are you ladies okay down there?"

We assure him we're fine, just excited. He looks at us like we're a little stir crazy, just laughs and shakes his head, and goes back inside. I don't think he wants to be a part of the crazy women group down on the beach.

"This calls for a celebration," I announce. "I'll grab a bottle of champagne and some glasses. And don't you dare tell Grace any details until I get back. And Cyndi, you're not going to believe this. Grace declared this day a holiday—'Grandma Needs to Relax.' And guess what? Now that you're going to be a grandma, you're an official part of this holiday!"

We all scream in excitement.

Lucas pokes his head out again. "Are you sure you're okay?"

We all laugh and reassure him. He still doesn't want to get involved and goes back inside. Smart man.

I run as fast as I can to get the champagne and glasses. I make it back down to the beach in record time. Not sure what that is, but for a 62-year-old, post-menopausal woman, it was pretty darn fast.

I pour the champagne, and try to come up with a toast.

"To Cyndi, the most non-conventional grandma God has ever created!"

We all laugh and yell "cheers" all around.

"Okay, now we have to have some details. Spill it," I tell Cyndi.

"Well, Alex called a little bit ago. You saw me on the phone. I was kind of surprised to hear from him. Like I told you, he didn't really like my last husband, so we kind of drifted apart. Not that we had any big arguments or anything, but we just let our relationship slide. I don't think I've talked to him since last Christmas. So this noon, out of the blue, my phone rings, and it's Alex. We chat a little, and it sounds like he's in a really good mood. Surprisingly, the conversation was pretty natural and relaxed, which was a great feeling.

Finally he says, 'Mom, I have some news. You're going to be a grandma.'

I screamed, literally screamed. He said, 'Mom, it'll be okay. You don't have to be called Grandma if you don't want to be. I just thought you'd want to know.'

I told him I screamed because I'm beyond excited, and that baby better call me Grandma because that's all I want to be called."

"When is his wife due?" I ask.

"In January. And here's the best part. Alex asked if I would consider moving a little closer to them. His wife's parents have both passed away, and he said they would love for their child to have one grandparent around. And that's me!"

She is beyond excited, and Grace and I are so happy for her. We fire questions at her. Are they going to find out the sex of the baby? Has her daughter-in-law been feeling well? Was this a planned pregnancy? Did Alex seem excited about it? Will your daughter-in-law work after the baby is born? When Alex says he wants you around, how close is he talking? How soon do you think you'll move? What are your plans?

Cyndi's brain and mouth are running a mile a minute.

"He wants me to move to Denver. Oh my goodness, I'm going to have to pack up my place in Florida! I hate moving! Maybe I'll just sell everything and start over. I have got so much to do!"

She's getting so worked up that she's almost at the distraught stage.

I tell her, "Oh Cyndi, you have time. None of this has to be done right now. You have until January. So we're going to take this afternoon to settle you down. Just forget about all of the details and soak up the sun and the joy. This is amazing. But remember, it's "Grandma Needs to Relax" day. Try to focus on the fun and forget the details for just this afternoon. And while you're at it—here's another glass of champagne."

We all laugh because it's just one of those afternoons that is made for laughter. Today there is no napping, there is no reading, there are no worries—there is only perfect contentment. The way it's supposed to be.

CHAPTER 49

GRACE

I call Mike with the news. He just laughs.

"Now that's something that's hard to picture–Cyndi as a grandma."

I laugh with him. "It'll definitely be unique. But I'm so happy for her. I think this will give her a little focus."

"What did Lucas say?" Mike asks.

"He doesn't know it yet. He wisely decided to avoid the crazy women on the beach today. Ellie and I are having Cyndi and Lucas over for dinner tonight so she can tell him and we can celebrate."

"What do you think his response is going to be?"

"Who knows? I guess we'll find out soon enough."

Lucas and Cyndi arrive at the same time, each carrying a bottle of wine. Ellie is apologizing about the meal.

"Sorry guys, it's leftovers from the weekend. Hope you weren't expecting a gourmet meal."

Lucas smiles at her, "Your leftovers are better than anything I could conjure up. No apology necessary."

We sit down on the porch to a variety of appetizers. A perfect accompaniment to the wines they brought.

Lucas remarks, "It looks like you women were having the time of your lives today on the beach. What gives?"

Cyndi explodes, "Oh Lucas, I just found out I'm going to be a grandma! Isn't that the best news ever? I am so excited I could just burst!"

Lucas stands up and gives her a hug. "Cyndi, I'm really happy for you. Congratulations!"

As he's saying this, Ellie and I look at each other. I think it hits us at the same time. What does this mean for Lucas' and Cyndi's relationship? Interesting. But this is a fun evening of celebration, and I don't think anyone's putting deep thought into future plans. We toast the new grandma, we eat our leftover hamburgers, and sit and talk, laugh and relax.

The next morning we look out to see gray skies and rain. Wow, the weather forecasters actually got it right for once. I've often said that if I was wrong in my job as often as the weather forecasters are in theirs, I would've been fired a long time ago. But since they have it right, the inevitable has to happen. We have to clean up the weekend mess. Yuk! Ellie and I divide up our duties, as we keep the washer and dryer going nonstop for the next nine hours. Wouldn't it be nice if you could have weekend guests and then command them to do all the cleaning before they could leave? Not very gracious, but it's a thought.

I'm a little down in the dumps today. The dreary weather always does me in, and the thought of our summer being over in a week or so puts the nail on the coffin. Ellie doesn't admit it, but she's feeling the same way. I know Mike is working today, but I give him a call anyway. He can tell I'm down.

"I think I'll come down for the day tomorrow. I won't be able to stay, because I have to work again on Thursday, but at least we could spend the day together. Maybe go out and celebrate Cyndi's good news?"

"Oh hon, you don't have to do that," I respond. "But if you insist," (we both laugh), "it would be nice."

"It's a plan. I'll see you in the morning."

I tell Ellie, and she's fine with that.

"Mike's right, let's go out to eat and celebrate."

Mike arrives the next morning. My husband's here and the sun is shining. The combination of those two things is going to make for a great day. Mike and I take the jet skis out for a spin around the lake. As we ride past the campgrounds, we see that they're packed, even though it's the middle of the week. Everyone is squeezing in their last vacation before school starts. I'm sure there are many moms that are just counting down the days until their kids are back in school, with an almost giddy anticipation. I was never one of those moms. I was always so sad when Jason and Emily had to go back to school. No more sleeping in, no more lazy days–to go back to a schedule was drudgery for all of us.

But I haven't had to think about that for years, so I'm not going to worry about it now. But it's that pervasive feeling of autumn that I don't like. As far as I'm concerned, there should only be one season, and that's summer. And I know, we're idiots for not moving somewhere that always has summer, like Arizona, California, or Florida. But as much as I hate fall, I love family more. This is where our family is, so this is where we'll stay. And for today, it's great. I just need to keep focusing on the positive and deal with fall when it actually gets here.

We take a nice long ride and eventually make it back to the cabin. Mike puts his jet ski on the lift, while I finish off my ride with some 360's and other tricks. If anyone had been sitting behind me, they would've been long gone. The rush of adrenaline this gives me is exhilarating, and I laugh out loud because this is one of my favorite things to do. I gave up skiing, but there's no way I was giving up jet-skiing. That would be like putting me out to pasture. Mike is just shaking his head as I drive my jet ski up onto the lift.

But he's smiling as he says, "You just love this, don't you? Good for you, babes. It's so much fun watching you do something that you love so much."

Cyndi and Ellie are sunning on the beach.

Cyndi yells at Mike. "Did you hear that I'm going to be a grandma? Can you tell I'm excited?"

Mike laughs. "Yeah, I can tell! Tonight we're going to celebrate. Murdo's at six."

Mike and I walk over to Lucas's cabin to tell him tonight's plan. He thinks it's a great idea. Mike asks him how his back is doing, and they start talking about different exercises, different meds, different therapies. Boring. I walk over to our cabin, grab a bottle of water, and join Ellie and Cyndi on the beach. The next hours just fly by as we fill Cyndi in with all of our "grandma wisdom." Oh my goodness, she even brought a notepad down to the beach, and is writing all of this stuff down.

I finally say, "You don't need to take notes. Just love this baby and let the parents be the parents. That's about it. You'll do fine. And you'll love every minute of it."

As much fun as this is, we look at the time and decide it's time to clean up for dinner tonight. We tell Cyndi to come over at five for drinks and appetizers before dinner. Ellie runs over to tell Lucas the same thing.

We're sitting on the porch as Lucas comes walking over. It's five o'clock on the dot—Lucas is one prompt guy. Cyndi isn't here yet, which is a little unusual. She's usually early, because she just can't wait to get the party started. We're drinking our wine and eating our cheese and crackers when she comes walking over. Hugs all around as Ellie pours her a glass of wine.

Lucas gives her an extra-long hug and says, "Hey Grandma, have you come down from cloud nine yet?"

She hugs him back and replies, "Not yet. This is the most exciting thing that has happened to me in a long time. Oh, besides spending the summer with you guys. By the way, sorry I'm late. I was on the phone with Alex."

We all tell her not to worry about it, it's no big deal. There is a mix of emotions playing over her face.

I ask her, "There's nothing wrong, is there? You seem a little subdued."

"There's absolutely nothing wrong. Everything's good. But the reason that Alex called is that there's a condo for sale in their neighborhood. He said it would be the perfect home for me, but things are selling fast, and he wants me to come out and see it. So I'm going to look for a flight out tomorrow."

Lucas looks a little thoughtful and then finally asks, "So you're seriously thinking about moving to Denver?"

"Why not? I have nothing in Florida. A few token friends but nothing beyond that. Nothing like what I found here this summer. My ex-husband left me with a nice house there that I can sell in a heartbeat, and enough money to buy whatever I want within reason. So yeah, I'm going to do this. When Alex called me, it was like I was given a lifeline, a purpose for my life. I'm going to take advantage of that, because I don't have a whole lot else going for me. I know it's sudden and unexpected, but somehow it feels right. I like that feeling."

Ellie smiles at her. "Cyndi, go for it. You're right—this is your once-in-a-lifetime chance." And then Ellie laughs, "And don't screw it up!"

We all laugh at that, because the possibility definitely exists.

I look at the group and say, "This was supposed to be a celebration tonight, but it's turning out kind of sad. Bummer. But you know what, let's go out and turn this back into a celebration. Our end of summer 'last hurrah.'"

We drive to Murdo's and enjoy an evening out on their patio, watching the boats and kayaks float by. The food is good and the company is better. Lucas and Mike ask Cyndi about the upcoming grandchild, but the reality is, guys aren't into it and don't know what questions to ask. Ellie and I laugh at some of their awkwardness. We watch the sun set and head back to the cabins. You can tell that Lucas' back is giving a little bit of trouble. He tells us that he's going to call it a night.

Cyndi asks him, "May I come over for a little while?"

"Sure," is his response. "Good night you guys. It was fun."

We watch them as they walk off together. Awkward.

Ellie just shakes her head. "I'm going to bed. See you in the morning."

Mike and I sit down for a little while. He says, "Well, that evening turned out a little different from what I thought it would be. That is the true definition of 'mixed emotions.'"

I agree with him. It was supposed to be a celebration, but it could end up being a "goodbye night," depending on when Cyndi flies out. Summer is winding down, which is sad enough, but there are other emotions involved. At one point we had such high hopes for Lucas and Ellie, and as annoyed as we were with Cyndi to start, she's become a fun friend. Kind of a melancholy end to a promising day.

And then to make matters worse, Mike tells me, "Grace, I have to go. You know I work tomorrow morning, and it's hard to get up so early to make it back in time."

I don't give him a guilt trip because it's his job, and I'm his mostly-retired wife. I get it. But it does put one more damper on the evening. As he's getting ready to leave, we see Cyndi walk back to her cabin.

Mike smiles. "It'll be interesting to see what becomes of that relationship. Personally, I don't see anything long-term. Lately it seems like it's more of a friend thing."

I tend to agree with him. I give him a kiss and hug, tell him to drive safely, and wave as he drives off.

ELLIE

Last night was weird. A mixture of highs and lows. And who would've predicted a few weeks ago that the thought of Cyndi leaving would be a low. I bring my morning coffee out on the porch, enjoying the view of the water. This coming weekend is Labor Day weekend, the unofficial end to summer. How sad. But the more I think about it, I realize that this doesn't have to be the end to my summer. I really have nothing to go home to. I could stay here all fall, and even winter if I wanted.

I realize that Grace is probably ready to go home. Mike has been great about the whole situation, but I'm sure he's getting sick of the drive and would like his wife at home a little more. I do know that I have some thinking to do. Do I want to keep my home in Iowa, or should I move to Sioux Falls to be closer to Mom, Grace, and some of the kids? Change can be hard, and the older you get, the harder it gets. But I do think I'm too young to settle for a mediocre life. This summer has taught me that there's more out there.

I see movement over at Cyndi's cabin and walk over to see what's her latest news. I see a packed suitcase by the door.

"Hi Cyndi. What's up?"

"Oh Ellie, I'm so glad you stopped by. Guess what? I have a flight out of Sioux Falls to Denver today at one."

"Really? You're leaving us?"

"Only for a few days. Alex wants me to look at that condo, and if that one doesn't work, there are other properties for me to look at."

"Are you coming back? Tell me you're coming back!"

"That's the plan. I don't have time today to pack up all of my stuff, so I'm coming back to do that. This isn't a long good-bye; only a short one."

"Do you need a ride to Sioux Falls? I could drive you."

"Nope, I've got my rental car that I can just drop off at the airport."

I tell her she has to come over to our place if she has a minute.

"Grace would kill us if I let you get away without saying goodbye to her."

"I'm all packed and ready to go. I have an hour to kill. I'd love to spend that hour with my new best friends."

Don't know if people form "new best friends" at our age, but I'm willing to go along with the sentiment. We go over to our cabin, run up the stairs, and shake Grace awake.

"You've got to get up," I tell her. "Cyndi is leaving."

It takes a few minutes, but she's finally awake and functioning. We head downstairs as we wait for Grace to put on a little more appropriate attire than her pajamas. Because her pajamas usually consist of nothing. Gross.

"Mimosa time. We need to do a pre-flight toast!" I announce.

Cyndi's mimosa will be orange juice with just a splash of champagne, since she has to drive. Grace's and mine will be just a little bit on the other end of the spectrum.

We raise our glasses. "To summer friends!" We all yell cheers and clink our glasses. And that's when the tears start.

Cyndi talks first. "I don't know where to start. I don't know if you've noticed, but I can come on a little strong."

Grace and I look at each other and smile through our tears—that's an understatement if ever there was one.

"A lot of women don't like me. I don't know if they're jealous of my looks or think I'm shallow or think I'm after their husbands. I'm not sure. But you two took the time to get past all of that and included me in your family. You will never, ever know how much that means to me. I have to honestly say that this has been the best summer of my entire life. And that is no exaggeration."

Grace and I reach over to give Cyndi a hug, and then I tell her, "Cyndi, I have to say, we didn't know what hit us on that first day at the beach. And also, for a number of days after that. You make quite a first impression. And maybe you should work on that, because this is one time in our lives that our first impression was totally wrong."

We all laugh when we think back to that first week. Only a month ago!

Grace agrees. "Cyndi, you made this month fun. To be honest with you, I think Ellie and I would've been totally bored with each other by this time. You do bring life to the party. And that's a gift for which you never have to apologize."

Cyndi looks at her watch and informs us that she has to go. Big, rib-crunching hugs follow.

I ask her, "You're coming back, right?"

She smiles and says, "Oh yeah, I brought way too much stuff along with me when I came. And some of those clothes and shoes are mighty fine. I'm coming back for them."

And then her eyes well up again and she tells us, "And I'm coming back to see the two best friends I've ever had in my life." And with that, she walks out the door.

CHAPTER 50

ELLIE

Grace and I give each other a hug and shed a few more tears. Who would've thought that the person that we thought was going to ruin our vacation made it the most fun? I look at Grace and smile.

"She is something, isn't she?"

Grace initially smiles, but then her smile turns into a frown. "So where do you think she and Lucas ended up? Are they still a thing?"

"I have no idea. But the fact that she didn't go over to say goodbye to him this morning makes me wonder. Actually, their whole relationship makes me wonder. Obviously he's not ready to commit to anything."

"Well, speak of the devil, here he is," Grace says as Lucas comes walking up.

I'm cringing, hoping that Lucas didn't hear us talking about him.

"Did Cyndi just leave?" he asks.

"Yes. You didn't see her at all today?" I ask.

"No. We said goodbye last night. And she'll be back in a few days. So what are you two beautiful ladies up to today?"

We pour him a mimosa as we discuss the plans for today. Nothing new—beach, sun, books, maybe a jet ski ride. We are really boring people.

And that's what we do—beach, sun, read, ride the jet skis. Not boring, but it is if you talk about it. Grace and I haul our leftovers from Murdos out of the fridge for our dinner. Plenty of food. Who could ever eat the portions that these restaurants serve in one sitting? Not us, which is a good deal, because we love leftovers.

Grace is in a funk tonight. She's thinking too much. The cicadas are buzzing, the sun is setting way too early, and she knows summer is coming to an end. This is a bad time of year for her. She'll be fine in a month or two. It's just this transition that she doesn't handle well. And the end of this summer will probably be harder than usual. Being here at the cabin has been great for her, but when you have high highs, you also have low lows. This will be a low month for her.

"You know what, Ellie, I'm going to call it a night. I have a new book to read, so I'm going to just read until I fall asleep."

Well, that's an oxymoron. If she has a good book, there won't be any falling asleep. If it holds her interest at all, she'll be reading it all night. But that's okay—her choice.

I'm sitting out on the porch, drinking my glass of wine, when I hear a noise. It's completely dark outside—the sun set over an hour ago. It's Lucas, knocking on the porch door. I invite him in and get him a beer. Tonight is a little cooler. I'm sitting under a blanket, and throw one to him.

He laughs. "Are you kidding me? It's still in the 70's."

He's right—I laugh too.

I ask Lucas, "What do you think of Cyndi leaving? Are you surprised?"

"Well, I would've been, before this whole grandmother thing came into play. Wow, that really took her by storm. But good for her, because it has given her something to focus on."

"I do think that's a good thing for her. But what about you? Does this affect any future plans you might have had?"

I can't believe I have the guts to ask that question, but I'm done tip-toing around the subject. Let's just get it out in the open.

Lucas thinks a little bit, and he must've decided to just be frank with me, because he says, "You know, Ellie, I'm sure you wondered what Cyndi and my relationship was. 'Are they serious?' 'Are they just having fun?' In the beginning, Cyndi was looking for a relationship. No surprise to you, but she came on pretty strong!"

We both laugh.

"But as I told you, I wasn't looking for a relationship. It took a little while, but she finally believed that I meant what I said. After that, she stopped coming on to me, and we just had fun. Nothing serious. I never so much as kissed her. I thought you might want to know that," he smiles.

"I do want to know that," I smile back. "Thanks for telling me. I'll admit, I was curious how far things had gone between you two."

"Well, I will tell you, there is one aspect of our relationship that's going to shock you."

"What's that, I ask?" Not sure if I want to hear this or not.

"You'll be surprised to know that Cyndi is a great listener."

"You're right–I am surprised. Actually, I find that very hard to believe."

"She was curious about my past, just as you were. I shared the whole story with her. And believe it or not, she had some great insights."

"Really?"

"Once she knew I wasn't interested in her in a romantic way, we just started talking more. She shared some of her background, and I shared mine. Remember that night that she told us she had a psychology degree? Well, let me tell you, that woman put some serious work into that degree. And she had lots of insights into my personality, past decisions I've made, and future decisions that I should make. It was really interesting."

"Well, you're right–that is shocking. Who would've thought?"

We sit there for a minute and then a smile comes to my face. "So, just curious, what are some future decisions that she thinks you should make?"

Lucas smiles too. "Well, for starters, she thinks I should be dating you."

"What? Are you kidding me?"

Lucas laughs. "That was her 'professional opinion,' even though she was the first to admit that she's not a professional."

"And what's your opinion of her 'professional opinion?'"

"Hmm, I think it might have some merit."

"Well, I certainly do, but what about your earlier reservations?" I get totally serious as I'm saying this, and Lucas gets serious too.

"Let's just say those reservations are still there, but maybe they shouldn't be guiding my life. I don't know. To be honest, I'm just plain scared. But maybe I just have to get past those fears and truly try and make a life for myself. So, with that being said, Ellie, will you go out with me tomorrow night?"

I try to keep from screaming, but a little squeak does make its way out of my mouth. "Lucas, I would love to."

I feel like I'm on a TV show, accepting a rose. Thankfully there aren't another 25 women around that he's asking out too. It's just me. I'm the person he's asking out on a date. And I couldn't be happier.

After Lucas leaves, I go running up the stairs. I peek in on Grace. As expected, she's not sleeping, and she motions me in.

I jump on the bed and tell her, "Well, I've got some news!"

"You do? Spill the beans!"

"You are not going to believe this, but Cyndi and Lucas weren't having an affair. She was giving him advice. Almost like counseling him!"

"What? Cyndi? Impossible! Are you kidding me?"

"Yep, that's the story. Can you believe it? Who would've thought?"

I proceed to tell Grace everything that Lucas told me. We go over every delicious part of the conversation.

But I tell Grace, "I'm not going to get ahead of myself. We are talking about one date. But it is pretty exciting, isn't it?"

We scream like two middle school girls and hug each other in excitement. We spend the next hour conversing, once again, like middle school girls. We are pathetic and we know it. But at this stage of our lives, it's kind of fun to act like teenagers again.

GRACE

Early in the morning, I call Mike with the good news. Predictably, he doesn't shriek like Ellie and I did last night, but he is pretty happy with the news.

"Wish I could be there with you guys. It's a bummer that I have to work again tomorrow, but I'll head out the second I get off work on Friday morning. Any big plans for the holiday weekend?"

"No, but hopefully it will be spent with the four of us together. Maybe it's time to make some more jerk chicken and hang out at the shack. The way it was intended to be."

"Grace, don't get your hopes up. We all love Lucas, but this is just one date. It might be too much for him to make any type of commitment."

"I know, but I'm the eternal optimist, right? I just feel it in my gut that this is the real deal."

"I hope so too, but hon, don't push too hard." Then he laughs and says, "But we will try our best to make the whole 'family package deal' look pretty darn attractive."

I laugh at that as I tell him goodbye. "See you Friday!"

CHAPTER 51

ELLIE

I change my clothes umpteen times. The good news is that Yankton doesn't have much for upscale dining, so wherever we go will be casual. I try putting my hair up—does that make my neck look skinnier? Or does that make me look older? I put my hair down—do I straighten it or let it go curly? The heck with my hair—it's prematurely gray and Lucas has seen it a hundred times.

Next up, I need to make a final decision on what I'm going to wear. A sundress, or jeans with a spaghetti strap top? It's hot out today—skip the jeans. A sundress it is. Green, to match my eyes, or golden yellow, to show off my tan? Grace hears me rummaging around and comes into my room to check on the progress.

"Oh, good grief, girl, throw something on, finish your makeup, and be done already! This isn't a blind date. He knows what you look like—the good, the bad and the ugly."

She looks me over and states, "And here's a plus, right now you are looking very good."

She comes over and gives me a big hug.

I tell her, "I'm so happy right now, but the reality is—maybe things haven't changed that much. Maybe Cyndi tried to talk him into something that he's still not ready for. This could just be a continuation of a doomed relationship."

Grace, also known as Little Miss Sunshine, gives me a pinch on my cheeks.

"Well, missy, that is not something we're even going to talk about. You're going on a date, and it's going to be awesome. Don't think otherwise!"

We hear Lucas knocking on the porch door. We come running down the stairs with me in the lead. I must say, I'm pretty excited about this date. As much as I try not to be, I just can't help myself.

"Hey Lucas!" we both yell. Grace asks us if we'd like a pre-dinner drink, or any appetizers.

Lucas says, "Well, if you don't mind, I'm kind of hungry, and I think we should just go. If that's okay with you?"

"Absolutely," Grace tells him. "You guys go and have fun."

Lucas leads me out to his car. He's turning this into a true date by leading me around to the passenger side and opening my door for me. Nice. I ask him where we're going.

"I'm kind of in the mood for Mexican. Are you okay with that?"

"Perfect."

There are two Mexican restaurants in town—both of them spectacular. Even though I don't know how the night will turn out, at least I know we'll have had a good meal.

He pulls in at Malina's Cantina. Once again, he's a gentleman and opens the car door for me. This is nice, but not necessary. I can open my own door—and it's a whole lot quicker that way. Grace and I have talked about this many times, and it kind of bugs us because we are not patient people.

We walk into the restaurant and are greeted warmly. Lucas is even greeted by name. Pretty cool. We're seated at a private booth, and both of us order margaritas. We make small talk until our drinks arrive, and then things start to get a little weird. An elderly couple walks out from the kitchen in the back and comes over to our table. Lucas stands up and they proceed to give him a big hug. The lady starts crying, and so does Lucas.

All of a sudden, it hits me. These are his parents-in-law. I have been in this restaurant numerous times, but when Lucas told me his story, I never put any thought into which Mexican restaurant Lola's family might own. I feel so stupid.

Lucas introduces me to Malina and Alejandro. I stand up and give them a hug. There is only a rare occasion that I'm ever at a loss for words, but I have to say, this is one of them.

I finally just say, "It's so nice to meet you."

That's it, Ellie? That's all you can come up with?

They are very gracious and courteous. They make a little small talk with me, and finally I have my wits about me and ask them, "Would you like to sit down with us for a bit?"

They just smile and say, "Oh no, you're with Lucas. We're just glad to see him here with a lady. It's about time."

Lucas looks at them and says, "You're right, it's been a long time. But I did want to introduce Ellie to you. I'm so glad you were here tonight."

They smile, give Lucas another hug, and make their way back into the kitchen.

Lucas looks at me. "You know, this wasn't fair to you. I really wanted you to meet Lola's parents, but why I didn't tell you in advance, I have no idea. I'm so sorry. I don't know what I was thinking."

"I don't know what you were thinking, either, but here's what I'm thinking. I think you just bestowed on me one of the highest honors you could have ever given me. To think that you would want me to meet them means more to me than you could ever know. I am overwhelmed." And with this, the tears start to fall.

"Oh Ellie, I didn't mean to make you cry. And why didn't I tell you in advance? That was so dumb of me. What an idiot. All of a sudden this afternoon I got this urge that I wanted you to meet them. It just felt really important to me. I'm so sorry. Obviously I ruined this evening."

"Are you kidding me? You just made this the best evening ever. Do you know why? Because you made it apparent that this was important to you. That *I* am important to you. I don't know what Cyndi talked you into or what's changed in the last week or two, but obviously something has, and I really like it."

"Well, it wasn't only Cyndi."

"What do you mean?"

"Your mom. I sat by her at the campfire the other night. She is the sweetest lady. We got to talking, first about small stuff, but then more serious stuff. What it comes down to is this.

She told me that I will live out the rest of my days in a meaningless, lonely life unless I'm willing to love again."

"She said that? I am so sorry! Usually she's not that blunt."

"Oh no, it didn't come across like that at all. It came across as someone who was very concerned about me and only wanted the best for me. When a person like that, with loads of life experience, tries to give you advice, you better take it. And the best part of it is, I knew it was spoken with love. Not only for you, but for me too. Who wouldn't take that to heart?"

I reach across the table to take his hands. And then the waitress (Lola's niece, I later learned), comes to take our order. Talk about bad timing. We order—a seafood chimichanga for me and a burrito for Lucas—and try to continue our conversation. The spell has been broken, but Lucas tells me we'll come back to this later.

I tell him, "Let's enjoy the night. Beginning with this wonderful dinner."

The dinner is absolutely delicious, and we thoroughly enjoy it, just as I knew we would. Once you meet the owner of a restaurant, you enjoy it even more, because now there's also a personal investment involved. The waitress brings us another round of margaritas, and about the time we're finishing them off, out come Malina and Alejandro with a dessert to share. There's a candle burning in it, so they walk out slowly to bring it over to us. Now we insist that they sit down with us, and this time they comply.

Lucas asks, "What's the candle for?"

Malina smiles shyly, "To celebrate a special night—the night we got to meet Ellie. And to remember all of the birthdays we never got to celebrate with you—yours, Lola's, and Lily's. We remember each one every year."

Oh man, bring on the waterworks. Lucas and I are both crying, and Malina and Alejandro, as stoic as they're trying to be, are both openly crying now too. Lucas reaches over, grips their hands tightly, and then blows out the candle.

"I'm so sorry that I've neglected you. It was just too painful for me to see you, and it reminded us all of how much we've lost. But I've been seeing lately that that was a mistake. We need to be reminded—not of the fact that they're gone—but of the fact that they were a beautiful part of our lives. They made our lives so much better, even though it wasn't as long as we would've wanted. And, Malina and Alejandro, I want you to know that I also take full responsibility for Lily's death. I wasn't around enough. Lola was floundering and overwhelmed, and I didn't help her. That's on me. I guess time does heal all wounds, because I've forgiven Lola—it wasn't totally her fault. We bear that blame equally, because we weren't the best parents we could've been. Can you ever forgive me for my part in this?

Malina cries, "Oh Lucas, we've never blamed you. In our hearts, we've already forgiven you, because you weren't really responsible."

"No, Malina, that's not true. I do bear some responsibility, because I spent way too much time away from Lola and Lily. Lola was young, Lily was a handful, and I didn't give Lola the support that she needed. So for that, I do ask for your forgiveness. But you know what? This has gone on for way too long, and I just think it's time for some healing. Let's do this together. I won't be a stranger, and I'd love to spend some time with you."

Alejandro gives a big smile through his tears. "Lucas, nothing would make us happier."

Malina smiles in agreement and says, "Ellie, we don't really know you yet, but if you're a part of Lucas' life, then we want to include you in ours too. Many years ago, it would've been so painful for us to see Lucas with another woman, but now we're just so happy to see that he has someone in his life. We never wanted him to be alone. This is good, si?"

"I hope so," I respond. "We've only known each other for the summer, and who knows where this will lead, but I am just honored to have gotten to meet you tonight. You seem like wonderful people. And I have to tell you, I've eaten here many times, and you make the best seafood chimichangas!"

We all laugh together.

"Oh, and your margaritas aren't bad either!"

Alejandro calls to one of the waiters walking by.

"Another round of margaritas, on the house."

When the drinks arrive, Lucas raises his glass.

"To my wonderful 'second parents,' and to the future, whatever it may hold."

We clink our heavy glasses and all say "salud" to that.

As we drive back to the cabins, Lucas reaches across and takes my hand.

"Tonight was an emotional night for me. And once again, I apologize that I didn't give you any warning. This afternoon, all of a sudden, I just had this overwhelming desire to introduce you to Lola's parents. It just felt like the time was right, and it was really important to me. Thank you for being so gracious."

"Are you kidding me? This will rank as one of the best dates ever. Because it meant something–something really important to you. And if it's important to you, it's important to me. The fact that you let me into this part of your life is something I haven't been able to imagine recently. I didn't know if we'd ever get back on track. And so I need to know, are we? Are we back on track?"

As Lucas is pulling down the driveway to our cabins, he's silent. Honestly, I blew it. I pushed too hard and he's pulling back. Why can't I just be patient? He lets go of my hand to put the car into park, and turns off the engine. I stay in my seat, wondering if this is the end of the date, or if we'll sit and talk a little. I'm getting a little close to the "being emotionally drained" part of the night. But Lucas suddenly jumps out of the car, runs around to my door, and opens it for me. Enough of being the gentleman!

But then the unexpected happens. He grabs me up out of the car and pulls me into his arms. He looks into my eyes, and then proceeds to kiss me. I guess he's done being the gentleman, because this is no gentlemanly kiss. Instead, this kiss sends me reeling. In my wildest dreams, I couldn't imagine tonight ending up this way. I was hoping for it, but didn't really expect it.

We walk up to his cabin and go inside. The kiss continues as we make our way to the couch.

"Lucas, you know I can't stay tonight, right?"

"I know that, and I respect that. But in the meantime, we can make out just a little, right?"

"Oh yeah, that we can do. And maybe even talk a little in between. But can I just clarify things? Are we building a relationship, or are you going to pull back tomorrow? Because I don't want to go back to this roller-coaster of emotions. I can't handle it."

"I think we can officially say that tonight is the night that we start building a relationship. September 2—the night we became a couple. You might have to be a little patient with me at times. I still have some demons to get rid of. But I think this summer has already been a good start to that. Thank goodness summer isn't over."

"I second that. I have to say, this summer has been one of the best but also one of the most frustrating seasons of my entire life. By the way, you're responsible for both of those emotions."

Lucas laughs, "Yeah, I guess I can take responsibility for that. But I promise, it'll only keep getting better from here." And he seals that promise with a kiss.

CHAPTER 52

GRACE

This is one long evening. I'm sitting out on the porch, reading a really suspenseful book, but even this book isn't doing it for me. I keep waiting to hear Lucas' car coming down the driveway. I so hope this evening is going well for them. But who knows—it's anybody's guess.

My phone rings; it's Mike.

"Have you heard anything from Ellie yet?"

"No, not yet, and it's driving me crazy!"

"I have to admit, it's driving me a little bit crazy too. Keep me posted if you hear anything."

"I will, but if you don't hear from me tonight, I guess that would be good news. I think it would mean that things are going well."

"I agree. One of those 'no news is good news' scenarios. Bye, hon, I'll see you tomorrow."

I continue on with the suspense novel on my book reader. The sun set a long time ago and it's pitch black out when I finally hear the car coming down the drive. The engine turns off and things are a little quiet until I can finally make out the shape of Lucas opening his door. Darn it, where's the full moon when you need it? I quickly snap my book reader closed so they can't see I'm on the porch. I'm not proud of my eavesdropping, but this is too important to miss.

I can barely make out the shape of Lucas walking around the vehicle and opening Ellie's door. From then on, things are a blur. I assume Ellie got out because then all I can see are two people standing very closely together. This goes on for a while and then I can see them walking into Lucas' cabin. Interesting. I guess the evening wasn't a total dud.

"Okay, enough of this," I say to myself.

I get ready for bed. I decide I'll read for a while—probably a long while. When Ellie comes upstairs, and I know she will eventually, I'll let her decide if she wants to talk or not. Her call.

It's after midnight when I finally hear her coming up the stairs. My light is on, which she can see under my doorway, so she knows I'm awake. But I hear her going into her room and shutting her door. Oh bummer. I so wanted her to come in and give me the play-by-play action of the evening. She's going to make me stew until morning? So unthoughtful of her! What does this mean? Did it go well? Did it go horribly? Is she crying her eyes out right now? Do I go in and check on her?

I finally decide to be an adult, and let Ellie be an adult, so I don't go and bug her. Morning will come soon enough. Maybe for her, but I'll be up half the night wondering what happened.

I'm still half-sleeping when I hear someone come in my room. Due to room-darkening shades, I'm not sure what time it is. I peak one eye open, about the same time someone plants a kiss on my cheek.

"Hey sleepyhead." Mike rubs my cheek and then gives me a proper kiss.

"Wow, you must've gotten off work on time."

"Just the usual. I drove straight from work. It is ten-o'clock—time for you to get up. Did you talk to Ellie at all last night?"

"No. She came in after midnight. I was hoping she would come and fill me in on how things went, but she went straight to her room. I guess we'll get to quiz her together."

I smile at that thought. This will be so much fun. Hopefully.

Mike slaps me on my behind and says, "Get your butt out of bed. I'll make some breakfast."

"Yippee," I drawl. He laughs and heads downstairs.

I quickly throw on some clothes and head down shortly after him. Ellie is sitting by the island, drinking which is probably her umpteenth cup of coffee this morning. I take a quick glance at her—happy or sad? Umm, I'm thinking happy.

"Okay, spill it. How did things go last night?"

"Okay," is all Ellie has to say.

What? That's all I'm going to get out of her?

"Are you kidding me? You come in after midnight and you're just going to say it was 'okay?' You owe us more than that!"

Ellie starts laughing. "I knew that would drive you crazy. Actually, it was more than okay. Way, way more than okay."

Mike and I sit there waiting to hear details. Ellie starts slowly.

"Well, you know that Mexican restaurant—Malina's Cantina?"

Mike and I nod our heads. We've been there more times than we can count.

Ellie tells us, "Well, the owners, Malina and Alejandro, were Lucas' parents-in-law. Lola's parents."

"Seriously? Why didn't we ever put that together? Pretty dumb on our part."

"That's what I thought. Lucas brought me there to meet them. It was very special, very emotional, and very meaningful. They are the nicest people, and you could tell they were so happy to make contact with Lucas again."

She proceeds to tell us in detail about the whole evening, from arriving at the restaurant, to the time spent there, to arriving back home, and the kiss by the car. Things get a little fuzzy after that, and I don't blame her for not going into play-by-play detail. We get the picture. And it looks like a pretty rosy picture, at that. Mike and I go over to give her a hug.

"We're so happy for you!"

"I have to admit, I'm pretty happy for myself too. And here's another interesting thing. Lucas wasn't only getting advice from Cyndi, he was getting it from Mom too."

"Mom? Really? That's not like her."

Mike says, "I told you I overheard her at the campfire, and she was telling him to get his act together.

"I told Lucas that usually Mom isn't that opinionated, and she isn't one to interfere. But evidently she told him at the campfire the other night that it was time for him to move on and bring someone into his life. And it sounds like he really took it to heart."

"Mom, the matchmaker. Who would've ever guessed?"

"I don't know if she was truly trying to be a matchmaker. I just think she saw that he was lonely and felt bad for him. You know she can't stand to see anyone unhappy."

Mike agrees with that.

"She could be sick and dying, and still be trying to make all of us kids happy. The eternal optimist."

We hear a little knock at the door, and Lucas comes walking in. He has a big smile on his face, and walks right over to Ellie and gives her a kiss. Mike whistles and I cheer. Lucas takes a fake bow.

Mike states the obvious. "I gather that things have changed a little, and we couldn't be happier for you. I think this calls for a celebration."

He heads to the fridge and pulls out a bottle of champagne.

"I think we'll forego the orange juice. And I also think we should've bought stock in this champagne company!"

We laugh as Mike pours the four glasses. We hold them high, not sure who should be giving the toast. We look at each other, and then Mike and I say together, "To Lucas and Ellie."

Nothing more needs to be said. We clink our glasses, take a sip, and then all start talking and laughing at once. What a beautiful way to start the Labor Day weekend.

I finally have to ask. "Okay, Lucas, what's changed? We like you. We like you a lot. But we're very protective of Ellie. She hasn't had the easiest life, and we would hate to see her get hurt—again. Tell us that's not going to happen."

Lucas takes a minute to answer.

"You know, I would've never have seen this happening. I was content. Not happy, but content with my life. But sometimes things get placed right in front of you. Call it serendipity, call it fate, call it people being placed in your path, or call it God working in mysterious ways. I don't know. But this summer was something that I could've never imagined. And as much as I initially tried to fight it—sometimes you just have to give in. That sounds terrible. It sounds like I'm succumbing to some terrible disease. That's not it at all. But after years of thinking that I'm not deserving of any happiness—maybe I am. And that's a feeling that's been foreign to me for a long time. It's taken me this whole summer, and it might take me longer, but I feel like I'm ready to start living life again. And from where I am right now, I really want that life to include Ellie."

Oh my. Could he have come up with a better answer? Mike and I look at each other and smile. We couldn't have asked for more. And with that, we move in for a four-person group hug. We've been waiting for this all summer.

CHAPTER 53

ELLIE

The four of us are relaxing on the beach when we catch a flash of hot pink out of the corner of our eyes.

"Hey guys! I'm back!"

Ellie and I quickly jump up to give Cyndi a hug. Lucas and Mike are a little slower on the take, but they get up too and greet Cyndi warmly.

"I've missed you all so much! Tell me what's new. Have you missed me? I have so much to tell you! And I'm so excited to spend the weekend with you!"

We all laugh. What would our weekend be without Cyndi? And to think that just a month ago we were quite anxious to get rid of her. Sometimes things grow on you, kind of like cancer. Oh, that's harsh. She's so much better than that.

"How's your son and daughter-in-law doing? Did you have a nice time with them?" I ask.

"It was great. Things started off a little awkward since it had been a few years since I had seen them. But things warmed up rather quickly and it didn't take long before we felt comfortable with each other, just like the early years when they were dating. As I told you before, we didn't have a major fight or anything. They just didn't like my second husband so it was easier to drift apart."

Grace asks, "I know you told us before, but what's the due date again? Are they going to find out what they're having?"

"She's due on January 7, and they just found out last week that they're having a girl. I'm so excited! Can you imagine all of the cute pink things I'll be able to buy for that little sweetie?"

"Hold on there, grandma. Don't go overboard. You are the mother-in-law, and some girls can get a little prickly when they're having their first baby. Just be smart and take your cues from her and your son."

"I know–you're absolutely right. But it'll be hard to hold back."

Lucas asks, "How'd the house hunting go? Any luck?"

"Alex found this really cute two-bedroom condo just four blocks from their house. Close, but hopefully not too close. I think it's going to be just perfect. I get possession of it in three weeks."

Mike says, "Wow, that's fast. And speaking of fast, you sure made it back here in record time."

"Well, I knew that Labor Day Weekend was basically your last hurrah here, so there was no way I was missing out on that. Plus, my rental agreement at the cabin only goes through next Tuesday. Time's a'wasting! What's our plan?"

My response: "I'm thinking beach, boating, food and friends. Who needs anything more than that?"

Absolutely no one.

Grace asks, "What's on the menu and agenda for dinner? I could run into town for whatever we want."

Lucas responds, "You women really don't want to cook tonight, do you? How about Charlie's pizza, delivered, on me?"

"You read my mind, Lucas. I wouldn't mind not cooking and just being a beach bum tonight."

Grace and Cyndi agree with me.

And then Grace asks, "Cyndi, just wondering, do you cook? I guess we've never gotten to put any of your culinary skills to the test."

Cyndi smiles. "I make a mean macaroni and cheese, straight out of the box. That's about it. Or cereal is always a good go-to in a pinch. I could bring some over for breakfast tomorrow if you'd like. I even have a variety for those with a discerning taste."

We laugh.

Grace tells her, "Actually, I am a bona fide cereal connoisseur. I'd take that any day over a big breakfast."

Mike groans. "The story of my life. She makes my favorite meal of the day into something to be endured rather than enjoyed. Ugh—it's so annoying!"

"Just another one of my amazing talents, thank you very much!"

We continue our afternoon with bantering, laughing, and easy conversation, with an occasional jet ski ride thrown in to cool off.

Lucas declares it's time for pizza and drinks.

"Okay, whoever wants may hit the shower, or if you want to stay sweaty and sandy, that's fine too. But I'm ordering the pizza soon, so none of this 'I take an hour to get ready' stuff. When the pizza's here, we're eating, no matter how you look!"

Mike shoots him a look. "How do you get by with that? I've been trying to tell Grace that for years, but it never seems to work."

Lucas winks. "The women are still in the 'trying to impress' me stage. They'll do whatever I suggest."

We three women look at each other, and all come up with the same idea. We run into the water and proceed to splash Lucas mercilessly.

Mike gets caught up in the torrent of water and yells, "Hey, I'm just an innocent bystander!"

You're never innocent," Grace yells back.

The water fight takes on new intensity as the guys run into the water and start dunking us. It gets intense until Grace, Cyndi and I finally call "uncle." We'll always be out-matched and over-powered by those big men. We all come sputtering up out of the water and onto the beach.

I tell Lucas, "Well, I guess you blew it. I was going to get all showered up and smell really nice, but now you're just stuck with 'stinky, sweaty' me. I guess the 'trying to impress you' thing has reached the end of its lifeline. Too bad for you!"

We all decide to stay sweaty and sandy, because we're starving. The pizza is delivered, the drinks are plentiful, and the night is perfect, because it's a holiday weekend. No--actually, it's perfect because we're with people we love.

————————

GRACE

Big surprise—I wake up to the smell of bacon. I come down the stairs and see all four of them sitting around the island.

"Cyndi, you traitor, you're eating bacon and eggs. I thought you were a cereal girl!"

"Oh, I never said I wouldn't eat a big breakfast, I just don't like to make it. And here's some Cocoa Pops for you, by the way."

"Thanks so much—they're one of my favorites!"

Cereal *and* chocolate in one tasty breakfast? Jackpot!

Mike tells us, "Okay, guys, time to make a decision. Beach and jet-skiing, or boating and water-skiing?"

A unanimous decision—boating it is. Not that it's a momentous decision, because we'll do the other option tomorrow. Coolers and beach bags are packed, and the day commences.

And what a beautiful day it is. The sun is shining and the water is calm. The whole mood is one of relaxation. Nothing pressing, no worries, fun music, good-natured teasing, great food—everything we envisioned, and more, when we first started this summer vacation. But there is a just a touch of sadness hanging in the air. No one talks about it and we avoid the whole topic of "summer's end," but it's there. I feel it intensely, because that's just the way I am, but I think everyone else senses that same feeling of melancholy.

We spend the evening eating dinner by the shack, and then Mike lights a roaring campfire. No kids are around so we don't have to make s'mores—yay! We can just talk and relax. Mike and Lucas are in some deep conversation about Mike's backyard deck project. The humongous deck that is costing us an arm and a leg but will be beautiful and well worth it when it's done.

Cyndi looks at Ellie and says, "I was just noticing today that you and Lucas seem to be a little closer than when I left. Am I just imagining that?"

Ellie smiles. "No, you're not imagining that. We are, and I hear I have you to thank for that. Is that true?"

Cyndi smiles right back.

"I wouldn't go that far, but I did give him a little nudge. When I first showed up this summer, I thought he'd be a great catch. And he is–just not for me. You two are perfect for each other."

I'm in total agreement, and then the three of us get into a little girl-talk, until the guys put a stop to that. From then on it's just a matter of five friends enjoying fun conversation and an impressive campfire. What could be better?

CHAPTER 54

ELLIE

If there is one thing that has made this summer better than we could've ever imagined, it's the weather. South Dakota summers can be awesome, or they can leave much to be desired. This one is the best we've had in a long time—if you love hot weather. And Grace and I do. Thank God for the sunshine.

That's what is running through my mind when I get up this morning. Another beautiful day for the last one that the five of us have together. Cyndi will be leaving tomorrow, which is Labor Day. I know Mike has to leave tomorrow also, and Grace and I haven't really talked about what our departure plans are. We're going to have to discuss that at some point. I go downstairs to find Mike and Lucas drinking big mugs of coffee, and I proceed to join them. Mike and I will be making our signature breakfast, and Grace will be eating her Cocoa Pops. Everyone's happy!

Our plan for the day is what we talked about yesterday—beaching it and jet-skiing when we want. And that's exactly what we do. What a fun day. Cyndi is in "refrigerator cleaning mode," so she supplies us with more food and drinks than any of us need.

Mike finally says what has been going through our minds all day. "I hate to be the spoil-sport here, but Ellie and Grace, we have to come up with a plan. Those jet-skis and the boat have to be winterized and put into storage, and we need to close up the cabin for the winter. This time it's all going to be done right, so we don't come back to a mess like you did this summer."

We're all pretty quiet, with thoughts of the end of this magnificent summer coming to an end. Grace and I look at each other. I know the look—we both are on the verge of tears. Until Cyndi breaks the spell.

"Well, I have some news!"

We all just look at her. What now?

"Mr. Jansen contacted me yesterday. He and his wife would like to sell the cabin, so he gave me first chance. I bought it!"

"What?" we all shriek.

"I was thrilled when he called. I couldn't imagine not spending next summer here with all of you. I'm selling my house in Florida. Even after buying the condo in Denver, I'll have plenty of money left over to buy the cabin. It'll be great living by my son and new granddaughter, but this is where I want to spend my summers. You're not getting rid of me yet."

Grace and I go over to give her a big hug.

"We're so happy! Summers wouldn't be the same without you. This will really be something to look forward to."

This definitely takes the mood from Mike's depressing realism to something we're all excited about. We spend the next few hours talking about all of the possibilities of our future summers together, including remodeling Cyndi's cabin. Another project!

We come up with a massive amount of ideas, rejecting some and finalizing others. This will be a blast. Mike and Lucas try to put a brake on the brainstorming, but they know it's useless. They also know it will involve some work for them. The rest of the day is spent talking about the future, our friendships, and the awesome summer that we've had.

Labor Day–the unofficial end to summer. I know we can have a lot of really nice days in September and even October, but somehow this day is always climactic in that respect.

The four of us walk over to Cyndi's place to say goodbye. We know it's not forever, but next summer seems like a long time away. She has all of her bags by the front door, and Mike and Lucas offer to take them to her car. Good thing–they weigh a ton.

The three of us just look at each other and melt into a puddle of tears. Why are goodbyes so hard for those of us who are really emotional? It's a mixed blessing–those big emotions give us great joy, but also deep sorrows. And probably everyone has those same feelings–they just don't show it as easily.

"I love you guys so much," Cyndi chokes through her tears. "You will never know how much this summer meant to me. You made me feel like I'm a semi-normal person!"

We all laugh at that. "And you are. Semi-normal. Not totally normal," Grace says as we try to lighten the mood.

We walk with her to her car. Hugs from everyone, and we all wave as she drives off.

Lucas says, "Well, she certainly made our summer interesting."

We're all in agreement on that point.

"Time for our last mimosa of the summer," Grace tells us.

We fill our glasses and go out to sit on the porch.

Lucas informs us, "All summer long, you ladies would talk about having champagne. But champagne only comes from France. This stuff comes from California. What you were drinking was sparkling wine."

I give him a slap across his leg. "Well, way to spoil the mood! We know that, but champagne sounds so much more sophisticated than sparkling wine."

The bantering continues as the four of us reminisce about the summer. We're all so comfortable with each other, like we've been a part of the same family our whole lives. We don't even go down to the beach. We spend the whole day on the porch, relaxing and conversing, telling old stories and looking forward to creating new ones.

Mike finally calls it a day.

"You guys, I'm so sorry, but I have to be at work in the morning. Ellie and Grace, let me know what your plans are this week, and whatever needs to be done here, I'll take care of it."

Lucas pipes in, "And I'll help. After all, I am the guy your mom hired to look after the place."

Grace adds, "And look how poorly that turned out!"

"Hey, I was only hired to maintain the outside. None of that crap inside was my fault!"

True. We say goodbye to Mike, and Grace heads inside. Lucas and I spend a long time on the porch, talking about our pasts, and dare I say it—beginning to plan our future. We're sitting together on the patio couch, and it feels so natural and comfortable. Probably too comfortable, so I finally force him to go home. We're not ready yet to take it any further. That's okay. It's only going to get better from here on out.

——————

GRACE

"As much as I hate to say it, we need to start closing this place up. Summer is over. Should we start cleaning today? How long do you think it will take us?"

Ellie responds, "I have no idea."

"Me neither. So do we start room-by-room? Do we do a deep clean, or do we do that next summer when we come back? I guess we need to do some cleaning, but whatever we do, it'll be dusty and a little dirty by next summer. I'd say let's do what we need to now, but do a really deep cleaning in the spring."

Ellie is looking a little wistful, staring out at the water.

"Hey, earth to Ellie, did you hear me? As much as we hate for this to end, I do need to get back to my husband and my life."

Ellie turns and looks at me.

"Grace, you don't have to do anything here. Because I'm not leaving."

"What?"

"I'm not leaving. What do I have to go back to in Iowa? An empty house, a few distant friends, no family there? I've talked to Mom, and she said I can stay as long as I'd like. I'm staying. This has been the best summer that I've had in many years. And not only that, but I think Lucas and I have a relationship on which we can build. I don't know yet if it's a forever relationship, but I feel like I have to stay to see what it can be."

"Oh Ellie, I think that's amazing. I always felt so sorry for you after Will died. This summer has really opened up new horizons for you. And you're right—there's nothing back there for you."

We look at each other with love in our eyes, as the tears fall down our faces. What a summer it's been—a summer of all the best things in life—sunshine, relaxation, friendships, family, and most of all, love. Who would've thought that this would be one of the best summers of our lives?

"But why does it seem like we're saying goodbye to each other forever?"

"Well, we're not—don't be ridiculous! We'll see each other in the next week or two. It's just a new era in our lives. Maybe the best era ever. The years come and go, and I think that what we've got coming up in the future is just as good, if not better, than what we've ever had before. Who could imagine that this stage in our lives might be the best ever? We're always going to be sisters, and also best friends, and nothing's ever going to change that."

I look at Ellie and we fall into each other's arms.

We hug and cry and I finally say, "Ellie, I don't mean to be abrupt here, but if you don't need any help with cleaning, I'm going to go. Putting this off any longer isn't going to make it any easier. Mike wants me at home, and I really want to be with him. Who knows what our house looks like?" I continue with a laugh. "Actually, I'm sure it's fine because he's a better housekeeper than I am. This has been amazing, but my life is at home with Mike and the kids."

"I get it. And I'm so grateful to him that we had this summer together. Who would've thought how this would turn out? My goal was to spend the summer with you, and that was everything I hoped for, and more. I was so lonely, and you gave me something to think about other than myself. But then, meeting Lucas--it filled an empty spot. A spot that I didn't think would ever be filled again. Grace, I am so hopeful. Lucas and I talked a long time last night. I think this is it. We both do."

"Oh Ellie, nothing would make me happier. You know, someday when we're older and grayer than we are already, I hope we look back on this summer and think, 'This was the summer that changed Ellie's life forever.'"

"That would be wonderful, wouldn't it? I can't be 100% sure of that right now, but there is hope. And that in itself feels very special. That's more than I've felt in a very long time. And for that I have to thank you. You made this summer possible in the best way ever."

"No, you did. It was your idea—all I did was show up."

"But that's the thing—it's all about showing up, and you did that. I couldn't have asked for more. How about same time, same place, next year?"

"You've got it. You couldn't keep me away. I love you so much."

"And I love you more. I couldn't have made it through these last years without you."

We look at each other, forcing smiles as the tears seep out.

Ellie brightens up a little as she asks me, "So, before you leave—one more toast for the road? Champagne—or sparkling wine?"

"Definitely champagne."
Ellie fills the flutes as I watch. We raise our glasses.
"To my summer sister!
"To *my* summer sister. The best ever! Cheers!"

EPILOGUE

GRACE

Mom's birthday is December 15, the same as her mother's. Our wonderful, fun-loving, amazing Grandma Grace. No one could laugh like that woman could, but when our family members get together, everyone would be able to tell that we all come by our laughs naturally. And we laugh often, which I've always believed is a great thing to do.

Mom is going to be 89 tomorrow, and we're going to celebrate. It won't be a big shindig like we hope to have next year for her 90th. But we're still going to celebrate, because life is too short and tomorrow isn't guaranteed. Mom has always hated the fact that her birthday is in December. The absolute worst thing, she always tells us, is when she got birthday presents wrapped in Christmas paper. What an insult! Mom doesn't get upset about too many things, but that's one thing we've heard about on more than one occasion. And the thought of a combined birthday/Christmas present, well, that ranks right up there with the Christmas wrapping.

We're at the cabin, which has a totally different feel now than it does in the summer. We have a nice fire going, even if it is in a gas fireplace. The view out the front porch is not the summer view we're used to. The lake is icing over. It's a cold, dreary look. Not my favorite.

Ann has come from Iowa, Katie from Arizona, and Dan from Michigan for the special occasion. None of their spouses came. Too close to Christmas with too many obligations. No one blames them, and you know what? It's kind of nice to be here with Mom and just us five siblings. It's been a while. We laugh and tell story after story. We've heard them all before, but they're still as new and funny as the first time they took place. We reminisce about Dad, and know that he would be so proud of us all. We miss him, but we know that we'll see him again someday.

We ask Mom what she'd like for a special meal and she gives us the typical response, "Oh, whatever. Don't go to any fuss."

Mike is coming in the morning. And Lucas? Well, he's right next door.

ELLIE

I can hardly sleep. It's going to be a big day. Grace and I bought all the food for today, even though Mom told us not to go to any work. We got a bouquet of flowers for her from the local flower shop, and a beautifully decorated cake for the occasion from the local bakery. Mom is going to love it!

I finally decide to get up and make a pot of coffee. Dan gets up and joins me. As it starts to get light outside we can see that it's snowing lightly. Nothing to ruin anyone's travel plans—just a light dusting. Even though we're not big snow fans in our family, it is kind of pretty. Slowly the house comes to life and we all sit around the kitchen island. Mike comes walking through the front door. He must've come right after his night shift. He gives Grace a big hug, gives Mom a big hug and wishes her happy birthday, and then there are hugs all around. When Mike met our family, he couldn't believe how much we hug.

An hour or two later the nieces and nephews start flocking in, with lots of "Happy birthday, Grandma!"

Many more hugs and kisses are exchanged as more people show up. Mom is so happy to see each and every one of them. The cabin gets louder and crazier as the day progresses. If this was summer, we could overflow to the outdoor porch, lawn and beach. But this is fun too, even if it's a little too noisy to hear all of the conversations. The kids run upstairs to claim their spaces in the bunkroom, and hang out and play games up there. Grace and I are constantly going to the pantry and fridge to replace the food and beverages. That's an ongoing task. News flash—the Andersons love to eat and drink!

GRACE

"Okay, Ellie, it's time."

We make our way upstairs. We talk about being summer sisters, and how this summer was the best ever. I thank her so much for the great idea—I'm so glad we did this! We talk about some of our favorite memories together, not only this summer, but over the years. We laugh when we talk about Cyndi. She definitely made the summer interesting. The truth is—we can't wait to see her again next summer. We talk about Lucas, and the progress he made over the summer. What a sweet guy. We share tears of joy and tears of sadness when we see how far everyone has come. Thankfully, the joyful memories that we reminisce about far outweigh the sad ones. We fix our make-up before we go down—we don't want anyone to know that we were crying. Like we're going to fool anyone.

I go back downstairs and give Abby a nod. She picks up her violin and starts playing Canon in D. That song always makes me cry, and obviously I'm not the only one. I give Abby credit for being able to play a violin with tears running down her face. Lucas is standing at the bottom of the stairs with a boutonniere on his lapel and a big smile on his face. Ellie is wearing a gorgeous lace-covered dress and carrying a small, tasteful Christmas bouquet. She's beaming as she walks down the stairs. I've never seen her look more beautiful. The pastor takes his place and the wedding begins.

—————————

MOM

I guess you don't even know my name, but that's not important. Being known as "mom" is a testament to my best work—the loving, well-adjusted, successful children that Paul and I raised. So many families are distant from each other or just don't get along. To physically see and to always know that my family shares a loving bond—nothing brings more joy to a parent than this. This is quite the birthday, and I couldn't be happier. Having Ellie get married on my birthday just adds to the joy. Seeing your children content, happy, and loved is really the most important thing a mother wishes for in her life.

I have had a wonderful life with an amazing husband, five beautiful children, 15 grandchildren (sadly, dear Shane was taken from us much too early), and 41 great-grandchildren. They couldn't all be here today, but the smiling faces all around me demonstrate just how blessed I truly am. God is good!

ACKNOWLEDGEMENTS

To my husband, Harlan. Your love and support have made me into the woman I am today. You're my hero, and have been a hero to others throughout your career. I thank God for you every single day.

To my sister, Beth, and brother-in-law, Leon. Your love and joy for life, even in the midst of adversity and tragedy, is a testimony to all who know you.

To my children, Jesse and Erin, and my son-in-law, Chad. No mother could be prouder of her kids than I am.

To my seven beautiful grandchildren: Rachel, Connor, Landon, Kate, Teegan, Kennady, and Brynn. You will never begin to comprehend how much of a blessing you are in my life.

To Carmen, one of my dearest friends and also my biggest cheerleader. Your encouragement kept me going.

To MaryEllen, whose advice and experience helped me immensely in the publishing of this book.

To all of my friends who took the time to read this book while I was writing it. You gave me pointers, advice and encouragement along the way. Rose, Cindy, Kay, Dawneen, Carol, Connie, Larry, Karen–I'm indebted to you all.

Printed in Great Britain
by Amazon

27547418R00189